Short Stories from the Network Series

KATIE CROSS

KCW

Contents

Short Stories from the Network Series

YA Fantasy

Text copyright 2017 by Katie Cross

Cover designed by Seedlings Online at www.seedlingsonline.com

For information regarding permission, send a query to the author at katie@kcrosswriting.com.

Published by KC Writing. Visit the author at www.katiecrossbooks.com.

Introduction

Welcome to *Short Stories from the Network Series!*

SPOILERS DISCLAIMER!

This canon of short stories has been written specifically for readers of the *entire* Network Series collection. If you haven't read all the books yet —WAIT! The spoilers in these stories could ruin the experience, and parts may not make much sense. I suggest you start with *Mildred's Resistance* or *Miss Mabel's School for Girls*.

To the fans that have read the Network Series and come back for more, welcome back! I'm ecstatic you want to read more.

In this collection, you'll find short stories following Mildred, Marten, Derek, Angelina, Merrick, Camille, and Hazel. Revisiting these characters and learning more about them through telling their individual stories helped me remember why I love writing.

Now, it's time to enjoy those stories!

CHAPTER 1

Mildred

M ildred is—and always has been—one of my favorites. Writing the following scene was a delicate process. I always imagined she would need something to give her the strength to make her final decision. Mildred is a fickle witch. She has deep, varied emotions that she rarely betrays. Tapping into that while preserving her personality was one of my favorite challenges when writing Mildred's Resistance.

Doing so again was a real delight.

* * *

Over the years, Marten's eyes had shifted to a deep umber. She hadn't noticed—until now. Instead of hints of hazel and flecks of amber, they'd deepened into the satiny finish of a dark walnut tree. That loving, compassionate gaze had guided Mildred through a government overthrow, the loss of a child, and a lifetime of hidden love and lonely nights.

But it couldn't help her tonight.

"Are you ready for the Anniversary Ball, Mildred?"

Mildred released a long, coiled breath that had been sitting in her belly like a hot snake. Instead of examining the flicker of torchlight along the perimeter of the forest, she studied herself in the reflection of the window pane. Aged eyes. Wrinkled face. She'd never felt so tired. Or frightened.

What's on the other side of all this? Where will I go when life just . . . stops? She shook her head, pulling herself from the morose thoughts. Brooding wouldn't extend the hours of her life—just rob her of the few she had left. Even so, it felt wonderful just to *think*. To unroll the *what if's* and play a sort of game with herself.

What if I had never taken the job as a librarian?

What if Marten hadn't introduced himself the day we met?

And the strangest question of all: *what if I had never fallen in love?*

On the cusp of her life, she allowed herself the luxury of uncertainty. Had she made all the right decisions? Should she have chosen a different path? Would she change her decisions if she could?

Marten stepped to her side, staying a respectable distance away while in view of the window. He maintained their careful facade of indifference without thinking; they both did. She caught his gaze in the reflection of the window. His concern felt like a warm caress.

"No." She cleared her throat. "I am not ready for tonight."

"Derek was the right choice for High Priest, even if unpopular."

"That's not what I'm concerned about."

She turned, smoothing out a wrinkle in the front of his dress shirt, and strode away from the window. Marten spun around, but stayed out of reach. His brow furrowed.

"It's Mabel, isn't it?" he asked.

"She'll come tonight."

"Yes."

"She'd be a fool not to."

Marten frowned. "There's no other way for her to beat you, is there? You're too powerful."

She tightened her jaw. "No. There is no other way. She'll come."

"Do you think she'll attack or come in peace?"

"I had hoped she'd deal with me privately, but Mabel likes to make a scene. What more can we do? The Guardians and Protectors have prepared for a possible attack. But we just don't know." She spread her hands. "It's all we can do, Marten."

He closed the space between them with three long strides, captured her wrist, and pulled her close. The drapes slid across her windows, closing them in. A pang of remorse made her stomach queasy. Marten hated speaking about her bargain with Mabel.

"Talk to me," she demanded. "Avoiding it isn't going to change the fact that I shall die tonight, Marten."

He released her, as if he needed more air between them again. The suffocating feeling of saying *merry part* stole over her, and she didn't blame him.

"I don't like it, Mildred. We've played into her hands."

"No. She's played into mine. I'm not needed in the Network anymore, Marten. Derek is. He's the witch that the Network needs. Besides, I'm getting old. I'm tired all the time. I've served my Network my entire life."

He reached up and ran his fingertips along her face. "How shall I live without you?"

"The same as you did with me. One day at a time."

A rueful smile crossed his lips. "So pragmatic."

She closed her eyes and leaned into his warm palm. "I don't know what to expect on the other side, Marten. I don't know what death will bring. But I will be there, waiting for you, when you come to me."

He drew in a deep breath. She paused, wondering why it drew her attention. Her eyes fluttered open just as he released his breath.

"But there is something more," he whispered.

A hesitant edge made his voice breathy, yet sharp. She tilted her head to the side, regarding him with intense scrutiny.

"What is that?"

His expression had become all lines, like the faceted edge of a crystal. For a moment, she had a hard time recognizing him. And then for a terrible, breathless second, she thought of *that* night. Filled with pain and fire and blood. The night infinitely more agonizing than the loss of her mother, or her best friend Evie, or her brother Jorden. More painful than any trial by fire she'd survived in life's cutting game of politics, intrigue, and deep magic.

A long-buried memory raced to the front of her mind with surprising clarity.

I cannot bear to see its face, she heard herself say, gasping from the pains of childbirth. *Please, take it, Marten, to someone who can care for it better than I.*

As always, Marten had done as she commanded. The angry wail had trailed away, echoing in her mind, taking her heart with it. She shut the memory away, back to the depths where it had survived for all these years. The melancholy and regret swept through her and back out, leaving her on the sturdiness of logic.

Marten said nothing, but he seemed to understand everything.

"You want to tell me about the child," she said. There was no question, no fear. Only determined intention. Marten hadn't admitted it, but she knew that he'd tracked the child all along. It must still be alive. She would have seen his grief otherwise; one of her only comforts in the long, lonely nights.

"It's a blessing that we have this opportunity at all, Mildred. You could easily have died some other way and never known the extent of your own legacy."

"My legacy is the Network."

"In more ways than you'll ever know."

By instinct, she slipped her hand into his. As always, his were soft. Full of the same warmth that he bore deep in his soul. Her breath caught at his touch. It always had.

"Only you can allow it, Milly."

She cleared her throat. A thousand fears whirled through her mind. Would knowing provide relief? Or fester the grief and resentment she'd borne away into the deepest recesses of her heart? The ignorance and denial had been a sort of balm.

Marten turned, his head tilting back. A locked box rested on the highest shelf. She beckoned for it with a silent spell. It drifted down, motes of dust peeling away, and settled in her hands. She opened the box with a second more powerful, intricate spell. Nestled in the small wooden space lay two small scrolls. One bound with a dollop of black ink, one with periwinkle. Binding agreements with Marten and Stella.

She pulled them out. "You're sure about this, Marten?"

"Aren't you?"

Mildred studied the scrolls. The paper had become brittle through the years, and it cracked under her fingertips.

"I suppose I am."

"Our time is short. The dinner has started. Bianca will be here to speak with you soon, as you requested."

Mildred's incantation burned the scrolls with cool fire and tongues of ice. The flimsy parchment turned to ash and billowed to the rug below in gray plumes. By the time it settled, Mildred's mind had already moved on with breathless expectation. She wouldn't go to her grave an ignorant mother after all.

She clutched his hand.

"Who? Who is our child, Marten?"

He blinked.

"I wonder if I even need to tell you, Milly."

He meant that she already knew. But no. She didn't believe in that sort of ethereal thing, where a witch could *sense* the truth before she logically knew the facts. Marten knew that. So he must have meant to consider who she would *dream* of being her child. Someone at once strong, but logical. Powerful, but kind. A mighty witch.

One with power.

Leadership.

The thought struck her all at once, as if it came at her from every direction. It spread like warmth in her head, her heart, and deep in her spine. She sucked in a sharp breath.

"Derek."

Marten's lips lifted. His eyes sparkled. "Yes," he cried. "Yes! Mildred, he is our son."

The trembling fire that swept through her carried all the solidness from her legs. She sank into a chair. *Could it be true?* Her voice came out a raspy plea. "Are you sure?"

"Positive."

"Absolutely certain?"

"I've watched him grow from a distance until he joined the Guardians. From there, I mentored him as much as I could without drawing attention. Now that you know, can you doubt it? How could he belong to anyone else?"

Her mind spun back. It was so easy to see now. Marten's casual indifference about the recruits that year. His attention to Derek that he tried to hide behind a professional facade. *It's a busy year for recruits,* he said.

Ambassadors don't do much. I'm going to help. He studied Derek's every move, speaking with him like an easy friend.

Mildred's thoughts whirled. For the first time since the night she gave him up, tears smarted in her eyes. She stared at the wall, blinking them back.

"All this time," she said. "All this time, I. . . I've spent all this time with him. And I never knew."

Or had she known? Was there something to be said for the fluff of *mother's intuition* after all? This wasn't the first time she hadn't been able to apply the sturdy lines of fact to make sense of her life.

Marten gathered her hands in his.

"What a gift it is, don't you see? You spent years working with your son. You helped him find his calling in life. Whether you knew it or not, you *were* Derek's mother of sorts. Or as influential as one, at any rate."

Mildred swallowed around the heavy lump in her throat.

"Yes."

"Fate has a funny way of helping us out in the end, don't you see? Good witches really do prevail, whether we know it or not." His face fell. "At least, in *some* ways we win."

And in others we die, she finished for him silently.

Marten prattled on with more details, his face suffused with light and pride. She caught a random phrase here and there. *Top of his class, of course . . . Hand fasted a lovely witch. I never met her personally . . .*

Her mind tripped over itself. *Hand fasted a lovely witch.* She straightened. Derek had been hand fasted.

Derek had a child of his own.

"Marten! That means—"

Marten stopped his eager pacing. "Yes! Yes, Mildred. Bianca is our granddaughter."

She swallowed, recalling the fateful Esbat when Bianca had stumbled into the room, barefoot, of all things. Her wild hair. Dove gray eyes. The stubborn set of her jaw and sneaky confidence. Oh, yes. It all made sense now. Bianca had a streak of arrogance that perfectly matched her father.

And perhaps her grandmother.

"Difficult girl," she muttered, looking away. Her eyes stung. "Of course she would be mine."

Marten laughed, gripping her in his arms. The amusement faded from his gaze when he pulled away and pressed her aged, wrinkled palm against his face.

"Do you realize what this means?" Tears choked his voice. She wiped away a tear as it trickled down his cheek.

"Yes," Mildred said. She leaned closer, pressing their foreheads together. "It means that we have a beautiful family, Marten. And that we've had a lovely life with them after all."

His throat bobbed. "Yes, of course. But—"

"There's no one else I would rather give my life for."

He closed his eyes. "I cannot let Mabel kill you. I don't think I can let you go, Milly. Not after all these years."

"You must. For Bianca. For Derek. For our family."

Marten opened his soulful gaze on her, looking like an uncertain, frightened little boy. "Life will be no fun without you here trying to control it, Mildred."

Despite herself, she laughed. A tear trickled free. She couldn't stop it and didn't try. Until Marten joined her beyond the veil of this life, she wouldn't speak with him again after this. The thought would have terrified her, if not for a pair of flashing, defiant gray eyes lingering in her mind.

For Bianca, she thought. *I can do it.*

For her granddaughter.

CHAPTER 2

Marten

At the beginning of *Alkarra Awakening*, *Mildred has just promised Bianca that she'll remove the Inheritance curse once and for all. She knows what it could require of her when she makes that promise to Bianca.*

My curiosity, however, turned to Marten. How would he deal with such a horrible ending? Would he support Mildred in giving up her life to a witch like Mabel?

The following scene was an exploration of that question.

* * *

Air shimmered in the wavering heat of the Western Network. A drop of sweat trickled between Marten's shoulder blades and down his spine. He just wanted to get this horrible meeting over with.

The wiry, trembling witch that stood in front of him resembled a frightened praying mantis. Globe-like eyes. Thin, twiggy limbs that seemed to go on forever.

"My name is Nasir." The servant bowed at the waist. "I welcome you to our Network."

"I appreciate your generosity in receiving me."

Nasir's eyes darted over Marten's face, dropping to encompass his clothes, and then his lips tilted in a wary smile.

"The generosity is not mine, but belongs to Her Greatness."

Marten let that go without comment.

Nasir pointed to his feet. "You must remove your shoes. Her Greatness requires all visitors to be barefoot."

"Of course."

Once Marten finished removing the shoes, Nasir beckoned with a cupped hand. "Come. Our leader should not be kept waiting."

They moved through the subdued, earthy elegance of the Arck—the Western Network castle built into a mountainside of red rock—without a word. Torches illuminated the halls with burnished light, casting copper halos on the wall. Only a few servants moved past, their eyes averted and linen uniforms pristine. The hallways opened up to grotto-like rooms every now and then. The rest lay hidden behind closed doors.

Nasir swept to the right down a hallway, his long robe fluttering. He stopped abruptly, gesturing to the left with an outstretched arm. "Her Greatness's throne room."

Nasir advanced into a cavernous room. Two waterfalls plummeted several stories down the striated walls, creating a small creek covered by glass. On the opposite end of the circular room sat an elegant throne sculpted from differing layers of butter yellow and fiery red rock that rippled from the wall. At the center of a throne, a blithe smile on her beautiful face, sat Mabel.

Nasir dropped to his knees and touched his forehead to the ground.

"Your Greatness. You have a visitor."

Marten waited just behind Nasir, his hands folded in front of him. His arms itched. Sweat beaded on his neck and trickled into his shirt collar. The hot, dusty air of the Western Network made his throat tickle—he longed for a deep, cool glass of water. But he'd take no form of refreshment from Mabel.

He came for only one thing. This exchange wouldn't last long.

Mabel straightened, as if surprised. "Marten? What a lovely surprise."

"Is it?"

Mabel smiled with full, ruby red lips, though the haughtiness in her glacial eyes remained unchanged. Despite the heat, everything about her reminded him of the lakes of black ice boasted by the Southern Network. Cold. Dangerous.

Marten advanced into the room several steps, leaving Nasir on the floor behind him. "A lovely home you have here." He cast his eyes around the room, chilling in its austerity. He couldn't imagine what horrors she enjoyed committing from such a throne.

She waved a hand. "It's a work in progress."

"Indeed."

"You came on behalf of Mildred, I presume?" she drawled. "I can't imagine you'd venture to the Western Network for any personal reasons. Oh, wait. Mildred *is* a personal reason for you, isn't she? Our loyal, well-deserving High Priestess who never breaks tradition."

He ignored her attempt to bait him, but her confidence made him wonder what—or how much—she knew. Soon enough, it wouldn't matter. He swallowed past his dry throat where the words sat, nearly choking him. He could do this. He *had* to do this.

"I came to speak with you about the Inheritance curse you hold over Bianca Monroe," he said.

"Desperate, are you?"

Incredibly so, he thought, recalling all the many avenues he'd already explored to break the horrific curse. The relentless tenacity of an Inheritance curse was one of the many reasons they'd been banned from use in the Central Network. Nothing had come of his attempts, which left him here in the Western Network, at Mabel's throne, just as Mildred had predicted from the beginning. Still. He had to try.

"Not yet," he said. "But there's no reason to reach that extreme."

Mabel inhaled slowly, as if savoring a delicious scent. "What a lovely statement. It reeks of desperation. You're not a very good liar, Ambassador Marten. Isn't that your job as a diplomat?"

"Some would say."

Mabel leaned forward. "Mildred can't figure out a way to remove it, can she? Inheritance curses are quite fickle that way. If you are here, she must be willing to bargain. Then again, there's very little I'm willing to accept in exchange."

"An inevitability we already planned for."

Mabel smiled. "Perhaps you do have some skill as an Ambassador. What is Mildred going to give me if I set that brat free from her curse?"

The words stuck in Marten's throat again. *So many ways to fail,* he thought. Mildred had accepted her fate so readily, but he couldn't. He knew more about Bianca than Mildred could ever dream. A young girl's life rested on the success of this exchange.

Perhaps that was the source of his strength.

Bianca wasn't *just* anyone. How else could he give the life of the woman he'd desperately loved for decades to someone as vile as Mabel?

He pulled in a breath and set his shoulders, forcing the words from deep within his chest, where he'd buried them beneath his heart. Speaking them wrenched his very soul.

"Mildred will exchange Bianca's life for her own."

Mabel's amused expression smoothed out. "Interesting," she murmured. "So she *is* desperate. It appears you are a better liar than you led me to believe, Marten. Well done. I love a good puzzle."

Marten folded his hands behind his back and suppressed the urge to vomit. Nothing about this situation felt right. Mildred's offer gave Mabel too much power. Too much incentive. The passing moments while Mabel considered the offer felt like an eternity.

Mabel stood, the folds of her linen dress falling in graceful waves. The left side rose to her knee and cascaded in layers around a perfectly sculpted leg.

"I'll take the offer on one condition."

He waited, never taking his gaze from hers, but the words turned his blood to ice. *So that's it,* he thought with a fissure of his heart. *Mildred will die.*

Marten cleared his throat. "What is your condition?"

Mabel summoned her *Book of Contracts* from where it lay beside her on the throne and held it in the crook of her left arm.

"I dictate the time and place."

"No."

"You mistake yourself, Marten. This isn't your choice."

"Those terms are unacceptable."

The image of all the ways Mabel could kill Mildred sent his head reeling. He knew this game: Mabel would make it as public and humiliating as possible. Mildred deserved better. If she'd die for her Network—for her granddaughter—at least she should pick the terms.

"Fine," Mabel hissed. "Then Bianca dies."

His mouth bobbed open, silent. Mabel advanced forward several steps, eyes gleaming. "Mildred can't always get what she wants, Marten."

A whirlwind of memories slipped through his mind. Endless nights. Piles of paperwork and letters. Bleary eyes. The birth of their child—and Mildred's tear-filled face afterward. Marten said nothing.

"Mildred can wait. And she will. Because I'm the one who has the power here, not her."

Marten drew in a long, slow breath. Rage swirled in his heart, spinning with a mighty thrust of power. He could attempt to kill Mabel right now: but the certainty that he would fail and die in the attempt held him back. The magic of the Mansfeld Pact wouldn't allow an Ambassador to kill a witch while on a diplomatic mission. Besides, he'd be of no use to his family dead.

Mabel grinned at his silence.

"I'll be in touch when I have my answer." She waved him to the door. "Leave. Don't attempt to return. My West Guards will kill you on sight."

Marten clenched his jaw. *Do your job for Bianca's sake,* he told himself. *For your son, your granddaughter, and your beloved Mildred.*

"I understand and will inform Mildred," he said, maintaining a bland, even tone by sheer willpower.

Marten backed away. Sometime in their conversation, Nasir had disappeared. A layer of protective magic undulated above Marten, silent, but powerful. He couldn't transport home from her throne room, but he wouldn't turn around either. Their gazes locked as he stepped back. A flash of amusement moved across her lazy lips.

Very good, she seemed to be saying. *You're a fool, but not as big a one as I thought.*

Marten stepped into the hall, closed his eyes, and with a heavy heart, transported back to the Central Network. *Mildred,* he thought with a heavy lump in his throat. *My dear Mildred.*

Achieving a diplomatic outcome had never been so devastating.

* * *

Although short, this scene with Derek and Marten wields power.

Marten has known Derek as his son for all of Derek's life, even though Derek has no idea that his biological father checks in with him from time to time. (Or that his biological father is still alive, for that matter.) Derek, an angsty teenager stuck in an orphanage after his adoptive family is killed by disease, finalizes his rebellion by joining the Guardians early at fifteen years old.

Marten eagerly takes advantage of the opportunity to begin mentoring his son. This scene is how that relationship began.

* * *

Presenting a sword to any inexperienced witch posed dangers; but handing them out to pubescent teenage boys—some of whom hadn't even reached their seventeenth birthdays—was another matter entirely.

Marten, Ambassador for the Central Network, watched the new Guardian recruits with a practiced eye. Nearly all of them shuffled around in wide-eyed disbelief. Their spiny, gangly limbs seemed to go on forever.

Immature boys without much strength, he thought, *tsking* under his breath. *Some can barely lift their half-armor.*

The recruits didn't look at all like they could have passed the infamous Wringer and made it this far into training.

Except for one.

Derek Black, the orphan who had snuck into this group of Guardians at fifteen, had already made quite a name for himself. His fast smile and flattering tongue distracted the female witch in charge of the paperwork. She hadn't noticed or checked for enchanted dates on his paperwork. Despite his youth, Derek had used a complicated spell to force a Network scroll to lie about his age—a spell most adults couldn't do. Marten could have reported him to Liam, the Head of Guardians, but couldn't bring himself to get the boy in trouble. Derek needed an outlet. His personality and talent had been too big for that orphanage for years.

Marten kept a wary eye out for him but couldn't locate the dark hair and stormy eyes. He'd seen firsthand Derek running barefoot amongst the lions of Letum Wood like a savage. When the lions attacked, Derek transported away, laughing. He snuck out of the orphanage to climb trees, lifting heavy limbs and swimming in the mossy ponds to amuse himself out of boredom. Such a hellion would have immense skill in the Guardians. Not because of talent, or anything as ethereal as that.

Because of heritage.

"Derek," he murmured, as if to the solitary piles of swords surrounding him. "My courageous, fierce boy."

The uncertain, chattering group of recruits yesterday had transformed into quiet, sober boys today. Short hair cuts. New clothes. Weary eyes from a long night. They had been sorted, given uniforms, and thoroughly tested through a long run in the forest. Now they stood in the lower bailey in perfect formation. Liam strolled amongst them, his voice bounding off the stone walls.

"Every contingent is assigned to a Captain specializing in a certain skill. Archery, sword fighting, hand-to-hand combat, apothecary spells, and leadership. Each contingent will have six weeks in each course to learn . . ."

Liam's voice droned into the background as Marten slid deeper into thought. All the recruits blurred together from this distance. Steeling himself for another interminable wait—he'd watched Derek from a distance for almost sixteen years, he could wait twenty more minutes—he leaned back against the wall and sighed.

Twenty minutes later, the six contingents of new recruits broke apart in a fan, hustling to different places in the lower and upper baileys. One contingent headed his direction. Marten's stomach somersaulted.

The long-awaited moment had arrived.

A witch transported next to him, jangling his already irritated nerves. Marten clenched his fist as Liam coughed right next to his ear, slamming a heavy hand into his shoulder.

"Any questions, Marten?"

Liam's grizzled blond hair sprouted like the roots of an upturned plant in the sweltering summer heat. Sweat dripped down the sides of his round face. His nose stuck out in a knobby knuckle.

"No, thank you." Marten shook his head. "Your instructions were suffi-cient. I'll match the boys to their swords first, review the basics, and then split into one-on-one instruction periods beginning tomorrow morning."

Liam snorted as he stepped away. "Good. Give 'em a hard time. If you make 'em cry, I'll give you twenty sacrans. And thanks for the help. If there's anyone that can teach sword fighting, it's you."

He transported away just as Marten's contingent closed the final gap, still in formation. They halted ten paces from him.

"Contingent Leader," Marten called. "Present yourself."

Two feet approached with a distinct, heavy cadence they'd been taught the night before. New recruits were usually frightened enough to behave the first two weeks. But with a boy like Derek? One never knew.

A sweaty, thick-haired boy stood before him. Marten knew the defiant glint in Derek's eye the moment he saw it. Derek had not only wormed his way into the Guardians at fifteen, but he'd been chosen as Contingent Leader.

Impressive, Marten thought.

"Contingent Leader?" he asked.

Derek's fist thumped into his own chest in the Guardian salute. "Derek Black, sir. I lead Contingent Balto."

A pair of hazel eyes underneath a mop of freshly-cut, coffee-colored hair met Marten's gaze. They had a hardened edge, like most orphans. A continual invitation to test their mettle. A pang of guilt ached in his gut, but Marten pushed it aside. *We didn't have a choice,* he wanted to say. *We wanted you.*

But Derek didn't even know that his biological parents still lived. Marten comforted himself with the ugly truth: Derek had strength that would never have been unlocked without the trials he'd faced. Good things came from difficult circumstances.

"Hold out your arm, Derek Black."

He obeyed. Nothing about Derek seemed impressively different at first. But he'd set himself apart during the Wringer with one of the fastest finish times ever achieved. Not only that, but Marten suspected Derek had filched something from a Captain on a dare, earning the loyalty of many recruits.

Forcing himself to concentrate on the task at hand, Marten studied Derek's figure, still skinny from orphanage life. The sword Marten had commissioned would fit him perfectly. A bevy of swords, differing in length and weight, waited in the bins. But Derek wasn't just any witch. He deserved better than just *any* sword.

Marten ordered Derek to heft a few swords, testing them in the open space while the rest of the contingent watched. Derek demonstrated a silent, powerful respect for the weapons. Marten observed with pride Derek's natural grip, strong forearms, gritty determination.

Definitely his son.

"This one feels good." Derek flexed his hand around a sword that had been through several Guardian recruits. The edges had chipped. It needed a good polish and sharpening, something Derek would learn to do throughout Marten's six-week course.

"No," Marten said. "That's not a good sword for you."

A skeptical eyebrow rose on Derek's youthful face. He opened his mouth, then shut it again. His nostrils flared, but he said nothing. Marten reached for a sword tucked against the side of the bin. He lifted it by the hilt, extending it for Derek's inspection.

"I'm no Ensis," Marten said, "but I'd say this may be the perfect sword for you."

Derek's brow furrowed. "Sir?"

"Just try it."

Derek studied it for a full ten seconds before he accepted the blade, running the tips of his calloused fingers over the metal. Marten held his breath. He'd commissioned the sword specifically for Derek a year before, from a witch who lived on the fringes of society and rarely ventured in.

The sword had twice the strength as the other standard-issue Guardian swords and metal that rarely rusted or turned brittle. Next to an expert Ensis blade, it was the best sword that currency could buy in the Central Network.

By sight, nothing separated it from the other Guardian swords, of course. Derek would never know that he held a blade worth three times what his cohorts used. But with luck, it would endure throughout his whole career. And Marten swelled at this fledgling moment of being part of his son's life. Derek pumped the sword up and down, swinging it in wide arcs.

"It's light, sir."

"Yes. Some Guardians prefer a heavier blade, but I think you'll do best without. Heavy blades have their place, but not with you, I think."

Derek hefted it in one hand. He couldn't wield it the way the sword deserved yet, but that would come. Derek wrapped both hands around it, his lips puckered in thought.

"Light, but durable," Marten continued. "A fitting blade for a natural-born leader."

Derek's eyes snapped to Marten, then back to the sword. Marten straightened.

"It's a bit long for you now, but you have some growing to do still, I imagine. At your age, anyway."

Derek ignored that comment.

"I will be teaching one-on-one classes with the Guardian recruits this time around," Marten continued. "You and I will get to know that sword very well."

Derek rolled his wrist, spinning the blade in a wide circle. The sharp sides whistled slightly with the movement.

"Yes, sir. Thank you."

Derek hadn't taken his eyes off the weapon, giving Marten a chance to study him up close. Physically, he held no resemblance to Mildred except a fiery expression and the regal set of his shoulders. A hint of Marten's brother lingered in Derek's eyes. His strong legs, wide shoulders, and dark hair hailed from his family. Derek would never know it, but he looked just like his grandfather.

Marten pulled out of his thoughts to find Derek peering at him, one eye narrowed.

"Is something wrong, sir?"

Marten cleared his throat.

"No. Sheathe it, and strap it to your hips. Send the next witch. I will see you tomorrow bright and early for your first lesson. As Contingent Leader, you will be first. I expect you to be at the top of your contingent in terms of performance."

Derek re-sheathed the sword, strapped it to his hips, saluted, and departed. Marten watched him go with a tickle of amusement.

What a familiar swagger the boy had.

CHAPTER 3

Derek

A lthough *Marie and Bianca were close, Derek's influence really sculpted Bianca.*

I created him in the image of my husband. Derek will always be special because, in many ways, he is my favorite.

For some reason, it was important for me to know what happened during—and after—Bianca's birth. Marie was in a difficult position: if she has a girl, her family curse will continue. If she has a boy, the curse will be broken.

I imagined Derek, officially helpless just like any father, wouldn't take kindly to watching Marie suffer and not being able to fix it.

A frightening time for anyone.

* * *

Derek stared up at the ceiling, one arm propped behind his head, and tracked a dancing cobweb.

Outside, the rain drizzled on the thatched roof. The air smelled musty, like wet reeds and hay. Marie lay next to him, curled on her right side, lost to sleep. Yet, her nose wrinkled; her forehead furrowed. He leaned down, pressing a gentle kiss to her temple. She stirred, but didn't awaken.

The pregnancy had been difficult, but the added weight of the Inheritance curse had been intolerable. She hadn't moved from bed for almost a week, unable to bear the pain in her ankles and hips. He glanced at the potion bottle on the side of the bed, then back to the clock. Not time yet.

The worst of it will fade in the days after the baby is born, Hazel reassured him daily. *I went through the same thing.*

But he heard what Hazel didn't say. That the pain of the curse would flare up with new strength from now on. Marie's hands would ache. Her knees give out. Her body tremble with pain after standing for too long. Perhaps it would be manageable for a few years, but eventually Marie would endure constant agony twice that of her mother.

Marie shifted, rubbing her legs against the sheets as she sought a comfortable position. Derek tucked a stray piece of hair behind her ear, trapping it between two fingers. The silky strands ran across his skin, supple as water. Her eyes fluttered open.

"Ah," he whispered. "She awakes."

She turned away, a hand clapped over her mouth. "Don't talk to me," she said from behind her fingers. "My breath smells terrible in the morning."

He stretched out next to her, laying a heavy arm across her torso and molding her body into his. He nuzzled her neck.

"You smell like the first day I met you."

"Liar."

"Cynic."

A smile crossed Marie's lips. The sound of a clattering pan came from the kitchen, followed by a slamming cupboard. Marie propped up on an elbow, a curtain of black hair sweeping down her face.

The good gods, she was beautiful.

"Mama's already getting breakfast?" she murmured through a yawn. "But it's so early."

He didn't tell her it was hours past their normal wake time. What did it matter? They had the whole day to be lazy while listening to the rain and planning for the baby. Marie started to stand, but Derek kept her pinned. "I should help her," she said. "It's so hard on her hands—"

"Definitely. You're definitely going to be helpful in there, bumping into everything with your belly and tripping over your own feet."

Marie giggled. "My feet are several sizes bigger now, you know."

"You could swap shoes with any Guardian."

"It's all your fault."

"I'll give you my dress shoes as recompense."

Marie sank back into the mattress with a groan, kneading her fingers into the small of her back.

"Ugh. I feel like I'm still going to be pregnant for my thirtieth birthday."

"In that case, we'll need to get you a new bed."

She pushed him away and rolled onto her back with a grimace. Derek gave her space, propping his head on a hand.

"Are you trying to tell me that my breath is as revolting as yours?" he asked.

"No." She sucked in a breath. "My back hurts."

A knock at the back door rang through the little cottage. Marie froze, her eyes widening. Derek slipped off the bed, padded silently across the room, and lingered near the door.

The high, shrill voice of Jenine Clovis pealed through the air. His lips curled up over his teeth. Jenine. The self-declared town gossip of Bickers Mill. She'd been prodding around for a while, attempting to find out who the father of Marie's baby was. Marie had borne the gossipmongers with utmost patience, but she refused to tell them anything.

Which only made them more rabid.

"Who is it?" Marie asked, struggling to sit up.

"That old hag."

Hazel opened the front door, but not much. Undertones of their conversation drifted through the air, but he didn't strain to hear much of it. Within minutes, Hazel closed the door, her curving shoulders slumping with a sigh of relief. Derek pushed away, reaching for his shirt, but stopped. Marie's face had scrunched.

"Marie?"

She reached for his hand and squeezed it. "Derek, I think . . . something is wrong."

"Wrong?"

Marie bit her bottom lip. "Call my mother. Now. I-I think I'm in labor."

Years of training as a Guardian, a Captain, and then a Protector had honed his instincts and emotions into razor-sharp control. But all of that stalled. His mind looped around that word over and over again. *Labor. Labor. Labor.*

Now?

"Don't we have more time?" he asked. "I thought you weren't due for another week or two. I—"

"Now, Derek!"

He spun back to the door. "Hazel!"

Hazel entered the room seconds later, hobbling on arthritic feet. She cast one look at Marie, placed a hand on her belly, and shooed Derek out.

"Give us a minute," she sang, shutting the door firmly in his face with a spell. "This is my territory from here on out, not yours."

"But—"

"She'll be fine. Just fine."

Derek pressed his forehead into the door and closed his eyes.

Don't let anything happen to her, Hazel, he thought. *She's all I have left to care about.*

No. She's all I really have.

* * *

The hours dragged on in agonizing torture.

Marie went from talking, to silence, to moans, and finally to an occasional weak cry. He paced. Swore. Fetched water. Weeded the garden. Fixed a broken cupboard. All the while, the song of Marie's pain wavered in the background. For the hundredth time, he went back to the bedroom door.

"Let me see her, Hazel. Please, let me be—"

"Go for the midwife. We're close. We're very close."

He pushed away from the door, summoning the magic in his mind. In all his life, he'd never been so bloody helpless.

The quiet, aged midwife followed with just a nod. She'd taken a vow of secrecy weeks before; she would not betray his secret. They transported back to the little cottage right as Marie started to groan. The midwife bustled into the room, the murmur of voices followed, and the cottage fell back into strained silence.

Suddenly, evening had come. He paced through Marie's tremulous cries as the next wave came, dragging a hand through his hair. He pounded on the bedroom door with his fist.

"How much longer?"

"Soon, Derek. Very soon."

"You said that hours ago."

"Let him in," Marie said. "Please let him in."

He grabbed the handle and shoved inside without Hazel's permission, dropping to his knees at her bedside. "I'm here, Marie."

A wavering smile broke through the pain. He threaded their fingers together and draped an arm around her shoulders. The midwife worked at the end of the bed, moving Marie's ankles and speaking under her breath. The room was comfortably warm, draped with towels, fresh linens, and a pot of steaming water. Hazel inspected a gleaming knife by the fire.

Marie pressed her pale, sweaty forehead to his.

"I'm so tired," she whispered.

"I wish I could take it from you, Marie. I would take it all. You would feel no pain."

She put her fingertips to his face. A tear trickled out of her eye.

"I don't know if I can do this."

"You can." He pushed ropes of wet hair out of her face. "You must. Because we're going to have a child. A perfect, healthy child."

She laughed, half-sobbing.

"A boy," she said. "It must be a boy."

Derek kissed her. "Whatever it is, it will be perfect, because it's a part of you. You can do this, Marie. I know you can do this."

"Next round," the midwife said as Marie tensed. "Just breathe through it, Marie. You're almost there, love."

Half an hour later, the baby slipped into the world with quiet, steady cries. The midwife held the bloody, slippery thing as Hazel wrapped it in a fresh, warm sheet. Marie's arms lifted, shaking.

"A girl!" Hazel cried. "Oh, Marie. A perfect little girl."

Hazel passed the little bundle to Marie, who pressed her against her chest with misty eyes. The squalling, bloody, oddly-colored child calmed on Marie's skin, her swollen eyes slitted shut.

"The good gods, it's a girl," he said. "She's a perfect baby girl, Marie. Look at our beautiful daughter."

A rush of fear darted through Derek even as he felt a throb of irrevocable love for his wife.

A girl. We had a baby girl. We have a daughter.

The curse will continue.

He shoved the thoughts aside, determined to enjoy the first moments with this new, incredible life. The thoughts departed, but not far. They hovered like a pesky fly, just out of reach, while the midwife finished her work. Marie nudged the baby onto her breast. Derek watched, awed by how little—how complete—the child had come out.

"What should we name her?" he asked. "It has to have a lot of vowels."

"Vowels?"

"You know, for yelling. She'll be running through the forest like a hellion, and we'll have to call out after her, you know."

Marie chuckled softly, running a finger down the downy softness of the baby's hair. "What about Bianca?"

He ran the name through his mind.

"Not just Bianca. Bianca Marie."

Marie shot him a pained, rueful smile. "What if she doesn't want to be named after her mother?"

"We'll add it to the list of reasons she'll hate us when she's a teenager."

"Bianca Marie," Marie murmured. "I think it's lovely."

"Marie, this—"

Marie shook her head. "No," she whispered, voice thick with emotion. "I cannot speak of it, Derek. Not now. It's not important. The only thing that matters is protecting her from it. We have seventeen years."

A shot of protectiveness nearly overwhelmed him. He pressed his lips to Marie's thick raven hair.

"Of course, Marie. Of course."

Exhausted, Marie lay her head back against the pillow, wincing as the baby worked out how to suckle. Soon, the babe gave up. Her lips slackened, plump and sparkling. She twitched, releasing a vigorous cry.

"Take her." Hazel nudged him toward the child. "While we help Marie clean up."

"Me?"

Hazel's eyes sparkled. "Yes. You. You're the father, aren't you?"

"Er . . . yes."

Marie carefully passed the baby to him. He wrapped his arms around the frail bundle and carefully lowered into a rocking chair. Derek touched her tiny fingers, pulling the blanket more tightly around her until every inch of skin was covered except her face.

"Bianca," he whispered, "we'll win, baby girl. No one is going to take you from me. No curse, no witch. Nothing will be stronger than you and me." His eyes darted to Marie. "Except maybe your Mama. She's stubborn, you know."

He closed his eyes and pressed a kiss to Bianca's wispy hair.

"Nothing."

* * *

Mildred's appointment of Derek as Head of Protectors turned the tide for the Central Network against an unknown enemy that lurked in the shadows—although that wouldn't be obvious until later years. When the next scene opens, Derek has been a Protector for several years under a witch named Jeramy, the current Head of Protectors. Derek and Marie have been hand fasted for three years. Bianca is two years old. No one knows about his family.

In the following scenes, you'll meet a witch named Andrei. His novel, *The Swordmaker*, is slated for publication as part of *The Historical Collection*.

* * *

The silence seemed to cling to the snow.

Evergreen boughs, heavy with ice, drooped to the ground. Snow drifts higher than Derek's hip rolled through the loosely packed forest. The tip of his nose—no doubt red—prickled every now and then. Despite the cold, the air was dry. The snow like dust. Too cold to melt, it just whirled around, catching him in the eyes. Twilight had fallen, masking the winter wonderland in strange shadows and shifting light. If it hadn't been so eerily quiet, Derek could have appreciated the quiet majesty of such a forgotten place.

"There." A witch named Andrei pointed to a cottage in the distance. "That's the place. Ve have been vatching for days. Just in case."

Derek tracked Andrei's arm, which pointed to a slipshod shanty in the distance. The boards, warped from exposure and age, seemed to trip over each other, some lying at haphazard angles, others separated with large gaps. Whoever lived inside was likely dead from the cold.

"You're sure?" Derek asked.

"Yes."

"It'll collapse the moment we go inside."

Andrei lifted an eyebrow.

"Not everything is as it seems."

Andrei's thick accent, slant nose, and teardrop shaped eyes made him a prime example of a Southern Network witch. He wore thick pelts and furs across his shoulders with pride. Despite the danger of being outside on such a night—predators grew hungriest in the winter—he showed no concern. His thick pants were tied with sturdy twine and rumored to be reinforced with enchanted strands of special silk.

A witch transported into place on Derek's left.

"Not much of a place, is it?" Jeramy, the Head of Protectors and Derek's boss, murmured. His eyes darted through the forest, the ground, the shanty, and everything else. A dusting of snow glittered in his red hair. Like Derek, he wore the fur caps and woolen coats of the Southern Network. Instead of blending in, they looked more out of place than ever next to Andrei.

"Trust me. This is the place." Andrei's eyes glittered. He motioned to the dilapidated structure. "They take our young girls. Two are missing. Some have run away and not come back. One, Viktoria, vas just taken last night. My tribe is too frightened to act."

"Why?"

Andrei's nose scrunched. "They believe the gods punish them for not obeying the High Priest. That more punishment vill come."

Jeramy hitched an eyebrow. "Do you believe that?"

Andrei scowled. "Ve vant these bad vitches gone. You must do this. Our Netvork does nothing. Ve are not strong enough vith magic."

"Your Network has done nothing?" Derek asked. It had been a stroke of luck that he'd stumbled on Andrei hunting in the forest that morning. After hours of stumbling around, transporting from place to place in vain, Derek had believed he'd never find the missing girls. Then he saw Andrei peering at him from the trees. A few well-placed questions later and Andrei had guided him to the right place.

This place.

Andrei shook his head in a sharp motion, cutting back and forth.

"The Netvork does nothing for the tribes. They hate us. They lie. They take advantage of my vitches and try to take our silk and swords."

"The Network is the one buying the girls," another Protector, Nathaniel, muttered from behind Derek. Nathaniel's invisibility incantation disappeared. His umber skin, smooth and rich, hid him in the approaching night.

Andrei stepped back, startled, and studied Nathaniel. His thin eyes narrowed. "Is this true?"

Jeramy confirmed with a nod.

"Nathaniel has been following the buyers for a week now," he said. "Your local leaders are funding the kidnappings. We haven't been able to track them to your High Priest, however. I can't confirm that he knows he has witches crossing the Network border to steal our girls."

Andrei's wide nostrils flared. For a second, his face flushed red. He paused, allowing it to fade.

Derek stepped back, observing, while Jeramy explained their plans to invade the shanty and save the girls. Every now and then, Andrei inserted a comment or direction. The common language worked well. Even though Derek mostly knew the *Yazika* language of the Southern Network, Jeramy hadn't directed him to use it.

"We'll act once it's fully dark," Jeramy said. "An hour, give or take. Nathaniel, stay on the perimeter. Leave no tracks."

Nathaniel glanced at the trees.

"Acknowledged, Brother," he said before fading into another invisibility spell. The slightest wisp of snow drifted from the top of an evergreen nearby immediately after. Derek would have laughed if it weren't so cold.

Jeramy clapped a hand on Derek's shoulder.

"Derek, go to Andrei's so we know where to transport. Once we recover the girls, I'll follow your magic there." Jeramy turned to Andrei. "We'll transport them to your place." His eyes slid back to the shanty. "Better build up the fire."

Andrei nodded.

"I vill do this."

Jeramy's hand fell. His eyes locked with Derek. "I'm going to update the High Priestess. I have a feeling we'll need apothecaries. Meet me back here within the hour."

Jeramy disappeared with a whisper of magic. Andrei caught Derek's eye and motioned him closer with a jerk of his head.

"You are the vitch that discovered this problem, no?"

Derek hesitated. It wasn't that simple, but it wasn't that complicated either. Over the last month, he'd been researching reports of young girls in the Southern Covens of the Central Network going missing. It had taken him weeks of scouting, tracking, following hunches, and waiting in the cold forest, hoping to see *something*, until he'd finally caught sight of the criminals and followed them here. The scheme had been bigger than he'd expected, encompassing not just Central Network girls, but tribal girls as well. Perhaps more.

"Yes." Derek nodded. "I stumbled on it."

"I make swords." Andrei held up thick, knotty hands. "The best swordmaker that you vill find. Come. See them. Perhaps I have something for you. You vill not regret."

* * *

Derek followed Andrei through deep drifts without a word, soaking in the strange silence of the forest. Snow spiraled from a smoky sky in lazy circles. Every other step, Derek sank to his thigh. Andrei seemed to float on top of the drifts, aided by his wide netted shoes and lean legs.

A cabin made of hewn logs, nestled deep in the thick, silent pines, came into view half an hour later. Rough shingles layered down the steep pitch of the roof, leaving room for a generous attic. Evergreens loomed high and close around the cabin. The thought of a warm fire made Derek's fingers ache.

"This vay."

Andrei led him around the back where a hidden shanty, not unlike the one Derek would soon invade, waited. Andrei used an incantation to blow the accumulated snow away from the door and then shoved it open. Derek eyed it warily, but followed Andrei inside.

A blast of warmth welcomed them. Derek stopped abruptly. Despite the shoddy appearance from the outside, a full blacksmith shop filled a spacious interior. Bellows. Healthy fire. A stack of wood that rose all the way to the ceiling. Swords crowded every wall, nook, and cranny in glittering, metallic shades.

Andrei spread his hands. "My shop. Touch nothing."

"Impressive."

Andrei waved it off. The door closed behind them. He shucked off his heavy coat, revealing a silk shirt of deepest black. It flowed in long, beautiful lines down his lean arms and slender frame.

"Ve cast spells to make it look not-so-impressive outside." A brief flash of teeth illuminated Andrei's face in a rare, toothy grin. "Less taxes. The tax vitches don't come in. Just look."

Derek advanced into the room, eyeing the open rafters where strips of metal hung, glinting in the firelight. Tallow candles illuminated sconces along the walls, casting warm curlicues of light throughout the space.

"Do a lot of witches around here use those spells?" he asked.

"Most of the vitches in my tribe, yes. Others, too."

"Do you think the kidnappers are in your tribe?"

"No."

In the back of his mind, Derek accessed a familiar, often-used spell that only the Brotherhood of Protectors knew. It gave them the ability to send thoughts to each other without speaking. The closest approximation was transporting a thought into the mind of another witch. It gave no access to their mind, just the ability to mentally speak.

Things may not be as they seem at the shanty. He sent the thought to Jeramy and Nathaniel. *Likely magic on the outside. Could be different inside.*

Within seconds, Jeramy responded with a thought of his own. It came into Derek's head clear as a bell and quiet as a whisper.

Nathaniel, look into it. I'm just about to speak with the High Priestess before I return for the raid.

Nathaniel's voice immediately followed.

Understood, Brother. Will report in ten. All quiet here.

The warmth beckoned to Derek, so he stepped closer to the stone fireplace. Andrei stood at a wall cluttered with gleaming metal shafts. Wooden pegs held the various swords in place. The sultry room left space for Andrei to move freely while Derek hovered close to the flames, thinking.

After a minute of silence had passed while Andrei shifted through the room, mumbling to the walls, he turned to Derek.

"I have a sword for your daughter."

One second passed after Derek heard the word *daughter*, registered what it meant, snatched the front of Andrei's shirt, and slammed him into a wall. Before he could demand an explanation—how could a witch like Andrei know about Bianca when Jeramy didn't even know?—seven glinting swords pressed against his neck with the cool kiss of metal.

Derek froze.

How had Andrei pulled *seven* swords in such a short time? No one outside the Brotherhood had ever bested him with a weapon.

Andrei's eyes tapered into slits. "If you move, you vill die."

Derek opened his hand, releasing him. Andrei stepped back. The swords remained, pressing against Derek's skin with the lightest of pressure. Andrei studied him for a moment, his mahogany eyes dark and wary. A light, strange thrum of magic seemed to reverberate in the back of Derek's mind. One he'd never distinguished before.

Well, well, Derek thought, eyeing the swords. *How very interesting*.

"So . . . you're an Ensis," Derek murmured, swallowing. One sword retreated into Andrei's palm; the rest returned to empty slots along the wall. "A Swordmaker using the ancient magic."

Andrei held out a hand, his face a blank slate. Derek inferred his lack of rebuttal as agreement. "Your sword," Andrei said. "I vant to meet it."

Derek had a loyal sword that he'd trained with since he started the Guardians—a surprisingly well-built, agile thing that he'd been given when he joined. Most Guardian swords were functional, but not invincible, and yet his had never failed him. A strange puzzle he'd pondered often.

Derek pulled it free. Andrei grabbed it by the hilt and shuffled across the room with expert footwork, swinging the sword in wide arcs. Once finished, he returned it without a word.

"Can you tell anything about it?" Derek asked, driving it back into the sheath. Andrei shook his head once.

"Doesn't speak."

The Ensis, or Swordmakers of Southern Network legend, used an ancient magic to communicate with their swords. The swords responded like living things. According to lore, only certain witches had the talent, and even fewer knew enough to explore it. Rumors of the Ensis had faded in recent centuries with the oppression of the Southern Network leadership.

"You have an impressive workspace here." Derek glanced around. A rumpled blanket and flat pillow lay in the far corner. "Do you stay here much?"

"I live here."

"Here?"

"Yes."

"What about that house outside? It seemed quite large."

Andrei acted as if he hadn't heard. His smooth brow had furrowed into a pile of lines. He tapped his teeth together, alternately mumbling and jerking his head back and forth, as if speaking with someone—or some*thing*. Derek couldn't explain it, but he had the distinct impression that Andrei spoke to the swords.

Finally, Andrei held out a hand and whispered something so quietly Derek couldn't hear. A smaller, shorter sword hanging near the ceiling lifted itself free and drifted into Andrei's hand. He studied it, nodded in satisfaction, and extended it to Derek.

"This is Viveet. She belongs to your daughter now."

Derek pulled the sword from the sheath. The blade rang as it slid free. Andrei's placid expression didn't waver. Derek had no reason to trust him, but he did.

"And how do you know I have a daughter?" he asked as he swung

Viveet through the air. She sliced it without a breath of resistance. Andrei nodded to the sword with a shrug.

"The sword knows."

Etchings in the metal shone bright blue, climbing in an intricate pattern of leaves and twisting vines.

"They all know vat they vant. I tried to make it something else, but no." He sliced a hand through the air. "The sword vanted the leaves. So, I made leaves. She vill be bright, more agile, vith your daughter."

Derek ran the pad of his thumb along the edge of the blade. The metal felt cool and certain. Hummed, almost. The color spiraled up through the sword with twists, hidden nuances of color and light and hue. When he touched it, it felt like Letum Wood. Home. Safety. He knew, but couldn't explain, that this was not his sword.

Andrei gestured to it.

"The sword is patient. It vill vait until your daughter is ready."

Derek inspected it again. The blade was light, short—just the size for Marie, which meant it would eventually be perfect for Bianca.

"How old is your daughter?"

Derek hesitated. "She just turned two."

"Ah. You vill start her with a shield first?"

"Of course."

Andrei nodded once. "I vill trust you, then. You vill be good with this. You teach your daughter the vays of the shield, and then the sword."

"Andrei, I can't just take it."

"You must." He shrugged. "It is not for me to decide. The sword has decided. I obey."

Derek bowed only his head, holding it in place for three seconds before straightening. Andrei closed his eyes to accept the gesture of gratitude. Derek strapped the sword to his belt.

"Bianca will cherish it."

"She vill. Viveet vill require it. Now go back to your vitches. Find Viktoria. I vill vait here."

* * *

Less than an hour later, the rough animal hair of Derek's fur cap itched. The sharp sting of winter bit at his nose again. Cold seeped into his boots, attacking his toes. He longed to return to Andrei's shop. Or, better yet, to Marie, where the fire was bright but her smile brighter. He tried to ignore all the discomforts by setting his mind on the mission.

Get in. Save the girls. Get out.

Nothing had changed in the last hour, according to Nathaniel's report. He detected no magic in use around the shanty. No smoke streamed from the chimney, which concerned Derek. Were the girls inside without heat? Layers of snow, thick as frosting on the sparse evergreens, sparkled in the moonlight. Flakes fell in torrents now.

Jeramy appeared at Derek's side, his gaze hooded, so not even the whites of his green eyes showed.

"No magic in use to protect it from intruders," Nathaniel said from just behind them. "I haven't sensed any active spells, anyway."

"Me either," Derek murmured in agreement. The forest lay as dormant as a tomb. The unlikely possibility existed that a different, unfamiliar magic was in place, but he still would have been able to sense *something*. Or so he hoped. Yet, he'd felt nothing at Andrei's, and his shop was full of active magic. Unfortunately, Derek had learned long before that even being a well-trained Protector did not equate with being invincible. He didn't like the variables of this equation, but the decision wasn't his to make.

"I think they're rookies." Jeramy rubbed a hand over his eyes. "Incompetent. Trying to make a little currency on the black market."

"Rookies are wild cards," Nathaniel said.

Jeramy set his hands on his hips. "Indeed. There's no telling what they'll do."

Nathaniel punched his chest. "It's bloody cold out here. Let's go. I hate the Southern Network."

Derek silently cast a spell. A powerful, invisible layer of protection rippled down his arms, torso, and legs like a warm rush of water. It would provide at least twenty minutes of defense from most known, dangerous spells.

"Just like always, brothers," Jeramy said. "In and out. We were never here. Derek, get your hands on the scumbag. Andrei said he'll take it from there. Southern Network tribal justice is sufficient, I believe. They'll disembowel the witch alive and hang him from a tree for their gods to torture in the next life."

The three of them fell into their respective duties without another word. Derek transported to a rickety side door. Jeramy to the main door. Nathaniel disappeared underneath an invisibility spell. He would remain outside as backup while monitoring the perimeter. Derek and Jeramy would storm the shanty at the same time.

The magic of their protective spells and invisibility came with seamless, nearly undetectable strength. Despite years of experience, Derek's heart still pounded as he stared at the door, prepping the magic in his mind. His fingers tingled. His sharpened vision caught every detail.

Jeramy gave the signal.

As one, they used incantations to jerk both doors off their hinges, casting them into the snow with dull *thuds,* then rushed inside the one-room shanty.

Six girls lay on the floor in a limp pile of bodies. One girl stared at the ceiling, blinking slowly. Another's head lolled to the side, her breathing slight and infrequent. White powder dusted their faces. Bright pink circles flushed the apple of their cheeks. Their lips had been painted a bright, cherry red. One of them wore a wig of bright white hair, which had gone askew. All of their hands and ankles were tied, the skin underneath rubbed raw. A hazy smoke filled the air. Not another soul could be seen.

Six, Derek thought to Jeramy and Nathaniel, crouching next to the girls. *There were only supposed to be three.*

Jeramy swung a sword into all the open spaces, lest a witch attempt to sneak by with an undetected invisibility spell.

Andrei mentioned disappearing runaways, Nathaniel said.

Derek tugged a wig loose, revealing a girl with olive skin and thick brown locks. The younger girl next to her looked like a sister. *These two look like they're from the Eastern Network. This must be even bigger than we thought.*

Was it confirmed that the witch responsible for the kidnappings is here? Jeramy asked.

No, Nathaniel responded. *Just that the girls were here.*

Jeramy cursed under his breath, barely making a sound in the still house. *We can't leave the Southern Network for good until the witch returns. We'll get the girls to safety, but the mission isn't complete until the witch is taken.*

Agreed, Derek said.

While Derek felt for pulses—all were slight and faint—Jeramy kicked aside a moldy straw mattress. Paper lanterns, no bigger than Derek's palm, littered the floor. The room smelled foul, with a pungent sweetness beneath. Except for a tattered dress in the corner and discarded tins filled with crimson goo, the room lay empty.

Derek pulled the top girl off the pile. A fake wig of snowy hair fell away, revealing long blonde tresses. He pulled one of her eyes open. Blue. Stacey Vartan. One of the missing girls from the Southern Covens. His stomach churned. She wasn't much older than twelve.

He thought of Bianca at home, her soft black hair, wide gray eyes. She was just walking now, waving her chubby fists. The thought of someone doing something so atrocious as *this* made his rage boil. He carefully pulled Stacey off the ground and into his arms. Jeramy lifted a girl that fit the description of Jasmin, the other missing witch from the Southern Covens.

I'll follow you, Jeramy thought to Derek.

The darkness and pressure of a transportation spell took Derek's breath away. He didn't maintain the invisibility spell during transporting, and as he released it, a surge of power made the annoying pressure of transportation fade more rapidly. Less than ten seconds later, the High Priestess stared at him with tight lips.

"Good. That must be Stacey." She nodded once. "Where is Jeramy?"

"On his way."

Two apothecaries rushed to him. He transferred her into their arms. Stacey's head rolled back as the apothecaries whisked her to a bed near the fire. The High Priestess motioned with a jerk of her head.

"Good work. Leave."

Jeramy appeared, a body in his arms, just as Derek finished his transportation spell to return—including the addition of emerging from the transportation spell invisible again. Once he returned to the hovel, he paused. With both doors gone, the hazy air had cleared. It felt as brisk inside as outside. The four remaining girls had started to stir. The one from the Eastern Network sat upright, blinking, as if dazed. A thought from Nathaniel entered his mind.

Something's changing.

Derek already felt it. A slight twinge in the air. *Keep monitoring,* he thought. *I'll be back.*

The Eastern Network girl groaned as Derek plucked her from the pile and transported away just as Jeramy returned, reaching for her sister. When Derek returned to the shanty, only two witches remained. One sat upright, blinking. Her coiling ropes of silky black hair and narrow eyes fit the description Andrei had given of Viktoria. A smoky, drugged cloud filled her eyes, but her movements appeared purposeful. The last girl, a short, tiny little thing, no older than ten, hadn't stirred.

Strengthening, Nathaniel thought to him. *Whatever it is. I can't tell. It's changing.*

The low, strange percussion, so unlike anything he'd ever felt, forced Derek to pause. He stared at the remaining girls with a frown. The new magic felt too . . . bizarre.

I feel it, too, he thought to Nathaniel. *It's . . . different.*

Edgy. I don't like it.

Derek couldn't shake the strange feeling that something wasn't right.

Could it be tribal magic? Nathaniel asked. Tribal magic would explain why Derek had never felt it before—he'd never worked with the Southern Network tribes.

Viktoria's gaze drifted around the seemingly empty room, with doors ripped off their hinges, eventually landing on the smaller witch in confusion. She attempted to stand, but wobbled. Grateful to be invisible, Derek waited, observing. The smallest witch's eyes opened, caught his, and quickly shut again. His hand moved to the hilt of his sword. Her eyes had been clear.

And she'd seen him.

Derek felt a familiar shift in the magic. Jeramy had returned, invisibility incantation still in place.

What's going on? Jeramy asked. *Something feels different.*

Derek caught something out of the corner of his eye. Viktoria stared straight ahead in horror. He glanced down. His invisibility incantation had started to fade, slowly revealing his shoes, ankles, knees—

Impossible.

Stronger magic, Nathaniel's thought barked through their heads. *Expanding by the second.* Jeramy appeared piecemeal as well. Despite Derek's every attempt to recast the spell, nothing happened.

Something is forcing our magic out, Derek thought.

No spell can overpower Brotherhood magic.

Nathaniel's reply came with a chilling response.

No known *magic.*

The short girl on the floor opened her eyes again. Her hair had faded white as the driven snow. The skin around her eyes turned to bags. Derek swore. Where the short, young witch had once been, now an old hag, with deep-set wrinkles and glimmering black eyes, sprang to her feet. She bared her teeth, gripping one of the paper lanterns in her hand. It burned with a sudden white-hot flame. She threw her head back and started to chant.

Get out of there! Nathaniel screamed.

Jeramy threw himself at the hag. Derek barely had time to grab Viktoria before a percussive *boom* rippled through the cabin, flattening the walls. A blinding flash of bright light followed. Derek transported away mid-leap, Viktoria tucked under his arm. He landed at Andrei's, on his back, with a heavy *thud.*

A group of witches stared at him, chattering in a rapid, unfamiliar language. His ears rang. Black spots swam before his vision. The witches stopped talking as Andrei waded from their midst.

"You found Viktoria!" he cried, reaching for the girl. Andrei stopped in his tracks. He blinked. "Vat happened?"

Derek's mind buzzed. He had to get back. Now. He shoved a stunned Viktoria into Andrei's arms and disappeared without explanation.

Almost instantly, he was back at the destroyed shanty. The bitter scent of sulfur and burnt hair stained the air. Derek waded through tattered boards and snow, shoving them aside. Only bits of blood and skin remained from the old hag. Frantic, he forced aside a portion of the old door.

"Jer?" he called. "Jeramy?"

Nathaniel appeared from beneath a piece of wood not far away. He coughed. Blood flowed down his nose and over his upper lip.

"All right, Nate?" Derek called.

"Peachy. Where's Jeramy?"

Derek had been frantically trying to connect with Jeramy through the Brotherhood magic, but without response. Several paces away from the shanty, a familiar head of red hair peeked out against the snow. Nathaniel and Derek reached Jeramy at the same moment. Derek flipped him over.

"The good gods," Nathaniel muttered.

Blood poured down the right side of Jeramy's face. A gash covering his forehead filleted the skin above his eyes. Soot stained the rest of his face and neck. Derek grabbed his neck. No pulse.

The rush of adrenaline had started to fade. His knees collapsed.

We gotta go, Nathaniel said to Derek's mind. *Southern Guards will come after an explosion like that. Gotta go. Can't be found here. Can't be found across the borders.*

Derek grabbed Jeramy by the waist and transported back to Chatham Castle.

* * *

An hour later, a weary Nathaniel and Derek stood side-by-side, burned and battle-scarred, in the High Priestess's office.

Both eyebrows and part of Derek's hair had been singed off in the explosion. Smoke clung to his clothes. A blister had formed across the back of his neck, and an apothecary had bandaged the wounds on his face to stop the bleeding. The scent of burned flesh lingered in his nostrils. Would he ever smell anything else?

Marten stood at the window, his hands folded behind his back. He stared at nothing. Mildred showed no visible reaction as Derek recounted the final timeline. Once he finished, she gave a curt nod and rose to her feet.

"The girls have been reunited with their families and, after their withdrawal from the powerful sedative potions they'd been given in the Southern Network, will recover. You have achieved the purpose of your mission, and I commend your work and sacrifice."

A trickle of relief, so faint he almost missed it, moved through Derek. *At least we have that,* he thought to himself.

Mildred paused, swallowing.

"But I join you in your mourning and grief." Her eyes met Marten's for half a second. "The apothecaries were unable to save Jeramy. He was one of the most talented Head of Protectors I've ever had the honor of knowing. His loss will be, and is, keenly felt."

A rare edge of compassion softened her tone. Derek and Nathaniel both inclined their heads. Having a witch as implacable as the High Priestess reach out with sympathy brought Derek's exhaustion to the surface. Jeramy had been his Brother, his leader, and his best friend. The Brotherhood would never be the same without him.

Amidst the darkness of his job, so encompassing and deep, he craved good things. The warm arms of his wife. The bright eyes of his daughter as she ran around the cottage, wearing pants under her dress. A hearty meal and time to sleep. Laughter. Bianca's endless giggle as she ran the trails. All the simple pleasures that everyone else had in abundance.

His mind rolled through the memories. He'd already sent a note ahead, telling Marie to expect him. She'd have a warm dinner. Crackling fire in the hearth. Bianca would be sleeping, but would wake in the morning. She was already running with reckless abandon through the forest. Barefoot, like her Mama. He couldn't wait to scoop her up. To hear her giggle when he twirled her around—

"Did you hear me?"

Derek jerked back to the present moment. Mildred stared at him, her hands planted on her desk. Nathaniel glanced at Derek out of the corner of his eye.

"My apologies, Your Highness," Derek said. "I was thinking of something else."

She studied him.

"I see that. Marten, you may stay. Nathaniel, you are excused. Derek, you are not."

With a weary nod, Nathaniel shuffled out.

Rest, Brother, Derek thought to him. *You did good work tonight.*

At the door, Nathaniel glanced over his shoulder, pressed a flat hand to his heart in the Brotherhood sign, and then disappeared into the hallway. Derek shifted his shoulders. Now that time had passed, every muscle in his body reacted to the events of the night. The powerful blast had sent him reeling in more ways than one.

The door closed behind Nathaniel with a light *click*. The High Priestess sealed the room with a spell and stared Derek right in the eye. For being such a short thing, she had power.

"Derek, I'm appointing you Head of Protectors in the wake of Jeramy's death. Effective immediately."

His thoughts sludged through waves of confusion and disbelief. "Your Highness?"

"I didn't stutter, Derek. You will be taking over for Jeramy."

Head of Protectors? No. That couldn't happen. Literally *couldn't* happen. Tradition implicitly required that the Head of Protectors be unattached: no children, no family. Derek shook his head.

He had both.

"Forgive me, your Highness, but that's not possible."

The High Priestess didn't know about Marie or Bianca. No one knew. How could he tell her now without losing all credibility and trust? *Your Highness, I'm hand fasted and have been for years. I have a two-year-old daughter that is fierce and wild. I haven't told anyone because I won't put my family in harm's way.*

Given how negligent it sounded in his head, it would sound worse out loud. Despite his reservations, his heart responded to the call with a visceral cry. *Yes*, it seemed to say. *Yes. Being Head of Protectors is what we have strained and sacrificed for. This is our purpose.*

"You're hiding something from me," Mildred said. "I don't enjoy being refused. What is it?"

Her stern expression and short, wispy hair looked odd in the dim light. He struggled to grasp what he was about to say. There were only two ways this conversation with the High Priestess could go, and neither looked good.

"High Priestess, I have a feeling that you already know why I'm hesitating."

Mildred held her chin up. "I have an inkling."

Derek swallowed, careful not to break eye contact. He would give her no reason to believe he felt any regret or shame.

"I have a child, Your Highness. She's two years old. Her name is Bianca. She has gray eyes and black hair just like her Mama. She lives in

Bickers Mill with her mother, my wife of almost three years, and her grandmother."

"You've never mentioned them before."

"No. I haven't."

"Why?"

"To protect them. Tim's wife was murdered by a cursed witch that broke free from the Guardians while in prison. I won't let harm come to my wife or child because of my career."

Her calculating eyes regarded him for a long moment. She drew a long breath.

"I see."

He waited, giving her time to comprehend what this meant. She didn't need it.

"You could have accepted the position and easily continued hiding them," she said. "You didn't have to tell me. It's likely I would have never known."

The thought had occurred to him, but only briefly. "I would never lie."

"Isn't withholding the truth a lie?" she asked with a haughty lift of her eyebrow.

"Is never asking me if I had a family negligence?"

Her lips pursed and eyes sharpened into flinty daggers. He closed his eyes and pulled in a deep breath through his nose.

"Forgive me, Your Highness. My fatigue should not affect my respect for your position or your decisions. I meant no dishonor. You are not a negligent witch."

"Tradition states that I cannot appoint a Head of Protectors that has a wife or child."

"Hence my refusal, Your Highness."

"I have not accepted it."

Derek's response paused on his tongue. He felt a traitorous flicker of hope. If any witch were strong enough to ignore such a foolish tradition, it would be Mildred. But would she? There were so many ways he could help this Network. Traditions that needed to be rooted out. Ways the Brotherhood could circumvent the rising evils. But he couldn't while bound to the old laws and habits.

"If any Council Member, or any witch in our Network, were to find out that I appointed a Head of Protectors in violation of tradition, they'd be livid. Likely call for your removal, perhaps banishment. If you accept the position despite your family, the Network can never know about your family."

"I know."

"You are the only candidate that I trust with the safety of my Network —and myself, although that's secondary. While I have a great amount of respect for the rest of the Brotherhood, you are the best fit. What do you propose I do?"

Derek suppressed his amusement. She asked out of curiosity; he could sense that she already had a plan. Mildred never entered any situation blind.

"I wouldn't presume to make your decision, High Priestess."

"Do you want to be a part of your child's life?"

"Yes."

"Can you do that while being Head of Protectors?"

He hesitated. "I can."

"Do you want to try to do both?"

A heady rush of power filled him at the thought. Lead the Brotherhood? Every Protector's dream. Raise Bianca? Every parent's dream. He calmed the rising emotions through sheer willpower.

"Yes, Your Highness."

"How would you do it?"

"The same way I do it now. I give them everything that I don't give to you."

She pressed her lips into an even thinner line. "That's no way to be a father."

"It's all I have."

"I suppose something is better than nothing, isn't it?"

A flicker of something moved through her eyes. She looked away. For a long moment, Mildred stared at nothing, said nothing. Derek waited, breath held, for what she would say. After what felt like an eternity, she turned and met his gaze.

"My offer stands. Derek Black, will you be the Head of Protectors for the Central Network?"

What she asked meant more than he could comprehend after such a long night. Did she really trust him to this degree? Was he really going to accept this position? He held out an arm, clasping her own small forearm in his.

"It would be an honor, Your Highness."

"Good. Now go home to your family for three days of recovery. It will be a while before you see them again."

* * *

Fans have often asked me why Bianca started school two weeks late—if she wanted to be part of the Competition, why wait?

Others have asked why Mildred didn't just force Mabel to remove the Inheritance curse. I wrote this scene between Derek and Mildred before I finalized the novel to figure those things out myself.

This is what came of it.

* * *

Derek caught Mildred's discreet glance when he stepped into her office uninvited. Before more than a second had passed, she'd returned to her work without a breath of acknowledgement. He suppressed a smile. She never did waste much time.

He filled the office doorway with his usual stoic silence, waiting for her to acknowledge him. Any attempt to force conversation would only result in being shoved into the hall with a spell. She'd done it before. And made him wait an hour just to prove her point.

With a second cursory glance, she stood up, her gaze flitting over his blood-streaked arm, the dark stitches on his face, and his tousled hair. He brushed off her lack of sympathy without a second thought. Eh. He'd been hurt worse. Besides, it wasn't his worst showing. She'd had lesser reactions for greater injuries in the past, and then she had only mumbled about not getting blood on the rug.

"What do you require, Derek?"

A pile of parchments lay to her right, while three separate quills wrote on different scrolls in the air. How she managed to run three quills *and* write with her own hand, he couldn't fathom. But greater mysteries drove the High Priestess. Not the least of which was where her humor went. After years of running the Network, he imagined there simply wasn't time for laughing anymore.

Perhaps there never had been.

He stepped through the doorway and stopped a few paces from her desk. His stomach curled. Although he spoke with her on a daily basis, he'd never brought her a personal issue.

"I need to discuss a personal matter with you," he said.

Donald, her willowy, bleary-eyed Assistant, stood behind the desk to the right, waiting for her signature. She scrawled her signature in a few places, blew on it, and released the paper. The parchment scrolled back together and floated to Donald's outstretched hand. He nodded, sniffled his constantly dripping nose, and wafted out. The door closed with a quiet click.

Mildred turned to Derek. "It's about your daughter, isn't it?"

"Yes."

"I figured as much." She set the quill down. "It's been almost thirteen years since our last discussion about Bianca. I've been expecting this. Sit down. I can't talk to you while you're looming over me like that, looking as if you're about to die. She's starting a Network school, Derek. It won't eat her."

Derek obeyed, but not because he wanted to. "She has a meeting with Isadora in a week."

Mildred stopped, one eyebrow rising. "She hasn't met with her yet? School started this week."

He shook his head. "No. We applied to Isadora, but hadn't heard back. For a while, I thought hope was lost. I haven't slept in a month, I think."

Mildred's eyes narrowed. She seemed to think it over. "An interview is a good sign. Isadora knows what she's doing."

"But why wait until *after* school has started?"

"Likely it has something to do with timing and chances. Who knows? I have never questioned Isadora before. I won't begin now."

"I will."

"Well, stop," she snapped. "Isadora has her reasons."

Derek dragged a hand through his hair. "Fine."

"Isadora will know what's best. She understands far more than we do with her foresight. Trust in that, Derek."

He was less optimistic. "I'm willing to hope that's the truth." He shifted, feeling squirmy. "But if she doesn't admit B—"

"No. I will not go above Isadora."

Derek scowled. "Why not?"

"Isadora is the Watcher for a reason."

"But you are the High Priestess! You hold more power than her."

"Yes, and how would that look for Bianca?"

The conversation ended before he'd fully articulated his thoughts. Yes, he'd come here with the hope the High Priestess would throw him a bone. *Decades of service to the Network and you,* he'd planned to say. *Just make sure my girl gets into this school, and I'll do whatever you want.* But the hope withered like a wickless candle. Thinking the High Priestess would deviate from the rules had been foolish. He knew better.

Desperation, he thought, *drives witches to worse things.*

Derek stood up to pace. He couldn't reconcile Mildred being right with his inability to cope with it. The High Priestess regarded him for a long moment before shaking her head.

"I know what your plan is, Derek. You've spent Bianca's whole life training her in defensive magic. In shield work. You even started her on swords." She rolled her eyes. "Why a fourteen-year-old girl needs to learn sword work, I can't fathom."

"You never know," he mumbled, thinking of Viveet and Andrei and the beautiful sword that lay hidden in his office, waiting for his daughter.

Mildred spread her hands. "I wish I could do more. But I can't. Mabel officially tried to remove the curse when Hazel petitioned me back during the Rebuilding. It didn't work. May had a lot of power, and Inheritance curses are powerful, nasty things. Mabel claims that she can't undo it."

Derek glared at her. "She lied, High Priestess. We both know Mabel had enough magic. Mabel pretends to a weaker talent than her grand-mother, May. She's done that all these years to fool everyone."

"I know that, but I can't *prove* it, can I? I can't force a witch to undo something she's already tried to remove. Certainly not a Coven leader and a respected High Witch of a Network School. Mabel would be suspicious —as would others."

"It sounds like madness." He ran a hand over his sleep-deprived eyes. "Utter madness, sending Bianca in there on her own. I don't like it, Mildred. There has to be another way."

"Sometimes utter madness is our only hope. A hard lesson to learn, I grant you."

"I can't talk to Mabel about it, or she'll know that Bianca is my daughter."

"And you'll lose Bianca and Marie."

He scowled, cognizant of how powerful the shared secret had become. After all these years as Head of Protectors, what would the witches in the Network do when they realized he'd lied all this time? Technically, he'd never said he *didn't* have a family. But accepting the position and with-holding truth was just as good as lying.

"Just because tradition states the Head of Protectors cannot have a wife or family doesn't mean it was ever a written rule," he said. "Maybe it's time we start warming people up to changing traditions."

Mildred shot him a scathing look.

"Now is not the time. Not with Almack dying in the West, the Western Network gathering near the Borderlands, and Mabel keeping something up her sleeve that I can't figure out yet."

Derek studied his scarred, calloused hands.

"Sending Bianca to Mabel's school has been my plan for the last decade, ever since I realized how talented and smart Bianca was. But I hadn't fully comprehended how dangerous it would be until now. I feel like I failed her as a father."

Mildred leaned forward.

"You can't protect Bianca forever. You're doing what you must to give her the best chance. Do you see it like that?"

"No."

"Well, start."

He laughed, but it dwindled into a bitter scoff. "If it were that easy, I would."

"I can't guarantee you that Bianca will be accepted into Mabel's school. Isadora may see a different path. Besides, Mabel can smell foul play like a fragrance. Regardless of whether Isadora allows Bianca in or not, Mabel will turn her away if she suspects Bianca's just trying to win her way out of the curse. But maybe Mabel has her own agenda that will work in our favor."

Derek steepled his hands in front of him.

"You think she's going to use Bianca as a pawn, don't you?"

Mildred nodded. "I do. Her grandmother did it to some effect, but Mabel is more clever than May. I think that's why Mabel continues with the Competition. She wants to weed out the most talented, the most promising, and then use them in her rise to greatness. Among others things." Her eyes flickered to the door, as if someone lingered behind it. Her voice had dropped slightly.

"Use them how?"

"To kill me."

Derek studied Mildred's small eyes. Her aging body possessed such power. She was probably the only witch who could speak of her own murder without blinking an eye. Derek had his own reservations about her suspicions, which she had voiced once to him in the recent past.

"You still believe that's her plan?"

"Absolutely. She's been waiting for this opportunity for years. She's patient, and that's one of Mabel's greatest strengths right now. All she needs is for me to die. Then Briton can appoint her as Council Member, at the very least. High Priestess at the most. It's all quite simple, really."

"And yet it's not."

She nodded once to concede the point. "No," she agreed. "I don't plan on dying anytime soon, and she can't kill me herself and then claim the throne. The magic of the Esmelda scrolls prohibits it." Mildred eyed him. "Besides, I think I'm not the only witch that she fears getting in her way. She'll want a backup plan. Bianca could be it if she proves herself clever enough."

Derek read between the lines, but said nothing. Mabel had good reason to fear him. His neck tightened just thinking about Bianca anywhere near the vile witch. How could he send her right into Mabel's clutches?

"Are you prepared to see your daughter through this?" Mildred asked.

Derek rose to his feet.

"I don't have a choice, do I?"

"No." Mildred picked her quill back up and turned back to her parchments. "Welcome to life. Send Donald in behind you."

Recognizing a dismissal, Derek turned on his heel. He was halfway to the door when she called out.

"I'll keep track of the situation, Derek."

He gripped the doorknob.

"Thank you."

And so will I, he thought before stepping into the hallway and giving himself to the darkness of transporting.

CHAPTER 4

Angelina

Writing Angelina's story opened up many facets of May and Mabel that I hadn't discovered before.

Exploring new places—and witches—of the Eastern Network was a fun adventure for me, and it helped me set up parts of the novel from The Historical Collection, The High Priestess.

Learning Angelina's story surprised even me.

* * *

Thunder boomed with a reverberating crash through the soggy, black night.

Dazed with hunger, Angelina stumbled up a muddy path and around the back of the old manor to the kitchen door. She rapped three times. Her knuckles smarted. She dropped to her knees, landing in a puddle on the ground. Rain sluiced down her hood, which had long been soaked. Her teeth rattled beneath her chilled lips, tinged with blue. She cradled her pregnant belly with one hand.

Please hurry, she thought. *I'm going to faint.*

Seconds later, the door opened. A young, friendly witch with puffy hair and concerned eyes peered out. Angelina didn't recognize her at first glance. Flour streaks littered her apron and the front of her nose. Mother must have hired a new cook in the months she'd been gone.

"Can I help you?" the stranger asked.

Angelina tried to stand, but stumbled, sending a spray of droplets onto the hem of the witch's dress.

"F-f-food," she gasped. "I-I'm starving."

The unknown witch hesitated, as expected. Vagabonds, desperate for work, currency, and food in this abysmal Network, wandered through the trees constantly. No doubt hers wasn't the first knock and plea for mercy on a stormy night. After what felt like an eternity, the witch hooked her arm underneath Angelina's and pulled her to her feet.

"I'm Celia," she said. "Who are you?"

The door closed behind them. Warmth wrapped around Angelina like a long-sought embrace.

"A-angelina."

"Who?"

Angelina swallowed. "May's daughter."

Even in the dim light, Celia paled. Her mouth rounded into an *O*. "What? She has a daughter?"

Angelina's legs collapsed before she could respond. The room swam. Her ears rang. Celia's arm tightened around her back, keeping her from crashing to the ground.

"Come to the fire," Celia said. "We need to warm you up."

The next hour passed in a strange blur. Celia locked the door to the kitchen with a spell, set water on to boil, and stripped Angelina's rags free, sending them to a bucket filled with warm, soapy water. Angelina sat naked, wrapped in a thick blanket, before the fire. The baby squirmed inside her, as if it, too, recognized the warmth. Celia handed her a mug of hot broth. The warmth permeated her frozen muscles and bones, restoring her mind. As the blur of hunger and cold began to fade, she stared at the familiar kitchen. The sooty hearth. The wood pile. The old cupboards filled with spices and herbs. A burning curl of fear filled her stomach, thick as lead.

What have I done? Why did I come back?

After a half hour of silence, Angelina spoke first.

"Thank you."

Celia glanced up from the pile of logs. She sent four more into the fire with a spell and nodded once. In the background, Angelina's clothes ran up and down the scrubbing board with a spell, cleaning themselves. They twisted together, wringing themselves out, before flying to the other side of the room, where Celia draped them over the back of a chair near the fire.

"I'm going to assume that you and your mother aren't close," Celia said, her eyes darting to the door. Her voice lowered. Ah. Celia recognized the darkness in her mother. Not every witch did. Angelina turned away, back to the comfort of the flames.

"No."

"I've worked here three months and she hasn't once mentioned you."

The kind uncertainty in Celia's voice made Angelina's throat catch. How long had it been since she'd heard a gentle word? How many times had she been turned away, the door slammed in her face, her currency stolen, her cheek slapped? All because Mother didn't want her anymore. Everything she suffered angled back to May.

To Mother dearest.

Angelina swallowed. "To May, I don't exist anymore. She kicked me out before you came."

"What for?"

A hint of a smile lingered in Angelina's weary expression.

"Falling in love."

Silence swelled in the room. Angelina's mind filled with the warm, enticing memories of her lover at her side. David. His silky, blond hair. Eyes bluer than the summer sky. A soft touch on the back of her neck. Whispered promises in the sweetness of the night. As quickly as the irresistible memories came, a stony recollection replaced them. His pursed lips when she refused him. The burn of his eyes after a bottle of ipsum. The careless flick of his hand as she told him her good news.

I'm pregnant.

I don't care.

Had it been fate that led her to a witch as conniving as her mother? As if Angelina had clung to her hatred of May so much that she brought her back into her life through David. But she longed for love—thirsted after it like a dying wraith. David had been her chance at freedom. Her escape.

Until he became his own prison. Under his brutal hand, all dreams of *love* and *home* and *belonging* faded away. Her girlish thinking hardened into the bitter wound of unrequited love. She set her jaw. The pain of David's betrayal, so fresh, still stung.

Celia sent a pointed glance to Angelina's belly. "Does she know?"

Angelina closed her eyes. "Not yet."

"Where's the father?"

Angelina set aside the empty mug, her stomach growling for more. Celia passed her a piece of bread, which Angelina accepted gratefully. She shrugged. "I'm not sure. He wants nothing to do with me or the baby, which is just as well." Her lip curled up over her teeth. "He's a lech."

Celia swallowed, rubbing a hand over the back of her neck. "May's not in a very, uh . . . that is—"

"She's in one of her moods, is she?" Angelina scoffed, tearing a piece of bread off with her teeth. "Just my luck."

"I'm not sure what I should do." Celia twisted her hands together. "I'm not—"

"Don't worry, Celia. I'll get this over with now."

Angelina called for the extra dress Celia had brought with a spell and stood as it neared. Celia tested Angelina's wet clothes at the fire while Angelina dressed, luxuriating in the fresh cotton.

The broth and bites of bread had restored some of her strength. Although she wanted to eat as much as she could, she'd have to take it easy. She'd hardly eaten in days. Anyway, she couldn't eat much with this stone of dread sitting in her stomach, rolling around every time she thought of Mother.

Celia stepped forward. "But—"

"No." Angelina held up a hand. Celia shrank back. For the moment that her voice lingered in her own ears, Angelina heard May in the sharp, commanding tone. It felt good to have power. "I'll take care of this. You won't get in trouble."

Angelina set aside the bread, squared her shoulders, and steeled herself.

Time to face Mother.

* * *

51

When Angelina knocked, her hand trembled.

The cold, she told herself. *It must be from the cold.* A draft swept down the hallway of the first floor. It surprised her that May hadn't moved her office upstairs to Angelina's old bedroom in the attic, where privacy would be absolute. Then again, May could exert far more control down here.

And there was nothing Mother loved more.

A long pause seemed to pass after knocking. The soft shuffle of a dress, an opening drawer, moving papers, all sounded faint in the distance. Just before Angelina knocked again, May's cutting voice rang through the door.

"What?"

The door creaked as she pushed it open with her fingertips. Angelina stayed just outside, as May had always insisted. *If I haven't invited you in, don't come in.* Dim candlelight cast flickering shadows on the wall. Outside, rain poured down the window in waves. The forest would flood in such a deluge.

May stared at her from where she sat behind her desk, her eyes glittering in a pale, thin face. Plumes of black hair drifted around her neck and shoulders. Her attempts with transformational beauty never resulted in much. The only striking thing about May was her commanding presence.

A sense of heaviness in the air, like a dark magnet, seemed to pull Angelina inside. What was this strange feeling? So leaden. So thick. It pressed on her chest, making her breath hitch, before disappearing with a wisp.

Strange, she thought, tucking it away to understand later. With Mother, nothing was ever what it seemed.

Not a flicker of surprise, excitement, or regret moved into May's expression as Angelina stared at her. Implacable, as usual. Tonight, it stung deep.

She doesn't care. She never has. She never will, Angelina thought. *You're a fool to come back.*

May returned her attention to a scroll in front of her. "You're letting in the cold air. Either come in or close the door."

Angelina stepped inside.

May cast her another glance. Her shrewd, calculating gaze slid to

Angelina's belly and quickly looked away. Had there been a flicker of something there? A slight curl of her upper lip, at least.

"Well, the rumors about David leaving you are true. I can't say that I'm surprised."

Angelina put a hand on her belly. She bit so hard on the inside of her cheek it nearly drew blood. There would be many more verbal jabs. She only had to endure it until she had the baby, recovered, and could leave again. Assuming Mother would allow her to stay.

Which wasn't likely.

"Yes, May. David and I are no longer together."

"I told you he'd drop you."

Angelina lifted her chin. "I dropped him."

May rolled her eyes. "Whoever did it first doesn't matter. You're pregnant, single, and jobless, I presume? A fitting tribute to your aspirations. I told you that searching for love would end this way."

How delicious it must be for you to see me fail, Angelina wanted to say. A roiling ball of anger replaced her heart. She nursed it, feeling power in the rage. Hadn't Mother always done the same? Clung to her anger at Father, who had deserted them—no, he'd deserted *May*—when Angelina was a small child?

Instead, Angelina said nothing. Desertion by a parent wasn't the worst fate. Angelina had survived just fine.

May leaned back in her chair.

"Let me guess . . . you've come here to ask for help, to grovel at my feet. Now that you're desperate and have messed up your entire life, you want Mother to fix it for you. Don't you? Well, I won't. Not by a long shot. You'll have to learn the hard way that I know what I'm talking about. Maybe if you had learned that sooner, we could be having a very different kind of conversation."

Angelina's resolve began to dissipate. Perhaps she couldn't endure this for four more months. Death for both her, and her child, would be preferable to enduring her Mother on a daily basis.

"I simply came for a warm place to stay the night."

"You could have slept in the kitchen without seeing me."

"Perhaps I should have."

May pressed her hands to the top of the desk and stood. "Well, it appears you got what you wanted. Be gone before the girls wake up in the morning."

Angelina's burning heart flared with a painful burst of sorrow. No, rage. She shouldn't have been surprised at May's cold hauteur. What else had Mother given her in the past?

The final piece of Angelina's pride crinkled away. She could reduce herself no lower than this in life. Pregnant. Single. Homeless. No currency to even buy a loaf of bread, and swollen with child. Her mother, the only family she had left, refused to soften her plight. The clothes she'd shown up in weren't even her own. She'd stolen them from a lady wandering along the road, half-crazed with ipsum.

"That's it then?" Angelina asked.

May pulled a quill from the drawer and lifted the top from an inkwell. Thunder rolled in the background. Bolts of lightning flashed against the backdrop of Letum Wood, illuminating the haunted forest's outline. Rain lashed the windows and walls.

"That's it."

Angelina swallowed. Is this how it had been for father? Had May dismissed him without a single ounce of mercy or compassion? Had Angelina expected welcoming arms? Hoped for them, maybe. Perhaps May was right. Dreaming would only cause trouble.

Angelina placed a hand on her belly.

"You don't want any part of your grandchild's life?"

May scoffed.

"You are not my daughter. My daughter would have shown more skill and talent in magical pursuits. My daughter would have been trustworthy. My daughter would not have chased after the foolish notion of love. My daughter would have shown interest in continuing my legacy. In the wake of your failures, I will find my real daughter." May met her gaze. "You are nothing."

Oh, Angelina thought with a dizzying rush of hatred. *But I have a plan, Mother.*

May continued her work. The bitter smell of ink filled the air. The fire snapped. Angelina hesitated another full minute, just to give May one last chance to make this right. May's gaze drifted to the bookshelf and back to her desk. The heaviness in the air had eased, making it easier to breathe.

The quill never stopped moving.

I hate her, Angelina thought, curling her fingers into a tight fist. *I hate her more than I could have ever imagined. I will become great without her.*

Angelina squared her shoulders. She wouldn't speak with May again. Not ever.

"Merry part, Mother."

* * *

Three months later, Angelina stared at the manor from the depths of the trees. Her shoulders were gaunt and skinny, her face drawn and pale. Childbirth had a way of leeching the life out of a witch. Maybe even the soul.

The second month of fall unfurled around her with barren trees and the brittle skins of dead leaves. Winter breathed down her neck. Her breath puffed out in clouds. The brittle vines of ivy sweeping across the front of her old home scraped against the stones in the wind. Inside, girls would be scurrying to classes. Breakfast would be warm, plain. The taste of porridge filled her mouth. Her stomach grumbled, reminding her. *No food*, it seemed to say.

As if on cue, the baby squawked, one scrawny fist flailing around her face. The wind whipped by in a haunting tune. Angelina blinked, feeling every breath rise in and out of her chest. After giving birth by herself in the forest, using a sharp rock to separate herself from the baby, and old rags to keep the child from dying, she imagined she only had a few hours left to live herself.

"You wouldn't take me," she said to the old house, picturing May warm and safe in its depths. "So I'll die in your name. But maybe you'll take her. And she can be that daughter you would be so proud of."

Her daughter, a perfect little bundle of toes and fingers and wisps of blonde hair atop her soft head, slept in her arms. She hardly weighed anything and didn't squall like most babies. The child had blue eyes . . . but didn't all babies? Not like these. A bright, vivid blue. Such an odd trait had frightened her at first, but quickly faded into the blur of life. The babe slept restlessly, as if she were vaguely aware that Angelina couldn't keep her and didn't mind finding a new mother. She yawned on occasion, her eyes shut against the spiny canopy of Letum Wood above her. It seemed appropriate to leave her nameless.

Soon, Angelina thought. *She'll be hungry enough to be angry soon.*

Darkness seemed to descend all at once, casting a dreary, chilly blackness over the manor. Candles flickered in the windows of the school, ringed by a wrought iron fence and held captive by the circle of trees surrounding it. Angelina ducked when a shadow walked by the attic window, but it didn't matter. No one could see her. Certainly, no one would be looking for her, a lost soul in the woods. The very idea that she had returned was ludicrous, but she remained hidden all the same.

She leaned down until her lips nearly brushed the babe's ear. Strands of ragged, unwashed hair fell into the scrunched face. The baby stirred.

"I love you, little one. But I cannot keep you alive. I am not sure I will survive myself. If I abandon you to an orphanage, I may never find you again." Her eyes flickered to the house. A dark edge crept into her voice. "Your grandmother will keep you alive. Celia will find you on the porch and take you inside. May will not send you away; it would harm her reputation too much. No. You will survive here until I return."

All of Angelina's insides seemed to shrivel as she hurried up the path the moment the moon slid behind a cloud. *My child,* she thought. *My daughter. I promised I would be a better mother than my own. How can I abandon her?*

The scent of fresh bread floated on the air. Happy squeals drifted through the door as Angelina hesitated, listening. Such joy. Such youthful mirth. Did they realize how blessed they were?

As she untied the makeshift shawl anchoring the babe to her chest, her heart shrank in fear. *I cannot do it,* she thought. *I cannot leave her.*

A cold wind whipped by in a heartless reminder of what awaited her. A frigid death, likely. The cursed life of a vagabond in Letum Wood. Angelina peered back into the forest. Her arms felt limp, like an old rope. Her insides still cramped. If she knocked on the door, May would turn her away, baby and all. Celia would have to listen to her employer.

But May would take *just* the baby. Angelina could feel it. *In the wake of your failures,* May had said, *I will find my real daughter. Somehow.*

With one last kiss on the tiny, wrinkled cheek, Angelina swaddled the baby as tightly as possible and set her on the woven mat. She knocked hard, then dashed away, flittering back into the safety of the trees. Once out of sight, she whirled around, digging the tips of her fingers into the rough bark of a tree trunk.

"Answer it, Celia," she pleaded. "Answer the door!"

The baby stirred. A thin cry reached Angelina's ears. She bit her bottom lip until the metallic taste of blood filled her mouth. Just when she could bear it no longer, the door opened. A crack of light spilled onto the porch. The baby cried in earnest now. Celia stepped out, a hand pressed to her face. She reached for the small bundle, pulling it into her arms. Celia glanced out into the forest. Angelina shrank back.

I cannot keep you, little one, her heart cried. *I may not even survive this last, desperate spell into a different Network. But I will always care for you.*

With a choked sob, Angelina gathered the last of her energy and transported away.

* * *

Angelina landed in a puddle of mud.

She groaned when a sharp rock stabbed her ribcage. Darkness swamped the edges of her vision. Her arms gave way when she pushed up with her hands. Her fingers sank into another pocket of mud. In the distance, a horse whinnied. Everything appeared dim here, in the deepest forest. When she shoved her hand forward, gravel grated on her fingertips.

Yes, she thought in relief. *A road.*

Through bleary eyes, she could just make out a dreary fog lingering in the only open space nearby. She'd transported herself to a road. Or had she walked here? Her mind whirred, unable to remember. Using the tips of her shoes, and digging her fingers deep into the soil, she pushed forward. Her elbows snagged on a rock. Her knee scraped an exposed stone. The *clop* of the horse's feet drew nearer.

Must get to the horse and rider.

Movement by movement, she inched forward until she lay across the middle of the mud-slaked road. Exhausted, she pressed her cheek into the wet soil with a sigh. The sound of the horse's approach increased. She could almost feel the vibrations of the hooves. They'd run her over. They wouldn't see her in this fog.

But it didn't matter. Because only seconds away lingered sweet, sweet oblivion. Where the pain didn't hurt so much, and the darkness wasn't quite so unfriendly.

Just before Angelina slid into the welcoming chasm, she heard a voice call out.

* * *

Angelina woke to the feeling of sweet, heavy warmth.

She stirred beneath a pile of soft, thick blankets. Her legs felt deliciously refreshed, as if she'd slept for days. She luxuriated in the feeling for several long moments, marveling that her stomach didn't throb any longer. When she'd fallen asleep, she'd been stretched across a muddy—

She sat up with a gasp.

Sunlight streamed into a single room cottage with bright, whitewashed walls and an open window. A salty tang filled the air. In the distance, a bird trilled a distant call. Was that the ocean? She touched a hand to her hair. Washed. Brushed, even. It fell around her shoulders in loose brown locks. Slowly, Angelina slid her legs off the mattress of downy goose feathers and to the floor.

Did she dare hope her plan had worked?

"Ah," a voice said from behind her. Angelina's head jerked back to see a woman step into the room. She had rich black hair—just like hers, but this woman's eyes were as deep and dark as her hair. Pools of ebony. They studied each other in uncertain interrogation. Firewood levitated in the air behind the witch as she stepped toward a small fire in the hearth.

Dark hair and eyes, she thought. *A promising sign.*

"Merry meet," Angelina managed, her voice croaking. "Thank you for your assistance."

The witch responded with a string of unfamiliar words. The distinct, husky accent gave the witch away. Angelina suppressed a rush of joy. *I'm here,* she thought. *The Central Network is behind me. Let the plan begin.*

Angelina switched to the common language. "Do you understand me?" she asked.

The grooves in the witch's face smoothed out. "Yes. I understand and speak the common language. My name is Marcelina. My husband is Roberto." She inclined her head. "Welcome to our humble ocean home."

Marcelina. Roberto. Ocean home. Angelina had arrived in the Eastern Network on her last dying breath.

Fate, she thought. *The good gods are finally smiling down on me. I'm destined for greatness here. I can already feel it.*

Angelina's shoulders slumped in relief. "My name is Angelina. Thank you for helping me. Am I in Cupertino?"

Cupertino city sat just across the border from the Central Network, near the old dirt road she'd transported to. Or meant to, anyway. In her hazy, post-birth state, she wasn't sure where she'd landed.

The witch sent a pile of firewood to the hearth. It clattered, but gathered into a perfectly stacked pile. Marcelina clapped her hands together to shake the dust free, then reached down to grab a bucket near the door. "Lark," she said, propping it on her hip. One hand went to the doorknob, as if she meant to leave already. Angelina felt a stab of panic. She leaned forward.

"Wait. Please don't leave yet. Lark?" she repeated. "Where is Lark?"

Marcelina regarded her with narrowed eyes. Her chin lifted. "A little village off the southern coast, near the Southern Network. My husband found you on the road. He thought you were dead. When he brought you here, so did I."

Angelina sat back. "Oh."

"Feeling better?"

"Yes."

Marcelina's jaw tightened. "Then where's the baby?"

Angelina's breath caught. Marcelina didn't give her the chance to ask the obvious. "I've seen birth and blood like that before. You were drenched in it. One doesn't have to be a mother to know what happened."

A sudden wave of fatigue rushed back through her. Despite her heavy sleep, she felt as if she could rest for several days more. The sound of the baby crying on the doorstep rang back through Angelina's mind, but she shoved it away to think about later.

Angelina didn't realize how long she'd let the silence go until Marcelina's eyes narrowed.

"You didn't abandon it on the roadside, did you?" she asked, her eyes flinty. "My husband said he looked, but—"

"No!" Angelina recoiled. "No, I didn't leave my baby to die. M-my mother has her." She turned away. "The baby is safe."

I hope.

Marcelina softened infinitesimally.

"Sleep more if you need to." She reached for a loaf on the table and handed her several slices thick with butter. "When you feel better, you can eat again, but then you need to go. We're too busy to stay at home like this, and we don't have enough to feed another mouth right now."

With that, Marcelina disappeared outside.

Angelina stared at the bread on her lap, blinked, took a bite, and then lay back down, pulled the covers up, and fell back into a deep sleep.

* * *

The first weeks wandering through the Eastern Network slid by in an obscure fog.

Angelina let the days go, content to lose them like sand through her fingers. Life as a vagabond wasn't new; she knew how to hide from patrolling Guardians, avoid small villages, and dash into the bushes when wagons rattled by. She stole bread from windowsills, pulled water from private wells, and slept in the forests that occasionally dotted the coast. The gulls lulled her to sleep. She stayed warm with her shawl and bathed in freshwater streams as she found them.

Her days roaming the Eastern Network soothed her like a balm. Months passed. A year. Angelina's olive skin blended in like she'd always been there. She kept an eye on the headlines of their newsbooks—not even a newsscroll in her strange new world—and waited for her plan to fall into place.

She committed everything about this new world to memory, spending most of her time memorizing the language. The dialects. The way Eastern witches spoke with their hands instead of words.

She thought of her daughter daily. Was she eating bread and milk yet? Did Celia raise her as her own? More than her little girl, Angelina thought about the delicious wisp of darkness she'd felt in May's office. Oppressive. Distinct.

And very, *very* forbidden.

One mild day in the early spring, she strolled down a market along the pier in Temi, a sprawling city known for its fresh fish and hand-painted figurines of the legendary merfolk. Silvery, wet fish lay in piles on wooden crates. Limp, veiny shrimp filled a low pallet with their wiggling, translucent bodies.

Nearby, a witch with a twisted mustache skinned a shark with the head still attached. The smell of decaying fish didn't bother Angelina anymore. She closed her eyes, drawing it deep into her lungs.

The ocean, she thought. *The ocean sustains us. It is part of us. We love and serve the ocean.*

The witch with the sprawling mustache smiled.

"You understand," he said, his words thick and heavy, like the knife he used as deftly as a knitting needle. Angelina smiled and moved on. At the end of the market, she turned to leave when a newsgirl caught her eye, waving the latest newsbook. Her tiny ankles looked so thin, Angelina feared she'd collapse.

"Isobel!" the girl cried, running to Angelina's side. Ah. Sweet Sera. Angelina hadn't seen her in months. Sera called over her shoulder. "Abelie! Lia! Come quickly. Isobel is here!"

A group of newsgirls flocked to Angelina's side, murmuring her name over and over under their breaths. "Isobel. Isobel," they said. "The bringer of joy. She has come again!"

Angelina bestowed her brightest smile on them. "Yes!" she said, laughing. "I have brought you more good things. Your dear Isobel never forgets you."

She'd chosen her Eastern Network name carefully. The superstition ran deep in their culture that the meaning of a name foretold great or terrible things. Isobel, *Bringer of Joy,* would suit her long-term purposes admirably.

Using her favorite—and most popular—incantation, Isobel produced one small piece of candy for each child. Grasping with greedy, dirty hands, the girls snatched all the candy away, scattering into the nooks and crannies of the bustling market with giggles. Magic didn't create very delectable food—it always tasted bland and porous—but these poor street urchins didn't know the difference. Only Sera remained behind, sucking on the treat with a broad grin.

"What news do you have today, Sera?" Angelina asked, reaching down to brush the girl's hair out of her eyes. Like all newsgirls, she wore it chopped short, shorn as a symbol of her status. Orphans, most of them. Scraping by with barely enough to eat. But they were a proud lot. Angelina liked them immensely.

Sera brandished a newsbook. The thin pages flapped, trilling a soft song. "Something wonderful! The High Priest's son, Diego, has finally decided to search for a wife! The whole Network is talking about it."

Angelina's heart fluttered, borne away on wings of shock. Had it come? Her long-awaited purpose. She blinked. "Oh?" she asked, feigning disinterest. "Why is that wonderful?"

Sera's face fell. She dropped the paper back to her side. "But Isobel! The lucky peasant girl he chooses could be you. They even have a list of places he'll appear to meet with the peasants. You must go meet him."

Angelina ran the tips of her fingers down Sera's face. Whenever she saw Sera, she loved to imagine the little urchin belonged to her. That Sera was the daughter she'd left behind. That the empty ache of love inside her could be filled with Sera's adoring gaze.

But, no.

A mere dream. An illusion. Sera's beautiful green eyes, the exact shade of sea foam, were not her daughter's.

Sky blue, Angelina recalled, the image a wisp of memory.

"I'm a vagabond, Sera. Magnolia Castle is no place for a witch like me. When would I sleep under the stars? I would have to wear nice dresses and have food served to me." She pulled a disgusted face.

Sera giggled, then frowned. "But Isobel! You would have all the food a witch could want." She pressed a thin hand to her stomach. "Surely, you must want to try?"

Angelina put a hand under Sera's chin. She'd tried to take care of the little girl in the past—give her a cloak, some food, even new shoes—but the girl adamantly refused help. Newsgirls cared for themselves.

"Darling Sera, you are a special girl. Here's ten pence. May I keep this newsbook? Thank you. Go on. Sell many, many more and earn yourself a warm dinner tonight."

The girl accepted the currency with a nod, a sparkle in her eye. "Come back to see me, Miss Isobel?"

"Of course, Sera. Of course."

She watched the little witch scamper away, bellowing the headlines in the newsbook with an arm waving wildly. Angelina's eyes narrowed on the bolded headline. *The Impegno Begins*. Dates listed beneath it in order of appearance, ending in her favorite little hideaway of all. A sly smile stole across Angelina's face.

The Impegno begins . . . and so does my ascension to power.

* * *

While resting in a pocket of sand, tucked safely into her favorite copse of trees along the coast, an unusual sound struck Angelina's ears. She smiled, steeling herself for a short wait. After months of tracking the *Impegno*, her moment had finally come.

A bright sun still infused the sky as it sat on the edge of the horizon, spilling glowing white and yellow beams. She pushed up, the sand shifting beneath her hands. A few paces away, slinking along the trees, was a broad-figured shadow. Groping blindly, she felt for the stray branch she kept nearby and closed her fingers around it. The looming figure tripped over a vine, nearly tumbling to the ground.

"*Lacce*," a deep voice muttered. Angelina straightened. The stranger might not be the High Priest's son—but she doubted that. This would be his last stop in the *Impegno*. After weeks of traveling throughout the Network, any witch—highborn or not—would seek escape from the teeming crowd of females awaiting him in the plaza on his last stop. Even a would-be High Priest needed time to think. Angelina's extensive knowledge of the area made it obvious that if the young royal were to escape, he'd come here. The only isolated stretch of beach in the area.

Yes, she thought. *Come this way.*

The male witch stumbled into the small clearing only a few paces away. As if drawn there by a magnet, his eyes drifted to hers. Angelina's breath caught.

She'd spent over a year wandering the Eastern Network; enduring all four seasons without permanent shelter, working only long enough to earn currency to wander again. She knew each village on the coast by name. Had glimpsed the tantalizing Magnolia Castle and smelled the sweet, deep blooms of magnolia flowers that never died. She'd poured over books in libraries, memorizing historical facts, names, accomplishments. Committed the flowering language into the deep center of her heart. Sometimes it felt as if her integration into the Eastern Network had been so complete that she'd met every witch on the coast.

But never, in all her many wanderings, had she seen such *eyes.*

Arrested, the male witch stopped. Long, curved lashes, dark as coal, blinked once. He tensed, hands held out in front of him as if he were about to shove her. Angelina leaned back, away from him. She tightened her grip on the cudgel. Showing fear didn't prove to be that difficult. A witch of this size could get whatever he wanted by force.

Play it right, Angelina, she thought. *And you'll be a High Priestess before you know it.*

The long silence became almost unbearable as they sized each other up. His gaze drifted from her face, to her shoulders, to the exposed portion of her lower legs. His shoulders straightened, and he drew to his full, rather impressive, height and put his hands on his hips.

"What are you doing here?" he asked.

His accent rolled with the heavy, deep intonation of the northern part of the Network—a hopeful sign. But what if this wasn't the High Priest's son? The greatest weakness in her plan was that Diego might not wander her way at all—or she might not know him if he did. She'd never seen the real Diego with her own eyes. Few accurate paintings existed outside the castle's walls, and everyone in the Eastern Network had the same deep eyes and olive skin. If this wasn't Diego, she'd need to transport away before he came within reach.

Angelina lifted one eyebrow. "I could ask the same."

"I won't allow it. Tell me who you are."

Her eyebrows rose. Bossy and authoritative. Even better. She lifted her chin a notch. "No."

His nostrils flared. "No?"

Heavy branch in hand, she rose slowly to her feet. She wore the lesser of the two peasant dresses that she'd sewn herself—after stealing one from a clothesline in the desperate throes of her first months here. The folds of linen fell down her body in unflattering lines. She preferred it that way. Anyone who saw her thought her too skinny, almost powerless.

"No," she said. "I won't leave. This land belongs to no one. You can't order me off it when I've done nothing wrong."

His tension seemed to calm. He motioned to the bundle at her feet with a nod of his head. "You have supplies."

"You have arrogance."

To her surprise, a wry grin played across his lips. They weren't full, but thin and beautiful. Curvaceous in all the right places. He smiled like he knew something she didn't. Perhaps he did. Her suspicion relaxed. Diego or not, this witch had a handsome face and kind bearing. When he wasn't trying to boss her around.

"Yes." He bowed his head for a moment. "I do have too much arrogance. It's a failing I've sought to correct for years. My father would agree with you."

To her surprise, Angelina's initial annoyance began to fade. Her fingers eased slightly on the branch.

"Then perhaps your father and I should meet."

"You're a wanderer?" he asked.

"Yes."

His eyebrows rose. "And you like it?"

She spread her hands. "Some of us don't have the luxury of opinion. It doesn't matter if I like it. I must bear it."

His eyes darkened—if that were possible, endless pools of warm brown that they were. "Interesting. Where were you born?"

"Livorno," she said immediately, then smiled to soften it. "I grew up on the outskirts, near the hills, in a quiet little village known for our sheep and wool."

"Ah." His eyes illuminated. "I love Livorno. Such a sweet landscape. The heart of our Network, really."

She'd spent the most time in Livorno, a quiet, coastal town with charming houses and markets teeming with fresh fish. Artists flocked there in swarms, painting the rich architecture and ocean vistas. The finest paintings lined the streets. Angelina walked all day, watching the paintings change, speaking with the desperate, currency-poor artists. They were so alive with passion and talent, it didn't matter that they only ate a couple times a week. She thought of her mother, her blue-eyed child, and felt the same swelling determination in her chest.

She'd have her revenge, just as these artists had their paintings.

"Where are you from?" she asked.

"North of Livorno."

"Near the castle?"

His fingers twitched at his side. Did she imagine him becoming tense? "How did you know?"

"Your accent."

His brow furrowed. "Yours is quite strange. Not at all like those in Livorno."

She cleared her throat. In her effort to know the entire Network, she had never lingered in one place long enough to perfectly mimic the gentle rift and fall of their dialect. He was peering at her now. Her throat tightened uncomfortably when she realized he expected her to explain.

She shrugged. "I grew up in Livorno, but I've wandered for a long time now. I take from here and there."

He nodded, as if that satisfied him, and she let out a long breath.

"Are you a wanderer also?" she asked. Her heart skipped at his quiet smile, as if she'd told a joke. He glanced around ruefully.

"Not by choice. I came seeking solitude."

She smiled. "Ah. You're lost then?"

He cracked a smile. "Not yet, but I'm sure to be soon."

A delicious streak of anticipation ran through her. She hadn't had such lovely company . . . ever. The last time she felt so eager for conversation had been with—well, that didn't matter anymore.

That was part of her past.

"Are you hungry?" she asked with a warm smile. He pressed a hand to his flat, muscled stomach.

"Very much."

Angelina leaned over, cudgel in hand, and picked up the bundle at her feet. A fishing net, some line, a rolled bag with her change of garments, and a few other trinkets were tied together with aging twine. She draped it over her shoulder, then glanced back, amused by his stunned expression.

"Well?" she asked. "Are you coming?"

* * *

"So, you just . . . you just hold the line in the water like this?" Diego asked an hour later. "And the fish will bite the bait?"

They sat on an abandoned stretch of pier, half sunk in the water and bobbing on the waves. Her legs dangled over the side, exposed as high as the knee, and drifted in the warm water. The heady scent of the ocean, the endless expanse of blue, calmed Angelina. She ran a hand through her frizzy hair, shaking it away from her face. His jaw tightened. He turned his gaze back to the water.

"Yes," she said. "You're doing very well. Have you lived so long in the Eastern Network and never fished?"

A light blush covered his face.

"No. I haven't fished directly in the ocean like this. I've seen the fishermen out in their boats, and I've swum in the water, but never fished."

His eyes grew distant. What lingered in his deepest thoughts? Angelina made a noise deep in her throat.

"Interesting."

"Is this how you eat?" he asked.

"Mostly. Sometimes I offer to do laundry and buy food with the currency. Foraging in the forest at the right season always helps. I've killed a couple of rabbits."

"Rabbits?" He swallowed. "You killed and ate them?"

Her nose wrinkled, recalling the coppery scent of blood and the warm smear of it on her fingers. "Yes. It's not pleasant, but makes a wonderful stew with wild onions."

He leaned back. "You really *are* a wanderer."

"Indeed. Desperation drives witches to achieve many things they never expected."

Her throat tightened, but he didn't inquire anymore. They remained in a quiet stretch of silence. She studied him from the corner of her eyes. Fine, strong legs. The pants, though filthy, were good quality, with even, sturdy seams. His shirt showed signs of sophistication. A fan of lines indicated it had been pleated at one point. Buttons. Perfect buttonholes. The casual wardrobe of a High Priest's son.

Or so she hoped.

He could be a butler, perhaps? No, he was no butler. Although refined and dignified, he wasn't boring enough. Stable boy? She drew in a deep breath. No. Not a hint of horse lingered about him.

The fishing line went taut, then slack again. Angelina cast an idle glance at it. She hadn't told him that she'd gathered a few incantations from other, more bizarre, wanderers. Spells that made the bait more appealing to fish. Although the magic took up to twenty minutes to really take effect, the animals would come soon enough.

A coward's way of eating, she heard in her head. No witch in the Eastern Network approved of using magic to lure an animal to its death. The law forbade it. The Easterners respected their ocean far too much.

Well, she thought, rallying her courage. *Time to find out if this is my fate or not.*

"So, what's life like in the castle, Your Highness?" she asked, idly tugging at her line as if she suspected something on the other end. Nothing yet. But like all good things, they would come.

He sucked in a sharp breath. The sound of the wind drifted lazily between them. His entire body had tensed, as if waiting for a punch. After several moments of utter silence, the tension faded. He let out a long breath, as if releasing his angst to the wind.

"Magnolia Castle, like the Eastern Network, is a wonderful place. It is home. It is where I belong."

Not here fishing on a dock? she wanted to say, but pressed her lips together. The possessive catch in his tone, the sudden fire in his eyes, made her want to shrink away instead. Perhaps she didn't know what she was getting into. Could such a sharp, intelligent witch be fooled? Angelina swallowed. She—a witch from the Central Network—marrying the High Priest's son?

A fraud.

It would *kill* May if she ever found out. A lovely concept, shoving all that back in her face. *Look at me now, May,* Angelina would say. *I became something more without you. Who is the failure now?*

"Indeed," she murmured. "It shows."

His eyes sparkled, as if appropriately flattered. Angelina eased further into this new role. *It wouldn't be that hard,* she thought, *falling in love with such a steady, attractive witch. Not hard at all.*

"How did you know who I am?" he asked.

She grinned, drawing a design in the water with her toe. "You're very out of place here." She slipped him a half-smile. "How has your *Impegno* been so far? Found the witch of your dreams yet?"

His sober gaze met hers.

"No."

She blinked, taken aback by his straightforward answer. Her heart burned. "Oh," she said. "I'm sorry for you, then."

He glanced away, brow heavy. "It's not as easy as it sounds."

"The peasant girls aren't interested?"

"Terrified, is more like it. The city girls are too . . . amorous. I don't even know them, yet they shove their bosoms in my face. How can I choose a wife amongst the desperate?"

"You can't blame the peasant girls," she said with a shrug. "What you offer is terrifying."

He threw up his hands. "Why? I offer them everything. I offer them the *world*. But they don't want it." He turned away, flinging a hand as if throwing something away. "Or they want it too much, and I fear what they really desire. Because it's . . ."

She held her breath, waiting. "It's what?" she prodded gently.

His brow grew heavy. His hand rested in his lap, the line rest loose between his fingers.

"It's too much to ask that they would care for me *and* the Network, isn't it? That they wouldn't be hand fasting me for just my position. I want them to be passionate about improving the lives of our witches, but also about me."

"Too much for some, maybe." She returned her gaze to the ocean, taking comfort in its vast expanse. "But not for all. Maybe you're looking in all the wrong places."

"Oh?"

She gestured behind them, to a small fishing village not far away. Streams of smoke drifted from the trees. The distant sound of children shouting drifted occasionally over the crashing waves.

"These fishergirls grew up in the same village, with the same witches, their whole lives. To them, the world is quite small, and they're happy to leave it that way. Tearing them away from their family would be excruciating, at best. Disastrous, at worst. Can you imagine plunging into Magnolia Castle when the largest witch-made structure you'd ever seen is no bigger than the market in Necce?"

"Oh." His shoulders slumped. "I never thought of that."

"And the city girls want you for your title. Am I correct?"

He eyed her warily. "Yes."

"They're *almost* rich, yes?"

"Yes."

"So, you offer them—and their family—the most direct, lazy route to everything they've wanted, but has been out of reach. To those in the cities, love in hand fasting isn't the point. Ascension is."

He leaned back on his palms. "You're right. How do you know all this?"

She shrugged. "I watch. Witches are the same everywhere."

He grunted. His eyes had become an umber storm. He pinched all the fingers in one hand together, shaking it slightly.

"Then where is the pride for the Network?" he asked. "Why are none of these girls proud of being from the East? Of our bustling artist communities and lack of war? The peace we experience came because of my grandfather."

His fervor waned. He let out a long breath.

"The witches are starting to forget, I fear, what it was like before the Mansfeld Pact. The war. The death. The destruction of our economy. Blood running in the streets. No one is proud."

She reached over, putting her hand on top of his. "Perhaps they just don't *know* enough to be proud. You need to find the witches that know the Network. That aren't afraid of leaving home. That don't care about riches or expensive gowns. See? You're just looking in all the wrong places."

"What?" he asked, grinning. "Are you talking about a wanderer? Do you think my father would agree if I brought a homeless girl to the castle?"

Angelina recoiled. "Why . . . I—no! Th-that's not at all what I meant to say." She yanked her hand away. "I'm sorry, Your Highness. I shouldn't have touched you. I never meant to insinuate myself or—"

His amusement faded. He reached out, but didn't make contact. "I meant no offense. Truly, I was only teasing."

Angelina pushed her hair out of her face and climbed to her feet, managing a perfect curtsy. His eyes drifted over her form, sending a dizzying rush in her head. A gaze that long, with a little hint of color on his cheeks, couldn't be a bad sign.

"Please don't assume I meant myself, Your Highness. I'm certainly the last witch that could wear any sort of crown." She scoffed, plucking at her dress. "See what I wear now? I'm sorry. I must go."

He leapt to his feet. "Please, don't go. I don't want you to go. I was only teasing you, Miss—wait. What is your name?"

She stood just as a silvery fish leapt out of the water. The line in Diego's hands went taut and slid through his fingers. He grabbed it as if on instinct, his head snapping from the fish, to her, and back again.

Angelina backed away. "Thank you for the lovely discussion. It was wonderful to meet you, Your Highness."

"Wait!"

Abandoning her things, Angelina ran from the pier, the slippery sand loose beneath her bare feet. He followed. No match for his strong, sturdy legs, he soon overtook her, grabbing her wrist with his hand. His touch was extraordinarily soft.

"Please." He panted, swallowing. "Please, give me your name? I cannot bear the thought of never seeing you again. I will wander the whole Network again if I have to."

Angelina hesitated just long enough to see a flash of fear in his eyes. A feeling of confidence settled deep into her chest.

Ah, sweet Diego, she thought. *I have you right where I want you. We shall be great together, you and I.*

With a demure tilt of her head and a low curtsy, she whispered, "My name is Isobel, Your Highness."

CHAPTER 5

Camille

C amille has always had my heart.
It wasn't until I wrote War of the Networks *that I realized how much. I missed her after the Network Series finished, which is why I selfishly decided to write the love story between Camille and Brecken.*

Reconnecting with Camille through these scenes satisfied a desire I'd harbored since writing Alkarra Awakening.

I hope you love Camille and Brecken as much as I do.

* * *

Camille had never faced a forest dragon before.

Then again, who had? They were *supposed* to be legends. A flicker of darkness in Letum Wood caught her eye, along with a slitted yellow eye that faded into darkness. Camille swallowed back a building scream.

"Okay," she whispered. "Okay, okay, okay. We just need to get out of here, that's all. Will it come after us if I start running? What if I scream?"

"Don't scream." Her best friend Bianca held out a steady hand. "I don't think it wants to hurt us, and I'm not sure it's seen you. Back up to the other side of the hedge."

Camille obeyed, feeling marginally better when *something* stood between her and the giant monster. She closed her eyes. Her fists clenched so tight her nails dug into her palms.

I will not die before I've had my first kiss, she thought. *I just won't do it!*

Bianca hadn't moved. Her gray eyes trained forward, no doubt tracking the beast. If any witch could remain calm with a dragon running loose, Bianca could. Camille's hitched breath lessened. She'd be safe with Bianca around.

Surely.

"Go find a Guardian and tell him what's going on, Camille," she whispered. "Can you do that?"

"Y-yes. Right. Calm. Calm. Calm. I'm calm. I'm calm. Can't you just transport us out of here?"

Bianca's silky black locks swayed as she shook her head. "Transportation doesn't work when two witches are touching. Just run back to Chatham. As soon as you're safe, I'll transport over and meet you near the back door."

"O-okay."

Camille lingered for a pause. *But what about you?* she wanted to ask. Although eager to escape the leering dragon's gaze, she didn't want to abandon Bianca to her death. Even if Bianca loved this kind of thing.

Camille crept back through the field, the grass swishing beneath her as she forced each step. "Find a Guardian," she muttered under her breath, attempting an awkward jog. "Find a Guardian. Be safe."

She cast one last glance over her shoulder. Bianca stood in the same spot, her hair fluttering in the tepid breeze. The dragon loomed high above the hedge, his angular head flashing a deep blue in the sunlight. He bared his teeth. His head whipped to the right. With a little squeak of fear, Camille spun back around, her legs flying as she ran for the castle. Oh, *why* hadn't she learned transportation yet?

"Find a Guardian. Find a Guardian!"

The Guardians would flock around her at dinner after all this chaos *for sure*. They couldn't resist a good story. Rumors about dragons circulated the contingents constantly. Now, she'd not only seen one, but practically been eaten.

Panting, she crested the final hill leading to Chatham Castle, where butlers bustled around tables set for the High Priestess's spring luncheon. Servants rushed to and fro with shiny silverware and taut lips.

"Hey," Camille screamed, waving an arm as she ran. "HEY! There's a dragon!"

The dragon bellowed, releasing a plume of fire. Camille's feet tangled, and she fell to her hands and knees. She looked in between her arms. From her upside down perspective, she saw the dragon straighten, wings spread. Smoke billowed from his mouth. Bianca had disappeared.

"Bianca!" she screamed, shoving to her feet. The nearest butler stared at the dragon in wide-eyed fear, a flute of champagne slipping from his hand and crashing to the floor.

"Call the Guardians," she snapped to him. "Now!"

Camille sprinted back down the sloping hill. She threw herself between the hedges only to find a burly witch running for Bianca, a murderous gleam in his eyes. Camille stopped. Bianca didn't even flinch as he barreled toward her.

"Bianca!" Camille screamed.

The witch threw out an arm, reaching for Bianca's neck. A glowing ball of heat shoved between the two of them, forcing him back. He shrieked. The white light exploded into a hundred thousand shards, tossing Bianca and the witch like rag dolls. The repercussion rippled through the air, breezing past Camille and stirring her limp curls, heavy with the humidity. Bianca rolled toward the dragon, who seethed with broiling smoke.

Camille's heart leapt into her throat. "Bianca," she wailed, gathering her skirts. "Why are you always getting into trouble?"

With a deep breath for courage, Camille darted down the final slope to her best friend, eyeing the dragon in terror. The beast had retreated a few steps. His wings tucked back down against his back. His tapered eyes widened. He watched Camille with what appeared to be careful disdain.

"Easy, dragon," she pleaded, her hands trembling. Egads! Why were they so *tall*? "Just let me see my friend?"

He snorted, as if he understood. Ludicrous. Camille crouched next to Bianca's head, keeping the dragon in her peripheral sight.

"Bianca? Are you alive? Bianca! Wake up!"

Bianca moaned. Her head rolled to the side. The dragon shuffled forward a step, nostrils flaring as he leaned toward them. Camille stifled a scream.

"We're both going to die if you don't wake up!" The ground shivered as the dragon inched closer. Camille bit back a sob. "Wake up! I can't drag you up this hill. I'm not strong enough!"

Her eyelids fluttering, Bianca slowly pushed up to a sitting position. At first, she stared at the forest dragon, so close his heat radiated into Camille's skin like a second sun. Sultry waves emanated from his mouth, surging over them in long strokes. Sweat trickled down the back of Camille's neck. The dragon rumbled deep in his throat. Like an arrow, Bianca scrambled backward, putting herself between Camille and the beast.

"No harm here," Bianca said in a low purr. She ducked her head, but kept her eyes forward. "What happened, Camille?"

"I ran back to make sure you were okay. I screamed for the butlers, then when I turned around you were gone, and I was scared that something happened to you. I-I didn't know what to do, so I ran back!"

"It's all right. Where are the poachers?"

Poachers? What poachers? Two witches lay prostrate on the ground up the hill, black smudges marring their expressions. A strange stillness struck a deep chill in her bones. "Those two witches?" she asked, lifting a weak hand. "They're lying on the grass. I think they're knocked out. They might be dead!"

Bianca ignored it. "I'm going to stand up, and I want you to follow but stay behind me. Understand?"

"Yes."

"Here we go."

Camille averted her eyes when the dragon sniffed the air. Once standing, Bianca hesitated, glancing to the poachers. *Not a good time for sightseeing!* Camille wanted to scream. *Do you see the dragon breathing fire above us?*

"Bianca?" Camille asked, swallowing. "What about the dragon?"

"He won't hurt us. He won't. I can feel it."

"Are you mad? It's a *dragon*!"

"Maybe." Bianca hesitated. Before she could say another word, shouts broke the silence. Camille shrieked when five Guardians transported into the air around them, forming a human shield. The dragon recoiled with a grunt, nostrils flaring. "About bloody time," Camille muttered.

"Are you all right, Miss Bianca?"

A Captain strode toward them, his dark chocolate curls bouncing with every step. Camille lifted an eyebrow. *Oh, merry meet,* she thought. *I don't know you.*

"Yes," Bianca said, as if they'd been taking tea. "I'm not hurt."

I'm fine, Camille wanted to say, waving an airy hand. *Don't worry about me. I just ran back into the dragon's lap to save her life.*

She closed her eyes instead, drawing in a deep breath.

I'm safe now, she thought, repeating an oft-used refrain. *I'm safe. Someone out there loves me and is happy I'm okay, even if I haven't found them yet. I'm safe.*

When she opened her eyes, Bianca had paled. Her eyes were drawn. Like the dragon, her nostrils flared as she stared into the distance, lost in thought. Camille watched her with a mixture of awe and concern. Ever since her mother died months before, Bianca radiated a strange mix of rage and sorrow. Now, more than ever, she burned hot as a coal. Camille feared she'd be burned if she touched Bianca's arm.

The Captain motioned toward the castle. "Let's get you back," he said.

His eyes slid to Camille's for a brief moment. In that pause, her heart nearly stopped. *The good gods,* she thought. *He is the most beautiful witch I've ever seen.* He looked past her, as if he hadn't really seen her.

"Your father will be hearing of this by now, no doubt," the Captain said to Bianca, "and will want to see you himself. I'll walk you back."

The shrill voice of Aunt Bettina rang through Camille's head. *There's no one to check on you, Camille. Forgotten girl. An orphan once, an orphan always.*

She dismissed the stab of pain and jealousy, but it left a lump in her throat anyway. Bettina had never said words like that. Not really. Bettina had subtle disapproval down to an art. But Camille still *felt* as if Bettina said it. Determined to take her mind off it, Camille hurried her gait until she walked beside the Captain, feeling safer with him close. The rest of the contingent remained behind, scurrying to do the Captain's bidding.

"I'm Camille," she said. "I don't believe we've met before."

He grunted. She scrambled to keep up with his long strides. In the rapid movement, the metal plates of his half-armor jostled against the leather connecting them. With every swing of his arm, the symbol of the Guardian on his wrist seemed to flash. Most of her friends here at Chatham Castle were Guardians, but she hadn't met many of the Captains.

"I'm assuming you have a name," she drawled.

His gaze slid to hers from the corner of his eyes. "Brecken," he said. The name sent a thrill through her. What a delightful name. So rare. With a fun little twang in the middle. Breh—*cken*.

She paused for a moment, as if considering what he said. "Brecken suits you."

He ignored her.

Camille squared her shoulders. "Well, thank you for walking us back to the castle, Brecken. After encountering a dragon, it's nice to feel safe."

He kept his eyes ahead. Bianca had fallen behind by now. Camille sent a worried glance over her shoulder, but Bianca seemed lost in the same stubborn haze she'd been in since her Mama died. Camille would take Bianca back to the Witchery, where she could space out.

Then she'd go to Fina in the kitchen and scrounge up a lot of chocolate.

Her terror of the dragon began to fade. Camille let the harrowing memories go. Dwelling on it wouldn't help. Besides, it wasn't like she could write to anyone about it. Aunt Bettina would blame her for it somehow, and Angie would faint for three days straight.

Camille let several strides pass—*jikes*, but he walked fast—before she attempted conversation again. Some Guardians were so fickle.

"Where are you from, Brecken?"

A sure win. Guardians loved talking about themselves. Brecken wasn't likely to be different. Several beats of silence passed without a word from him. Camille blinked. "Uh . . . I'm from Hansham. It's a little village in Letum Wood. Lovely place. Excellent bakery. Have you heard of it?"

Two Guardians jogged up to Brecken, saluting as they slowed. He barked a couple of orders and the two continued on. One of them, Luther, departed with a wink. Camille's stomach plummeted in a downward spiral. *Oh*, she thought. *How awkward!*

Camille rubbed her fingers together as she half-ran, half-walked back to Brecken's side. What if Brecken had seen Luther take such flirtatious liberties? He'd think her brazen! Then she'd never find out anything about him.

A few days earlier, Luther had asked her to go with him to the Anniversary Ball—still months away—but she turned him down. Too early to say *yes*. Plenty of time for a genuine romance to bud up somewhere. *Someone to really care,* she thought with a discreet glance at Bianca, who frowned at the ground. *Like Bianca. Everyone cares about her. Her father. The High Priestess. Leda. Stella. But I'll find someone to fear for my life when I encounter a dragon.*

A one-time occurrence, hopefully.

The castle closed in with surprising speed. She only had a few minutes to appease her oppressive curiosity. She simply *had* to get one real response out of him.

"Do you have a favorite weapon?" she asked, half-panting. She pressed a hand into her side to allay a building stitch. "Most Guardians pretend they like hand-to-hand fighting best. Barbaric, if you ask me. Others say swords. The Archers sound really difficult to get into."

Did she imagine it, or did his grip on the hilt of his sword tighten? Was it awkward to walk so fast with one hand on his sword?

"I-I've been at the castle for a few weeks now," she continued with another poor attempt to hide her shortness of breath. "Isn't it wonderful here? The servants and the turrets and the dinners—oh, I can't even *talk* about the dinners. I haven't eaten alone once since I've come."

Camille snapped her mouth shut when Brecken's lips moved. His eyes narrowed. Every so often, he shook his head in a subtle way, as if talking to himself. Camille blinked as she realized he likely hadn't heard a word she'd just said.

Very odd.

A little prickle of annoyance flashed through her, then faded. *My fault,* she thought in disappointment. She shouldn't bother him while on duty. Although friends with many Guardians, she made a point not to bother them while working. She wasn't desperate, after all. Just lonely.

The Wall—several stories of rock and stone melded into an almost-impenetrable defense—loomed ahead. They'd pass under the arched doorway soon, leaving the field, the dragon, and the terrible day behind. Camille would be safe. Leda would listen to their story. Michelle would be concerned and satisfy Camille's need for someone to care. It would be comforting.

Except for leaving Brecken behind.

Well, she thought, pressing her lips together as Brecken peeled away with one last question to Bianca. *I'll just have to find a time to talk to him while he isn't working.*

She started up the Wall steps, her mind already whirling with plans.

* * *

Finding the right mealtime in the staff dining room required careful calculation. Fortunately, Camille knew just when to arrive so there weren't too many Guardians or too few.

She planned her lunches and dinners with precision. Eating with the same Guardians too often would create gossip amongst the servants. Unbecoming. Somehow, Bettina would hear. She always did. Even though the Guardians were just silly witches that made her laugh, Bettina would find something improper. In a world dominated by masculine arrogance, any touch of femininity sent Guardians reeling, especially pretty curls and a quick smile. Camille didn't mind a little careless flirting. So long as they kept their proper distance.

She waited outside the dining hall the next day, cloaked in an invisibility incantation. Idle chatter sifted through passing witches. She'd have to be invisible more often. The maids had far looser tongues this way.

"—nearly killed both poachers with her magic."

"Wasn't even wearing shoes, I hear."

"Derek will give the poachers Veritas, no doubt."

"Dragons? Honestly. I don't believe it."

"Local Factios members, I bet."

"Did you see the article? Dragons are back!"

She scowled. Blessed be. *Bianca wasn't the only one there,* she wanted to say, but bit her bottom lip. What did it matter? Any minute now, the first wave of Guardians would fill the dining hall with the intermingling scents of sweat and leather. Brecken should be amongst them.

She'd watched him from the Witchery turret as he trained, just to be sure.

Sure enough, Guardians flooded the hall minutes later. Once they settled at the tables with their food, Camille straightened her dress, pushed her hair away from her face, and removed the magic. With an eye on a far table, she piled a cucumber sandwich and fresh fruit on her plate. She sashayed through the tables, plate balanced on one hand. Brecken sat at a small table with one other Guardian on the far left.

Perfect.

Camille veered to the right.

Luther and Zeke called to her before she reached their table. "Oy! Camille! Over here."

"Camille!"

Luther waved a long arm. She lifted her hand with a vague smile. "Merry meet, gentle witches," she sang. A chorus echoed back, rippling down the packed benches. Zeke straightened. A blond Guardian named Ted cleared his throat. Another named Jameson looked away, but peeked back from the corner of his eye.

Camille continued on her path, alone. She settled on the end of an empty table large enough for six. By the time she set down her plate and smoothed a napkin on her skirt, two bodies flanked her. Zeke and Luther.

Just as planned.

"So, Camille," Luther said, tapping her shoulder with his. "How are you doing? Rumors have been flying, you know. Your friend danced with a dragon, apparently?"

Zeke sat across from her, tossing his stick-straight black hair out of his eyes. He smiled, quiet and reserved. Camille tightened her jaw, then relaxed. So what if Bianca always had the spotlight? She sank her fork into a piece of strawberry, slicing it in half. The heavy *clink* of the fork against the plate satisfied her.

"Yes, Bianca did encounter a dragon," she said. "But thankfully she came out all right. Only the poachers were injured."

"So . . . she didn't wrestle it?" Zeke asked, casting a sidelong glance at Luther. Luther cleared his throat.

"No!" Camille cried. "Are you crazy?"

Zeke slugged Luther, nearly sending him off the bench. "Told you."

"Oy! That hurt. Garret told me she wrestled the dragon *and* killed two witches."

"They were stunned." Zeke rolled his eyes. "Not dead. You'd believe anything, Luther."

"How do you know if they're dead or not?" Luther puffed out his chest. "You've been in the dungeons all morning."

"Yeah. Two poachers are down there, imbecile. Derek had a little visit with them not long after. You should have heard the screa—"

Camille cleared her throat. "Where did you hear the news? I thought the two of you hated reading the *Chatterer*."

"Guardian report." Luther shrugged. "The Captains have to write them up after incidents. Couple of witches read it out loud before the run today."

Camille turned her attention to a piece of cucumber, willing herself to be hungry. Not an ounce of appetite could compel her to eat when she dangled on the cusp of all the information she needed.

"Paperwork? Sounds boring," she drawled. "Not as fun as fighting off the poachers, I imagine?"

Luther guffawed. "Certainly not."

Zeke clucked under his breath. "Those stupid blokes sure got it when Derek interrogated them."

"Who was the unlucky Captain that had to do paperwork?" she asked, pushing the fruit aside and studiously avoiding their gaze. Zeke gestured with a nod to the other side of the room.

"Breck did."

A thrill skimmed her spine. "Breck?"

"Brecken. He was the Captain on duty."

Must not write very thorough reports, she thought, although Brecken struck her as the meticulous sort. A skill she couldn't even fathom bothering with. Why hadn't he included her in the report?

"Hmm," she murmured around a long sip of cool water.

With careful ease, Camille cast a careless glance at Brecken's table. He leaned forward, fork in hand, listening intently as the other witch spoke, waving his arms. Brecken commanded an undercurrent of purpose and single-handed attention. Like everyone else, sweat stained his collar and the tendrils of his hair. The dining room always smelled foul in the summer, thanks to all the stinky bodies after training.

Affecting as bored an air as possible, she waved for a nearby pitcher of water and an empty glass. It settled on the table. Luther reached to pour it for her, and she gave him a grateful smile.

"Is Brecken new?" she asked.

"No," Zeke said.

"Just quiet," Luther added.

"Captains like him. Guardians don't. Thinks a lot. Follows the rules." Zeke tapped the side of his head, leaving a few crumbs in the reedy black strands. "Real smart. Good with tactical planning, I've heard."

Luther's nose wrinkled. "He works too hard. Then we have to work hard. I don't like him."

Zeke and Luther laughed, as if he'd told a joke. Camille let it go, smoothing out a ruffle of annoyance. Steering the conversation onto Brecken so easily had been a small miracle. The two of them had attention spans the size of gnats.

"Where's Brecken from?" she asked with a sip of water. It trickled down the back of her throat, soothing and cool.

"Dunno."

She scowled. "What *do* you know about him?"

Zeke's brow furrowed. "Why d'ya want to know? Thought ya hadn't heard of him?"

Camille's shoulders snapped back. "That's why I want to know."

Luther tossed a hearty piece of meat pie into his mouth and chewed around it. "Aw, don't worry about that. Just boring stuff."

Zeke waved it off. "Hey, how do you make your hair so curly anyway?"

Camille staved off another burst of irritation. She just wanted some solid information about Brecken. Attempting conversation a second time would be tricky. She'd have to be successful, or fail without appearing too cheeky and bold.

Such a delicious challenge.

"Brecken's a bore, anyway," Luther continued. "He's on grounds duty, which means he patrols the perimeter of Chatham Castle. Walks through gardens to check security. Can't imagine anything more boring than that."

Camille ignored them. It sounded romantic and wonderful. Except in the heat. She'd rather walk the gardens in the fall, when her hair stayed in defined curls and her arms didn't sweat.

"That's where the poachers hid, you know?" Zeke said. "Hid in the gardens. Brecken would have found them soon enough. He was probably delayed smelling the flowers."

Luther snorted. "Or chasing burrowing gnomes in Fina's cellars. Hardly a real job!"

They both chortled again.

Camille folded her cloth napkin into a perfect triangle. Her plate of food remained untouched, pieces of fruit cut into varying sizes.

"I see," she murmured.

"Hey, Zeke." Luther shoved his shoulder. "Did you hear about the Guardians on watch last night? Swore they saw a red dragon. Said it was fierce."

Zeke snorted. "They lie. You can't see a forest dragon at night. They're too sneaky and dark enough to blend into any night sky."

"They swear it."

Camille leaned back as the two of them descended into a debate over whether forest dragons glowed in the dark. Her eyes slipped to the other side of the room. Brecken had leaned back in his chair, relaxing against the wood. He sat alone at the table now.

Her stomach dropped like a stone when he looked up, his gaze grabbing hers in a frightening embrace. She gasped. Brecken had eyes like the sky, even from here. His mass of curls spun around his head in loose abandon. For what felt like an eternity, they stared. Camille's stomach fluttered. Then a raucous group of Guardians walked between them, obscuring her view.

When they passed, Brecken was gone.

* * *

Days later, Camille dropped her textbooks with a groan.

"Why are books so heavy?"

Leda shot her a glare. "Treat your books like gold, Camille," she hissed. "They're worth far more."

"They weigh more than a dragon," Camille mumbled. "I would know! I practically fought one off."

"Quiet. The librarians will kick you out."

Leda carried four textbooks in her left arm, not counting the three in her bulging bag that swung at her hip. She'd drown beneath them any moment now. A nearby librarian passed with a *huff*. Leda smiled an apology to her and then pressed her lips into a thin line of warning as she faced Camille again.

"Can't you help me?" Camille pled in a quieter tone. "Leda, you know I'm terrible with algebra. Numbers and letters shouldn't mix!"

"No, I can't help you. I have too much of my own homework. Besides, the scroll Miss Scarlett assigned you is just a review. You can't fail. She just needs to measure what you already know."

Leda glanced to the other side of the circular room, no doubt worried she'd lose the table she claimed every day. Her books didn't fit on anything smaller.

"But Leda!"

"You can do it, Camille." Her expression softened. "I know you can."

Camille sighed and settled onto a wooden chair with a *plop*. "Right," she muttered. "Sorry."

Leda eyed her with her straw-colored eye, a lock of white hair spilling into her face, before disappearing around a stack of books twice her height. She'd study alone, on the other side of the library, like she always did.

You talk too much, Camille, Leda always said with a sigh. *Even when you think you're being really quiet.*

The dead talk too much for Leda, Camille thought, peeling open her algebra scroll. The columns of symbols and numbers made her nose wrinkle.

"Jikes," she said. "I'd rather face the forest dragon again."

Camille found a properly sharpened pencil. Rooted through the bottom of her bag on the offhand chance she'd hidden a snack. Smoothed out her homework scroll—which had a little fleck of dust she couldn't brush away—and glanced at the clock.

Only two minutes had passed.

Resigning herself to her fate, she dropped her chin onto her palm and skimmed the equations. The droll voice of Miss Scarlett rang through her head as she attempted to read them a second time.

Algebra Equation Review.

$$9x + 5x = ?$$

Camille bit her bottom lip, scrawling out a confident *14x.* "Easy," she said, moving on to the next.

Solve for x.

$$3x - 4 = 7 + 2x$$

With careful pencil strokes, she worked out the equation, and, with a little breath of relief, wrote:

$$X = 11$$

Maybe Leda had the right idea, Camille thought, straightening. *This is easy! I love algebra!* She buzzed through the next four questions, but screeched to a halt at the fifth. Blinking, she tilted her head to the side. "Uh oh."

$$13x / 5 = 20 / 3x$$

She gulped. "Oh, dear."
Uncertain, she moved to the next problem.

$$(2)(y-3)(5 / 2(y-3)) = [(10 - y)/(y-3)](2)(y-3)$$

Her eyes skimmed the page with growing trepidation. The equations went from challenging to impossible. Two equations didn't even have numbers. Camille rubbed her earlobe, taking in deep breaths. She'd fail. Miss Scarlett would make her retake algebra from the beginning, and she couldn't handle the thought of relearning it once more.

Bettina would be so disappointed in her—again.

Resolved to do her best, Camille pulled the scroll close, leaned forward, and set to work. Twenty minutes of attempting to apply what she *thought* she knew left her with a paper flooded with useless scribbles and a stubby pencil. She fumed for a full minute, staring at it with a heated frown.

"Forget it."

She shoved the scroll away. The satisfying sound of parchment tearing followed. With a passionate growl, she grabbed her algebra book and lifted it over her head. Flinging it across the floor would—

"Having a good time?"

Startled by the unexpected voice behind her, she jumped. The algebra book slipped from her fingers, crashing onto the top of her head with a heavy *thud*. She scrambled for purchase, managing to catch it before it hit the ground.

A pair of sky blue eyes slid into view, accented by thick chocolate curls. Camille's heart leapt into her throat.

Brecken!

A bolt of terror and elation ripped down her spine and left her knees in a mushy mudslide. Brecken's eyes tapered, flickering from the crown of her head to the book.

"You all right?"

Her cheeks flared a bright red. "Uh, yes. Fine. Thanks."

He plucked the book from her limp hands. "Why kill the algebra book?"

"It deserved it."

A hint of a smile lingered at the corner of his mouth. Her headache spread. With it came the ugly realization: she'd just dropped a textbook on her head. In front of Brecken. She'd have to play it cool a few minutes longer until he left or she could slip away—and speak with him later, when a pyramid of eraser shavings didn't cover her dress.

Snatching the book, she slammed it back to the table. The same librarian sent her a surly frown. Camille scowled back. Under his breath, Brecken chuckled. Or had she imagined it?

"I'm not in the mood for jokes," she muttered, rubbing the top of her head. "Go away. I need to figure this out."

"Homework?"

"Yes."

He stepped back, and she let out a breath of relief. *Go,* she thought. *Just go.* Maybe she could salvage the remnants of her pride. Oh, she'd never talk to him after this. It just . . . it wouldn't be worth it. She could find someone else to take her to the Anniversary Ball. Someone as deliciously mysterious had to be out there. She studied him from the corner of her eyes.

Well . . . maybe.

He'd already turned to leave when he paused. Camille's heart pounded. Why didn't he keep going? *Just go already!* she wanted to scream. He turned slowly to face her.

"Would you like some help?" he asked.

Her back stiffened.

"Really?"

He put his hands on the chair across from her. "Yes. I used to teach my brothers. I love math. I miss it, actually."

Camille sat there for several moments, staring at his hands. Firm. Long, sturdy fingers. A hint of callouses on the edges of his palms, like any devoted Guardian. But not Luther. Nor Zeke.

"But . . . why would you help?" she asked, unable to tear her eyes away from the wide palms and slightly bruised knuckles. Had he gotten into a fight?

He shrugged. "Why not?"

"Because learning algebra is miserable!"

"Only if you don't know what you're doing." The chair slid across the wooden floor with a scraping sound as he pulled it toward him and then sat down. This certainly hadn't been what she expected. Swallowing back a rise of nausea—she'd dropped a book on her head, after all—she pushed the homework scroll to him.

"I've been trying for almost half an hour," she said. "I can't figure it out past equation six. I *used* to know how to do up to ten, but I've forgotten. I don't . . . I don't want Miss Scarlett to think I'm stupid."

His eyes darted through the jungle of her failed attempts all the way down to the final equation—something she'd never dream of completing on her own. All letters? No numbers? How could that even be *math?*

Brecken set it down.

"Easy. I can help you with this. We'll do a review. Then you'll probably figure it out on your own."

She lifted her gaze to meet his, surprised by the breathless flare of heat in her chest. How could she tell him no? Brecken wanted to help her. The same girl he'd blatantly ignored after she chased down a dragon and saved her best friend. Did he think her stupid because she didn't know algebra? Did her hair look okay?

A simple review wouldn't harm anything, right?

With a hesitant smile, Camille nodded. "Yes," she said. "If you don't mind, I would appreciate some help."

Brecken nodded once. Camille wondered if he ever smiled—really smiled.

He reached for the textbook. "Let's start here," he said, thumbing through the pages. "We'll look over a few equations, and then you can work them out on your own."

Camille swallowed. "Sure," she said with a little sense of relief, uncertain whether she felt it because Brecken was finally giving her some attention, or because she had a prayer of not disappointing Miss Scarlett.

Either way, sitting next to him felt good.

And Camille loved feeling good.

* * *

"Leda. I'm horrible with algebra. He's going to think I'm really stupid. Why did I agree? How can I let him tutor me?"

Leda rolled her eyes. They strolled through Chatham Castle on their way back to the Witchery. Sunlight slanted through the windows, illuminating the air with dust motes. Camille's head pounded, whirling with numbers and letters and the exhaustion of studying. One of Fina's fizzy drinks and a solid brownie would pull her out of the funk of *thinking*.

Luther and Zeke would be off duty soon. Maybe they'd go for a walk with her through the gardens. She never had to use her brain much with them around. Except last time when they'd tried to throw her into a pond. Camille veered to a different plan.

"No, he isn't going to think you're stupid," Leda said. "From what you said, he seemed really eager to help you with algebra."

Camille's nose wrinkled. "I know. So weird."

"No, it's not," Leda snapped. "Some witches *like* algebra."

"I know," Camille grumbled. "So weird."

Leda sighed.

"Leda, algebra is not romantic." Camille clenched her book and scroll to her chest until it crinkled. Leda glanced over, frowning in disapproval. "There's no way to drift into other conversations. He was totally focused on those stupid letters. I tried to get him to talk, but noooo."

Leda sent the door to the Witchery turret open with a wave of her hand. "So, he's focused. That's not the worst thing for you, you know."

Camille opened her mouth to reply but stopped. Leda had a point. Bettina's voice drifted back through Camille's mind.

You need to focus, Camille. You could really achieve great things if you stopped flittering from one project to the next.

Camille sent the thought away with a frustrated growl. Leda's slippered steps pattered up the spiral staircase with dainty ease.

"Camille, why are you so upset about this? It's just Brecken. You aren't even courting. He's only helped you *once*. And it wasn't even a graded assignment. Just a review!"

"It's more than that. How will I ever get him to ask me to the Anniversary Ball?"

Leda lifted her brows. "What does the Anniversary Ball have to do with anything?"

"I want him to ask me."

"Why?"

Camille's mouth went dry. How could she explain it to Leda? It barely made sense to her. Something about Brecken's intensity and quiet movements had her mesmerized. Why did he care? What cogs turned behind his beautiful sky blue eyes? He struck a strange chord between the powerful Guardians and a focused intellectual. The aftereffects hummed deep inside her.

She'd never met a witch like him.

"Because I like him," Camille admitted quietly. "I just . . . I just really need him to ask me to the Ball. It's romantic. It's . . . it's a definable, real thing he can do to show that he's interested."

A small inner voice echoed through her head.

I just really need someone to care.

Leda stopped on the final step, one hand on the doorknob into the Witchery. Her bemused gaze cut through the darkness of the corridor.

"Just let him tutor you, Camille. If romance is real, it'll happen, right?"

Leda slipped inside the Witchery, leaving Camille on the steps, lost in thought.

* * *

The soft edges of spring faded into the sultry waves of summer.

Instead of being cool and refreshing, the fragrant air lay heavy and wet on Camille's shoulders. The unbearable heat crept into the castle throughout the day, increasing until she couldn't stand it. For now, the whole world felt uncomfortably warm. Wildflowers bloomed around her in velvety patches of deep color. She stood in the middle of the castle gardens, eyeing a bush of bulbous pink catclaws.

Any minute now, Brecken, she thought, tapping her right foot. *I have classes to attend.*

There would be nothing romantic about algebra lessons, but walking in a garden of wildflowers rang with passionate tension. Brecken would be on his rounds soon. She'd nab him then.

Her stomach growled. She longed for a drink of cool water. She'd already been out for an hour, wandering from flower to flower, jumping at every sound. What if Brecken did his rounds after lunch while she was in history class?

"What am I doing here?" she muttered, caressing the velvety petal of a dragon flower. "I'm insane."

The crinkle of Bettina's latest letter issued from her dress pocket. Her shoulders slumped. Perhaps she *should* work on algebra. She certainly hadn't accomplished much last night—four Guardians had invited her during dinner on a tour of the upper dungeons. She shuddered, recalling the dank air with only hints of sunshine from high slits in the walls. Below that, the true dungeons lingered, filled with horrible witches and no sunlight at all.

Sounds like life with Bettina, she thought, wandering to the garden opening. A rickety wheelbarrow blocked her path. Behind it stood a wizened old gardener with a bushy white mustache. His kind, wrinkled face lit up in a smile.

"Oh! Sorry, miss. Didn't see you there."

"It's all right."

Piles of weeds filled the wheelbarrow, topped by rusty trowels and hand-sized rakes. He steered the wheelbarrow with a spell. One hand pressed into the small of his back while he wiped his forehead with the other. He belonged in a plush, comfortable chair with stacks of books and a decanter of dark ipsum, not out here in the heat of the day.

"Are you here to weed?" she asked.

He chuckled. "Certainly not here to hold a Council Meeting. What's your name?"

"Camille."

"I'm Gerald. Old and ornery Gerald."

Camille smiled. "Do you need some help?" she asked, gesturing to the flower beds. Bettina often sent her outside to weed the garden in the summer. *Keeps your hands busy so your mouth stops for a while,* she'd always say. *Stay outside until my headache fades.*

Camille didn't mind the rough, earthy smell of dirt. She just didn't like it to linger beneath her fingernails forever.

Gerald paused, regarding her. "Help?"

"With weeding." She gestured with a wave of her hand. "I'd love to help, if you need it."

He muttered something she couldn't hear. All the weeds zipped out of the earth, collecting into a knee-high pile in the middle of the garden. Clods of dirt rained from the sky.

"Getting the weeds into the wheelbarrow is my problem," he said with a grimace. "My back flares up these days, you know. Can't scoop them up."

Camille brightened. "I can help."

She collected the weed pile and stuffed it into the wheelbarrow. The thick leaves itched against her skin, leaving a sickly sweet scent behind. She didn't mind.

"Thank you!" Gerald cried. "That will be much nicer on my back. Come on, then. Let me talk at you for a bit while we go to the next garden. I'm always seeking someone that hasn't heard all my stories."

He prattled about a trellis that needed fixing and a stubborn rosebush that wouldn't bloom, interweaving stories about his life as a gardener for forty years. Camille fell into his happy, mindless chatter with delight.

"And your wife just . . . up and left?" she shrieked, mouth slack. "You're joking!"

Gerald chuckled, grinning beneath his mustache. "Yes. I never demanded she make me dinner again. I went to bed hungry and alone that night. That was the last time." His brow fell. "Until she died two years ago."

Camille swallowed. "I'm so sorry you lost her, Gerald. It's terrible losing loved ones. But it's more terrible living without them every day."

His eyes sparkled. "Yes. It is. But life happens. We must accept it and move on."

"Will you tell me how you met? I love a good romance." She clasped her hands as they drifted past a tinkling waterfall. "Your wife sounds simply wonderful."

His eyes lit up. "Prepare yourself. It all started on my twelfth birthday, when—"

"Gerald," a familiar voice called. "Are you talking to the statues again? How is your back? I came to see if I could help."

Camille straightened up from a fresh pile of weeds with a squeak. Brecken stopped mid-stride, his eyes widening. The weeds dropped back to the grass. A stalk of leaves swung from a curl by her left ear.

"Brecken. There you are." Gerald lifted a hand in greeting. "This is my new friend Camille."

A current of panic raced through the air, swelling her discomfort. *No!* Camille thought. *My hair is messed up, and I'm all sweaty. This is not romantic!*

Brecken nodded, clearing his throat. "Merry meet, Camille. It's, uh, good to see you out here."

She peeped a quiet, "Merry meet."

"So, Brecken," Gerald said, clapping him on the back, "I hear you're having troubles with dragons lately?"

Gerald steered Brecken into conversation, giving Camille a moment to collect herself. Her mind spun. She always encountered him at the wrong moment! Instead of appearing composed and feminine, she looked like . . . Bianca. Weeds in her hair. Stains on her dress. Her fingernails rimmed with dirt. Brecken would think her an untamed forester.

Frantic, she shoved the weeds into the wheelbarrow, brushed the stems from her dress, and straightened. Brecken glanced at her from the corner of his eye and then looked away. His lips twitched.

"Merry part, Gerald," Camille said, calling on all her strength. She side-stepped away. "I need to get to class."

Gerald smiled with a toothless gap in the very front. "Thanks for your help, Miss Camille."

Camille squared her shoulders and started toward the hedge. Just as she passed Brecken, she hesitated. Should she take advantage of him arriving unexpectedly? She'd had their conversation all mapped out—if he'd have showed up as planned.

Merry meet, Brecken, she would have said. *It's beautiful out here, isn't it?*

Yes, but not as beautiful as you in that dress. Is it periwinkle?

Dove gray.

Of course. Your sense of style knows no bounds.

She'd trill a little laugh—not too much—and he'd offer her his arm. Their fateful romance would commence, vaulting them into an everlasting love that not even Bettina could mar with her ugly breath. Camille swallowed back her excitement. She'd just *die* with the romance of it all.

With a tremor deep in her heart, Camille opened her mouth. The words came out in a painful squeak.

"Lovely day to merry meet when the doves are so gray and beautiful."

The mad tangle of words filled the vacuum of air. A horrified panic filled her chest, making it difficult to breathe. What had she said? *Lovely day to merry meet? When the doves are so gray and beautiful?*

Camille sucked in a sharp breath. Heat flooded her face. Her eyes prickled. She tensed, waiting for a condemning laugh. Oh, how Luther and Zeke would tease her relentlessly! Her hands clenched in fear.

Seconds passed. Gerald's voice continued rolling in the background. The *far* background.

Camille glanced over her shoulder to see Brecken and Gerald twenty paces away, inspecting a hedge. "Possible breach, I think," Gerald said. "Screaming gnome, maybe?"

Brecken, his brow heavy and eyes narrowed, studied a strange hole in the bush.

Camille exhaled in relief. Brecken and his blasted concentration. He hadn't even heard her ridiculous foible. She sighed. Their faultless romance would just have to begin another day.

In the meantime, she had history class to avoid.

* * *

Camille sank into the hard library chair with a groan, dropping her head back. The domed ceiling soared high above. Her algebra book lay in front of her. She hadn't even opened her new homework scroll yet. Just the thought of all the letters and multiplications sent her mind spinning.

He won't come, she thought, eyeing a painting of a naked wood nymph. *He'll be busy. Or forget. Weed in my hair. There was a weed in my hair! Why would he come?*

She let out a long breath.

No. She shook her head. *That's not fair. He'll come. He won't leave me waiting. He's too kind to leave me guessing. Isn't he? I don't even know him.*

He probably won't come.

Her thoughts spun out in wild abandon. The librarians bustled around with the quiet rustle of skirt and book. Leda's table lay empty in the distance. Camille brushed Leda's absence off. Procrastinating was always harder when Leda glared at her across the room. She could loll around all day when Leda was—

"Ready?"

Camille straightened up to find Brecken settling into a chair next to her. His wild curls bounced, still damp and coiling around his ears. The broad cut of his strong shoulders seemed more apparent than ever the way his shirt pulled across his chest. Camille swallowed.

"Er, yes."

His eyes dropped to the book, her clean quill, and the blank, unopened scroll. "Were you waiting?" he asked.

"Uh, yes. Waiting."

His lips twitched, lifting to one side. "You didn't think I'd come, did you?"

A sheepish blush crept across her cheeks. "I wondered."

His brow furrowed into two deep grooves between his eyebrows. He leaned back in his chair. "Really?"

"Well, I just didn't know! I-I thought I wouldn't be a priority. You're a Captain, after all. I mean. You must be busy? Tell me more about what you do. I hardly ever speak with Captains, to be honest."

He gestured to the book with a hand. "I told you I'd come."

"I know. I'm sorry. I shouldn't have doubted you. I just . . . I worried that you'd forget. Bettina thinks I'm awfully forgettable," she added in a mumble.

She sank lower in the chair, nearly disappearing beneath the edge of the table. His expression froze in place until he softened with a flicker of amusement. "It's fine. But for the record, I don't forget things like this."

"Obligations?" she quipped with a light-hearted smile, pushing up in her chair.

"No. Algebra lessons. Let's get started."

Her face fell. Camille swallowed. *Sweep me off my feet, why don't you?*

"Yes. Thanks." She nudged the textbook to him. "Miss Scarlett wants me to work on ways to solve linear equations. She said that we'll do a more in-depth review of the basics than originally planned. I think that means I didn't do as well as she'd hoped."

Brecken made a noise in his throat, already intent on the textbook.

The words *graphing, substitution, elimination, multiplication,* and *factors* ran through her mind in dizzying whirls. Working out math problems that combined numbers and letters was bad enough. But having to put the problems into actual words made it even worse.

Brecken shifted closer, sending the musky scent of leather in her direction. He leaned close, pointing out a paragraph in the textbook with a tap of his finger.

"It sounds complicated," he said, "but it's really simple. A linear equation is simply $x + 7y = 15$. When you plot that, it makes a line.

That's it. Once you start adding in other variables, like exponents, it's non-linear."

He drew a graph. Camille's confusion cleared as he demonstrated the first example. Her lessons from Miss Bernadette rushed back to her. *This* was familiar. She did know algebra!

"Oh." She blinked. "That's it?"

He nodded. "That's it. Pretty simple, huh?"

"Well, when you put it like *that.*"

She spun the book back toward herself and re-read the paragraph. After asking him a few clarifying questions, and receiving his approving nod, a bolt of confidence set her thoughts flying. With quick slashes, she created a graph, solved the equation, and plotted the line.

"Ha!" she cried, setting the feather down. "Take *that*, Bettina."

"Great. Let's go to the next part."

The next paragraph killed her budding enthusiasm. Increasing amounts of letters and numbers—large and small—blurred her mind.

"Jikes. What's $y = mx + b$?" she asked, peering closer at the page. "There aren't even numbers!"

"Slope intercept form."

Brecken sketched out another collection of letters, numbers, and graphs one piece at a time. His easy instructions set Camille at ease. His steps built slowly on one another. She fell into the lesson with surprising ease. The low cadence of Brecken's voice lulled her into a world where algebra made sense. Without Miss Scarlett's intense gaze looming over her shoulder, her brain relaxed. For whatever strange reason, Brecken seemed to truly enjoy teaching algebra, and his enthusiasm wore off on her.

"Oh!" she cried. "So $f(x) =$ and $y =$ are the same?"

Brecken held up his hands with the widest grin she'd seen yet. Her small victory felt all the greater for his enthusiasm. "Yes! Good work, Camille. You got it."

Camille warmed to the sound of her name from his voice. He set aside a quill, glanced to a clock, and stretched his arms behind his back. Camille followed his gaze, startled to see an hour had passed. He scooted his chair back.

No! she wanted to say. *Don't go. We haven't even talked about your favorite food or game yet!*

"Well," he said through a yawn. "I better get going."

"Oh, but wait!"

She reached over, setting a hand on his arm to stop him. The feel of his skin against her hand sent a jolt through her. She withdrew with a sheepish smile.

"Sorry. I, uh, just wanted to thank you. Before you go. For, uh, helping me."

He smiled with that slight grin that made her knees tremble. The power of his full smile would melt her into a puddle.

"No problem."

"Do I owe you anything for your help?"

He recoiled. "No. Of course not. I enjoy algebra." A fleeting grin ghosted his lips. "Makes me feel like I'm hanging out with my little brother again."

Camille's heart sank. So, he was tutoring her out of a nostalgic sense of love for his brother? She brushed that aside. He'd given her a detail! She had to make the most of the opportunity.

"What's your brother's name?" she asked.

"Colton."

He elongated his arms above his head again. Camille fought to keep her eyes on his face, determined *not* to look at the sculpt of his shoulders or the way his muscled arms rippled in the light.

"Well, I appreciate it," she said, then glared at the book. "At least someone likes that stuff."

He stood up. "Just keep going. It'll click."

Her heart plummeted. The lesson really was ending so soon? Then again, he had given her an hour. Surely, he didn't get much time off. At this rate, she'd never win Brecken over or convince him to ask her to the Anniversary Ball. *Weeds,* she thought with bitter reproach, *in my hair. Chucking my book across the room.*

Absolutely nothing in their repertoire had a hint of romance.

She gave into her thoughts with a rueful sigh. Maybe romance wasn't as important as she'd always thought.

"When do you want me to come back?" Brecken asked, setting his hands on his hips. Her head jerked up.

"What?"

"When do you want to do this again?"

She swallowed. "You want to come back?"

He let out an exasperated sigh. "Camille, I just told you. I—"

"Tomorrow! H-how about tomorrow? Whenever works best for you. I can make it work. Whatever you need. I mean, whenever you need."

Brecken paused, his gaze narrowing as if in deep thought, before nodding. "Sure. I can come in the evening. After dinner. I'll just meet you here?"

Camille exhaled in relief. Even if all they had was another algebra lesson together—hardly a tangle of romantic tension—at least it gave her time with him. And all frustrations aside, Camille couldn't deny that she'd enjoyed the last hour of algebra with Brecken's help.

An impossible thought.

"Great," she said with a grin. "I'll be here. Waiting."

For your attention forever, she added with a silent quip, watching him stride out of the library with his easy gait. Then she dropped her head onto the table.

Romance is stupid.

* * *

"I just love shopping in Chatham City," Camille said a few days later as they walked along Letum Road, flanked by the deep emerald of Letum Wood. Horses passed, their jet-black manes glittering in the sun. Her stomach rumbled with thoughts of Miss Holly's Candy Shop and her mouthwatering sea salt caramels. Michelle and Bianca flanked her on either side.

"I'm almost out of caramels," Camille continued, "so we'll stop at Miss Holly's Candy Shop first. Then we'll get a few ribbons for my ball gown at the dressmakers."

Camille mulled over her ribbon dilemma as they walked. Henrietta insisted on a colorful ribbon to play against the ivory shades of Camille's ball gown. The purity of ivory marred by color? Unnatural. Like white, ivory could hold its own. *Simplicity,* Camille thought. *Leave the extravagance for the Ball itself.*

When Camille had suggested as much, Henrietta simply rolled her eyes.

Bianca peered at the forest, her raven-black hair fluttering off her shoulders in silky banners. Michelle squinted, her beady eyes nearly disappearing into her cheeks. After spending all morning writing a history essay, Camille looked forward to the buzz and excitement in downtown Chatham City. It would be just the thing to distract her from the ugly truth: Brecken still hadn't asked her to the Anniversary Ball.

Michelle and Bianca's conversation faded into the background as they passed into Chatham City. Tray, a Guardian with red hair and pale skin, winked at Camille. She ignored him. She wasn't brazen enough to respond to such blatant flirting in public. Besides, who of the Guardians could compete with Brecken?

None.

Chatham City swarmed with witches, piles of garbage, and bouquets of fresh flowers. Nose wrinkled, Camille navigated her friends through the streets. The high-pitched *clink clink* of the blacksmith's shop reverberated in her ear.

Camille jerked to a stop.

"Oh," she said. "What's going on here?"

A growing crowd blocked the street ahead, occupying the space with the scents of body odor and char. From a platform elevated above the milling witches, a thin witch waved his arms with belligerent passion.

"Our Protectors will soon be dying under his command if we don't do something about it!" he yelled.

Bianca's nostrils flared. "Clive," she muttered. "It's one of his rallies to get signatures against Papa."

Camille swallowed a sudden rise of fear. Everyone knew *Clive*. The Guardians always talked about how much they hated working for him in Chatham City. *Lazy*, they always said. *Doesn't really care about security.*

An unforgiving ideal, in their opinion.

"The High Priestess doesn't want us ta know, but the fighting has already begun! The Guardians are in the Borderlands even as I stand in front of ya—facing the West Guards."

"He's lying," Bianca hissed. "The fighting hasn't begun yet."

"Are the West Guards in the Borderlands?" Camille asked.

Bianca paused. "No . . . and yes. They aren't in the Borderlands, they're just along it on the other side of the border."

"No one's going to care whether they are fighting or not," Michelle said. Her eyes darted through the unknown faces. "The fact that they are so close is bad enough. Let's get out of here. I have a bad feeling."

Camille's stomach flipped. *I'm safe,* she thought, falling into the familiar mantra. *I'm safe. Someone out there loves me and is happy I'm okay, even if I haven't found them yet.* Feeling marginally better, she grabbed Bianca's arm. Bianca pulled away, stumbling when a wave of witches knocked into her.

"Wait," Bianca said. "I want to hear what he says."

Camille's blood rushed in her ears. Someone shouted a comment about Tiberius.

"Bianca, let's leave," she said. "I don't think we should stay. What if someone recognizes you?"

"Wait." Rage flashed in Bianca's gray eyes like lightning in a thunderstorm. "They're talking about my father."

Hisses and angry bellows rolled through the air. The sticky rage sent goosebumps down Camille's back. Such an audience would be outright violent if they knew Bianca had come. They *must* leave.

Camille shook her head. "I know! That's why we need to go."

"She's right, Bianca." Michelle stepped forward. For a moment, Camille felt safe next to her broad shoulders. *I am safe.* The feeling faded when spittle flecked the back of her neck from a boisterous shout behind her. Witches laughed. Every moment paused, passing in lifetimes while Bianca listened to the vile insults.

Please, Camille wanted to plead. *Let's go!*

"Bianca, come on," Camille said. "Come on!"

"Yes," Bianca finally said, swallowing. "Let's go."

Camille turned to leave, clutching Bianca's arm. Suddenly, her hand lost its grip, and whirling around, Camille caught a glimpse of Bianca's bare feet disappearing into the crowd. Anonymous hands shoved Bianca into the conglomeration of stained cloaks and old dresses, laughing uproariously at the sport.

"Bianca!"

"Bianca!" Michelle cried. Her voice died in the melee. "Bianca!"

Camille shoved into the crowd, attempting to elbow witches aside. "Let her go! She didn't do anything to you."

A glimpse of Bianca's dark hair caught Camille's gaze. Witches pushed Bianca back and forth, cackling like mad fairies, until one stopped and stood her on the ground. Michelle caught up to Camille's side.

"Jikes," Camille muttered. "She has the worst—"

Michelle paled. She grabbed Camille's shoulder. "Oh no."

"The good gods," Camille heard the witch say. "You're Derek's daughter."

Bianca elbowed him in futile attempts to wrench her arm free. "Let me go!" she growled. Michelle surged forward. Camille followed.

"Let her go!" Michelle yelled.

"She's not who you think she is!" Camille screamed.

The crowd had tightened to see the debacle, blocking their passage. Frantic, Camille attempted to drive through two males with thick bellies, but they didn't budge. The rancid scent of ipsum drifted from them in heavy waves, making her want to vomit.

"She's here, Coven Leader Clive!" someone called.

"Bianca!" Camille screamed. "Transport!"

The quick *crack* of a slap rippled over the crowd. Silence fell over the immediate area. Michelle gasped. Camille paled.

"Bianca slapped him across the face," Michelle whispered. Camille worked through the two drunken witches in time to see the crowd renew their onslaught against Bianca. They grabbed her hair. Her clothes. Tugged at her bare feet and ankles. The sound of Bianca's name floated through the crowd.

"Derek's daughter is here."

"Bianca Monroe!"

"Tell Clive!"

A female witch in a revealing dress that smelled like cheroots pressed in on Camille, giggling. "Bianca!" Camille screamed, reaching through the bodies. "Take my hand!"

"She looks like a real tart, doesn't she?" shouted the witch holding Bianca. "Just like her pretty Mama must have been!"

Camille held her breath.

No.

Through the press of bodies, she glimpsed Bianca's profile silhouetted against the crowd. Bianca had become oddly still. Her body tensed. Fists clenched.

"No," Camille wailed. "Bianca, keep it together!"

Someone reached for Bianca's neck, but she swung an arm around. Brilliant white light exploded with a crack over the heads of the crowd. The witch flew back with a bloodcurdling scream. The rabid crowd stilled.

Michelle grabbed Camille and hauled her back, shoving them both through the tightly-packed bodies. Camille kicked, punching arms and legs at the witches surging toward Bianca. Three witches tackled Bianca to the ground.

"Let me go! Michelle, we need to help—"

"We need to *get* help, Camille! Bianca's going to—"

A shimmering light exploded over the crowd. Camille heard screams just before a wall of air slammed into her, knocking her to the street.

* * *

Michelle stumbled. Witches screamed. Camille scraped her palms and knees on the cobblestones. Once she gained her breath again, she shot to her feet. Michelle straightened. Ten witches lay on the ground around Bianca like wilting petals. She lay in their midst, hands bloody, her expression twisted in pain. Camille scrambled forward.

"Bianca!"

"Camille, no."

A deep voice and firm grasp on her upper arm stopped her. Camille whipped around to see Brecken standing there, his brow creased. "Brecken!" she cried, grabbing his arms. "We must help Bianca!"

He shook his head, his lips pressed tight. "No. Merrick has her now. She'll be fine. I came for the two of you."

Merrick's lithe frame emerged from the crowd. He grabbed Bianca by the arm, helping her stand. Bianca wobbled, then took Merrick's hand and followed him through the stunned crowd.

"Come on, Camille." Brecken tugged her arm. "It's not safe here."

She hesitated until Bianca disappeared, then followed.

Stumbling through the thick press of witches, Camille held on to Brecken and Michelle's hands as they wormed through the chaos. The crowd had doubled since they arrived. Murmurs rippled through her ears as they hurried past.

"Wild girl."

"She's killed them, ya think?"

"Shouldn't have been here."

"No one wants them here. Exile Derek and his wild daughter."

Camille's despairing thoughts nearly overwhelmed her. She should have forced Bianca to leave! The crowd thinned as they passed Miss Holly's Candy Shop. Michelle released Camille's hand and watched over her shoulder as they half-jogged away, witches streaming past them to join the crowd. A contingent of Guardians marched through the arch, nodding to Brecken as they passed. When Camille stepped through the arch leading to Chatham Castle, she drew in a deep breath. Brecken still hadn't released her hand.

I am safe, she thought. *Someone out there loves me and is happy I'm okay, even if I haven't found them yet. I'm safe.*

"Madness," Brecken muttered under his breath, his gaze sparking like a firecracker. "She's stupid for even being there. Fool."

Camille jerked to a stop. Brecken spun around, his gaze dropping to their entwined hands. Camille released his.

"What did you say?" she hissed. Brecken paused, blinking. His expression hardened.

"Bianca," he said. "She's a fool for attending the rally. And you!" he cried, gesturing to both of them. "You were with her! Are you mad? Bianca's wild. No good can come of being friends with a witch that attends a rally like that."

"We didn't *attend,*" Camille said. "We happened upon it while looking for a ribbon, thank you very much."

"Then why didn't you leave?"

Camille's mouth bobbed for a second. She glanced to Michelle, who bit her bottom lip. "We . . . well . . . we tried."

"Right," he muttered. "Let me guess: Bianca wanted to stay?"

Michelle swallowed, averting her eyes. Camille put her hands on her hips. "No. She wanted to leave."

"Right away? She didn't want to hear what they said about her beloved father?"

"Well, I would have been curious too!" Camille snapped. "They're talking about her father, whom she loves very much."

"Yes, I know." Brecken advanced toward her a step. Camille planted her feet, meeting him scowl for scowl. "I respect her father, but I can't respect such a careless, selfish girl. Do you realize how many witches she put in danger with her uncontrolled powers?"

"It wasn't her fault!"

He scoffed, whirling around. His stride increased, covering almost twice the ground as before. Camille ran to keep up.

"They attacked her!" she said, grabbing his arm and wrenching him around. They skidded to a stop. "We were leaving, but the crowd started shoving her. She couldn't transport away because the witch held onto her. They attacked Bianca."

Brecken shook his head once in a sharp back-and-forth jerk. "Fine. They were wrong. But she never should have been there. Just like the poachers. I suppose they attacked her too?"

"Yes!"

"No. They attacked the *dragons*. Bianca interjected herself into the situation."

"The poachers would have killed that dragon!"

"You don't know that!"

Camille stomped her foot. "Yes, I do!"

"Don't you see, Camille? She's reckless and doesn't think situations through. She just acts. She threw herself at the poacher, who would have killed her. Maybe you too. And the crowd? What if they had turned on you for helping her?"

Deep inside Camille, a small voice whispered a faint agreement. Hadn't Bianca thrown herself into the situation to save the forest dragon? She could have gone for the Guardians alongside Camille. Camille exchanged a frantic look with Michelle, who half-shrugged, biting her bottom lip. Her uncertain eyes seemed to ask the same thing. Was Bianca wild and uncontrolled, too reckless to be safe?

"She lost her mother, Brecken," Camille said, running to catch up again. Her dress swished around her pumping legs. Her chest heaved. The edges of her binder stuck into her ribs, aching with every deep pant.

Jikes, but this wasn't ladylike.

"I know." He threw his hands in the air. "The whole Central Network knows her mother died."

"They don't know the half of it! Marie died in her arms. The Network didn't even publish the truth about it: they lied. Marie was murdered. Of course Bianca's a little out of control. If you keep talking about her like that, I will be too."

He whirled around so fast she slammed into him and then scrambled to shove him away.

"It's horrible what happened to her mother—whatever the full situation. That doesn't excuse her recklessness. The Guardians will have to subdue that crowd, which puts *them* at risk. She kept the two of you there, so that put *you* at risk. And Bianca may have killed one of those witches. That witch could have a family. Ever think of that?"

Camille stammered a dying reply. The frustration in his expression withered into wary resignation.

"She's not a very good friend if she's constantly putting you in danger." He ran a hand through his mop of sweaty curls. The wooden doors into the lower bailey stood only a few steps away. Somehow, they'd already made it back to the castle.

"Why do you care?"

He turned away, jaw set. "Because I don't want to clean up a dead body next time."

Camille growled under her breath and threw a rock at his back as he strode into the lower bailey.

Forget romance, she thought, stalking toward the front doors. *I hate him forever.*

* * *

Camille didn't talk to Brecken for a week.

She fumed while studying alone in the library, equations and polynomials whirling through her head in a furious snowstorm of algebra. How dare he not show up? How dare he say such things and then fade away, as if afraid of her?

Good, she thought, slamming her pencil onto the table for the third time that hour. *Let him be afraid.*

Just when she'd decided to pack her bags and stroll the halls—maybe Luther would distract her—a body dropped into the chair opposite her. For a moment, her heart sped up. Brecken! He'd come—she *knew* he'd come!

Leda released a sharp, long-suffering sigh. "Camille," she said, drumming her fingertips on the table. "We need to talk. You're sulking. You sulk so powerfully you pull bad weather in from the south."

Camille scowled. "Do not."

Leda gestured with a flick of her fingers to a rainstorm drumming the windows outside. Camille sobered.

"That's not my fault."

"I know," Leda said. "But it's still crummy outside, and I need a break. I know something is going on."

Camille studied her from the corner of her eyes. She knew Leda loved her. Leda just didn't *show* it very often. "How?" Camille asked. "How do you know something is wrong?"

"Because you're quiet."

Camille reared back. "But I thought you hated it when I talked? You're always telling me to be quiet."

"Do you ever listen?"

"No."

"Exactly."

Camille shook her head. Being friends with Leda was its own form of algebra. Camille stood up, shoving her homework scroll into her bag. At least Zeke and Luther were consistent; they liked inappropriate humor and teasing her. She'd go see them. No! She'd visit Henrietta and work on her Anniversary Ball gown. She'd be the most dazzling witch in the room. Then Brecken could watch from the sidelines, his heart breaking. He wouldn't take his eyes off her. But she'd just flick her hair over her shoulder as if she didn't care. Then, realizing what a fool he'd been to—

"Are you listening?"

Camille jerked to find Leda standing right in front of her, so close their noses almost touched. Camille pulled back, her eyes crossed.

"No."

Leda fidgeted, shifting like she had an unreachable itch. "I know I *say* I don't like it when you talk all the time, but the truth is . . . I kind of do. It reminds me of home, which is never quiet with my eight hundred siblings running around. Talking is . . . it's fine. Except when we're in the library." Her eyes darted around the quiet room, and she lowered her already quiet voice. "Then it's just annoying."

Camille straightened. "Really?" she cried.

"Yes," she hissed. "Now keep it down."

A grin split Camille's face. She'd never let Leda live this down. But her short-lived joy died. "I need to study algebra," she said.

"I know. You daydreamed through the lesson today. Miss Scarlett reprimanded you five times."

Camille grimaced. Any more disobedience and Bettina would find out in her weekly report from Miss Scarlett. All she needed was one more furious letter from her spinster aunt, bemoaning Camille's uncertain and tempestuous future. Brecken flickered through Camille's mind, but she shoved him back. *He* didn't deserve any thought time.

Leda glanced to the empty table. "Where's Brecken?" she asked.

Camille shrugged and turned away, picking at the cover of her algebra book with her fingernail.

"Camille," Leda said. "What's going on? Trouble in paradise?"

"No. Well . . . maybe."

Leda grabbed her arm, hauling her outside the library. She shoved her against the wall. "Spill. You'll never pay attention until you've talked it out, and you know it."

Relieved, Camille tilted her head back against the stone wall with a frustrated growl. "Brecken hates Bianca!"

Leda's ears perked up. A strand of white blonde hair fell into her eyes as she leaned forward.

"What?"

Camille recounted their conversation. Leda's shock faded as Camille ended on a breathy, "That's what he said. He thinks Bianca is a bad influence. How can I court a witch that hates one of my best friends?" She frowned. "Romance isn't what I thought it would be. This kind of rots, actually. Why do all the books lie?"

Leda quirked an eyebrow. "Camille, he's not wrong."

"Leda!"

Leda shrugged, spreading her hands. "What? Bianca is dangerous right now. The lessons with Merrick haven't been going as well as the High Priestess expected. Bianca almost killed several witches because she couldn't control herself. Brecken has a point. She didn't *have* to fight that poacher. Why didn't she just transport away to get help?"

Camille's mouth worked up and down. Her mind flooded with a rush of thoughts. *Why didn't Bianca transport? Why did she have to be the hero?*

"Well . . . I . . . I mean . . ."

"It's not disloyal, Camille. It's just true. You still love Bianca, but until she has her magic under control, just be a little more wary."

"Are you sure?" Camille asked, fidgeting with her dress. "It just feels wrong. Bianca is going through a lot right now."

"I'm sure."

"Then what am I supposed to do about Brecken?"

"Just . . . keep an open mind with both, I guess? I don't know. I don't even believe in romance. It's all mushy, gushy jumbo. Ignore him, for all I care."

"You could always—"

"No," Leda snapped. "I will not look into the future for you."

Camille giggled. "I know, Leda. I was just teasing you. I don't want to know what happens."

Leda rolled her eyes. "He's a witch, Camille. Not a force of nature. Love can't actually kill you, you know."

That's what you think, she thought, recalling the play of muscles across his back whenever he leaned forward to help her fix an equation. Camille gave Leda a weary, knowing smile. "Sure, Leda. I know that. I just . . . I'm just frustrated."

"You know that I don't care much about relationships, right? But even I can see that you just need to be yourself. Don't worry so much about everything else. I think Brecken will come around. Just . . . let it happen."

Camille's stomach sank. Leave everything to chance? Romance needed a little push. All her favorite romance books made that *very* clear. *How will I ever find someone to care if I don't make it happen?* Her heart floundered at the memories. Being herself hadn't been enough for Bettina. Or Angie. Or most of the girls at Miss Mabel's.

None of this made any sense. Maybe algebra wasn't the most complicated thing in her life.

"Maybe," Camille said.

Leda shrugged. "Just give it a shot. Try it. See what he does. Maybe if you relax, Brecken will feel more comfortable too."

Camille paused. As a tactic, it wasn't the worst idea. He certainly hadn't responded to her attempts at conversation while he worked. "Yes," she said. "I will try. Thanks, Leda."

"Are you ready to study now?"

"Yes." Camille exhaled. "I'll try."

Leda opened the library doors with a spell and slid inside, grumbling under her breath about needy, loud best friends. Camille followed with a new spring in her step, humming under her breath as she wondered what algebra equation she'd have to figure out next.

* * *

A lily pad floated on top of the murky pond in the Forgotten Gardens when Camille wandered up, arms behind her back, several days later. It hovered with such a light touch that it hardly touched the water. She wondered if she could ever live so gently.

In the background, the setting sun sank low in the sky, casting puddles of citrus banners over the treetops. Honeysuckle thickened the air. Camille sat down on the edge of a fountain, slid to the grass, and then lay flat on her back and stared at the changing clouds. She propped her hands behind her head and forgot decorum. And Brecken.

And her next algebra test.

Bettina's letter shifted in her pocket. *Miss Scarlett says you're showing improvement in algebra. That's relieving to hear. One doesn't want to fall behind the others. Your Aunt Angie has taken ill with what she thought was the plague, but turned out to be indigestion . . .*

Camille wished she could erase the letter. Aunt Bettina had perfected the art of saying—and loving—nothing. Having her say something, but also nothing, hurt most of all. After all Camille's hard work, Bettina couldn't just say *good job* or *I'm proud of you?* No. Of course not. Meeting expectations shouldn't deserve praise.

Show me rampant creativity or unbound intelligence, Bettina had said one day. *Then you'll earn my praise.*

Camille blinked, tilting her head back. Tears burned her eyes.

"I am safe," she whispered. "Someone out there loves me and is happy I'm okay, even if I haven't found them yet. I'm safe."

The words drifted away when a fat tear dripped down her cheek. Who was she kidding? She'd never be safe. She'd never be *okay.*

"Do you always talk to yourself?"

The unexpected, rolling voice sent icicles through her heart. With a gasp, she sat up. Brecken stood ten paces away, legs braced. His hair blew gently in the wind, looking like a wild storm on top of his head. She lay back down.

Traitorous heart, she thought as it pounded in her throat. *Calm down. We don't like him anymore.*

To her surprise, her heart listened. For a moment, she considered him with the same indifference she gave every other Guardian at first. "No," she said, waving a hand. "I was speaking with the forest spirits."

Brecken strode over, his feet swishing in the grass as he walked. She swallowed back the rest of her tears, wiping self-consciously at the moisture collecting beneath her eyes. *Of course* Brecken would pop up when she was lying in the grass, as unladylike as possible, crying about her horrid aunt.

Romance, she thought, *is a bloody lie.*

He lay down next to her in the grass. They stared at the slow creep of stars in the darkening sky. In the quiet, Leda's words caught up to her. *Maybe if you relax, Brecken will feel more comfortable too.*

Camille suppressed the urge to put her arms at her sides. She left them behind her head and left the blades of grass on her dress.

"I came to apologize," he said, clearing his throat. "I shouldn't have been so frustrated with you after the rally. There was a lot going on that day. I'm sorry."

"Sorry for throwing a rock at you."

He laughed. Slowly, then in great, rolling waves. The edges of Camille's lips twitched.

"You have good aim," he said. "It hit me in the back of the head."

Her gaze snapped to his.

"Really?"

He rubbed the spot, as if it still stung. "I didn't want you to know, so I didn't turn around. You should think about learning to shoot a bow and arrow. You might be better than some of our newer recruits."

The last of her laughter faded into the low warble of a songbird in the background. *Perhaps the lack of talking isn't so bad,* she thought, closing her eyes. Laughing had never felt so cleansing. A breeze brought the honeysuckle closer, wafting it over her. The Guardians kept her surrounded by constant noise. But the calmness of the silence spoke deep to a sliver of her hidden heart. She enjoyed it, riding it like a long wave, letting it brush her past idle thoughts and ideas.

"Why were you crying?"

Camille paused, wondering how to explain Bettina, or the crushing feeling of loneliness fracturing her heart in the quiet moments. She blinked. *Because I miss my parents, and I feel like I'm just missing ghosts. I don't know their voices. I've forgotten their faces.*

"Because I'm sad that my Aunt Bettina doesn't know how to love anyone. Or anything."

Brecken stirred. "That makes you sad?"

"Yes."

"It just . . . you can just say that?"

Her brow furrowed. She turned to face him. "What do you mean?"

He half-shrugged. "I mean . . . you can just say that you're sad?"

"Yes. I'm sad." She spread her hands. "It's pretty easy."

"Oh."

"Are you ever sad?"

He blinked and fell into a long stare. "I suppose so. I would never just say it, though."

A note of defensiveness crept into her voice. "There's nothing wrong with saying it. I'm sad. That's all there is to it."

"I agree," he said, brow furrowing. "I admire you for being brave enough to know it, express it. There's something . . . intriguing about witches who feel so openly."

"You would never speak about how you feel?"

"I wouldn't even think *to* feel first."

Camille sighed, looking back to the changing sky. Dark, deep violet hues crawled across the canvas now, scattering the remnants of daytime. Stars glittered with lonely winks, as if blinking back tears. Did she *feel* so freely? What would *not* feeling be like? She pictured an empty box and shuddered.

"Are you going to the Anniversary Ball?" she asked.

He shook his head. "No."

She expected her heart to plummet, but it remained, solid and strong. *Of course you aren't going.* She couldn't even pretend to be surprised. Dancing didn't suit him—so brooding and focused. Ignoring the inner voice screaming, *but what about romance?* Camille tucked a hair behind her ear.

"Do you prefer swords or arrows?" she asked. To her surprise, his eyes narrowed in thought. She'd stopped attempting such inane questions long ago, quickly realizing that he'd never divert from algebra for a different subject. She hoped he'd answer tonight. He'd sought her out—that counted for something. Expecting Brecken to step into her desire for a romantic love had been immature—maybe a little selfish. But being his friend felt like the right thing.

"Swords," he finally said, jarring her from her thoughts. "I'm not that good with anything else."

"Running or hiking?"

He paused. "Hiking."

She nodded. "That's what I thought."

Another stretch of silence drew out. The hiccup of pain caused by Bettina's letter didn't feel so encompassing with someone lying next to her. Even if they didn't touch.

"If you could go anywhere," he asked, tilting his head to the side as if to regard a new star, "where would you go?"

Home, she thought. *I'd go home. Whenever I find it, that's where I'd go.*

"Somewhere cool," she said instead. "Not so hot. I don't like how my hair looks in the humidity. Also, I get tired of sweating."

He chuckled.

"What?" she cried. "I wasn't joking!"

He sobered, but had to roll his lips together to suppress another chuckle. "I know," he said. "I know. I just . . . I think it's funny that you admit these things. Out loud."

"You asked," she grumbled.

They fell into a steady, easy conversation for the next hour. Darkness crept over the field, overtaking them both. Just talking to him felt wonderful. She'd never imagined such easy conversation with a Guardian.

When a distant horn blew, he let out a long breath. "I need to go," he said. "But thank you for talking with me. I've enjoyed our conversation."

Camille smiled. "Me too."

He stood up, holding a hand out after her. She accepted, a thrill zipping through her hand and into her toes when their fingers touched. As soon as she gained her footing, she pulled her hand away.

"I'll walk you back," he said, stuffing his hands in his pockets. She nodded. They strolled out of the garden and across the grounds. Camille stared longingly at the cool grass before slipping away, allowing it to disappear behind the hedges. What a lovely evening.

When they reached the lower bailey, Brecken nodded once. His eyes appeared soft in the torchlight.

"Goodnight, Camille."

"Night, Brecken."

She started up the stairs, looking forward to slipping her shoes off and letting her binder loose. What would Leda say about her late night? Michelle would likely be asleep already. Her early shifts—

"Camille, wait."

She stopped, glancing over her shoulder to see Brecken a few steps away, one hand held out. He dropped it back to his side, his jaw working up and down.

"Yes?" she asked.

"Tutoring again?" he asked. "I-I mean . . . Can I tutor you again? I've missed our time in the library together."

"Sure." She shrugged. "That sounds great."

"Tomorrow. Same time?"

She nodded. "See you then."

Camille left him standing on the stairs leading into Chatham Castle, the glittering stars spraying in the sky behind him.

* * *

The weeks of summer slid by in a lazy blur of ivory silk, Witchery nights, and stuffy evenings with Brecken in the library. Camille's incompetence in algebra smoothed into confidence. Brecken's guiding comments came less frequently, and he even drifted into conversations about Guard duty, burrowing gnomes, and Camille's rampant love of pastries.

"So," Camille drawled when he dropped into the chair one sultry evening in the third month of summer. "I brought a surprise!"

She yanked a cloth off two bubbly cups of Fina's special fizzy water. "It's watermelon flavored!" she cried. "Fina squeezed fresh watermelon juice inside just for me. It's so good, Brecken, you'll die. This will be my third glass. Okay, fine. Fourth." She pointed. "Don't judge me."

Brecken didn't reach for a glass, even though she already held hers. He stared at a knot on the table, unblinking, his hands in his lap. She straightened.

"Breck?"

He shook his head. "What?"

She motioned to the cup. "Fizzy water. Do you want some?"

"No. Let's just get started. What are you learning tonight?"

"The quadratic equation." She frowned and shoved the book to him. "Miss Scarlett reviewed it, and I practiced with her, but I'm still confused. She said something about an incomplete square?"

"Completing the square."

"Sure. Whatever. My point is—"

"No," he snapped, driving a hand through his hair. "*Not* whatever. Completing the square is an algebraic method. You have to learn how to do it."

Camille leaned back. "Ooookay. Didn't mean to upset you. What's wrong, Brecken? You seem . . . haggard."

Her eyes drifted over him. Stains littered the front of his white shirt.

Bags drew his eyes into his cheeks, making him appear gaunt and weary. He rubbed one eye with a fist and mumbled under his breath.

"What?" Camille tilted her head. "I can't hear you."

"Just get your homework scroll, already," he snapped.

Camille's hand hovered over the scroll, then dropped back to the table. "Brecken, if something is bothering you, I can figure this out on my own. Leda will answer my questions as long as I don't ask in the library. I think," she added in a mumble.

His brow furrowed. For a long stretch of time, he just sat there, staring at the grooves in the table top. What felt like an eternity later, he drew in a deep breath and lifted his gaze to hers.

"I'm leaving for three months, Camille."

The air left her lungs. Camille felt as if she'd been kicked in the gut. *Leaving?* She had so many questions she wanted to ask. Yet, she licked her lips and attempted to pull herself back together. Somehow in the interim of life and studying, Brecken had become her good friend.

The pieces of realization drifted slowly into place. No matter how much Brecken felt like hers when they spent time together in the library, he wasn't. He belonged to his job. A job with increasing danger. *West Guards in the Borderlands,* she thought, recalling articles in the *Chatterer*.

Brecken, Captain of the Guard.

"Oh?" she asked, trailing into a squeak.

He growled, sinking lower in the chair. "My contingent was reassigned to the Borderlands for a three-month duty. I leave next week."

Camille's hands fell into her lap. "I see," she murmured.

"I have to do inventory, order supplies, communicate with the other Captain, and plan our departure." He gestured to the table with a helpless lift of his hand. "I won't have time to help you in algebra."

"Of course not. I understand."

His heavy brow deepened. "That's it? That's all you have to say?"

For a moment, Camille plunged into her jumbled thoughts. *You may miss the Anniversary Ball, and that would break my heart. I'm angry that you're leaving. But I just want you to be safe—even if you'll never be mine.*

She swallowed it all back.

"What do you want me to say?" she asked, forcing her voice steady. "I-I-I'm not sure what this means."

"Nothing." He turned away. The legs of his chair squeaked as he shoved away from the table, nearly clattering backward. "Merry part, Camille."

She shot to her feet.

"Wait!"

He stopped, shoulders tensed. A nearby librarian hissed at her to be quiet, but Camille ignored her, at a loss. Was he irritated with her? Except for their argument after Clive's rally, she'd never seen him anything but focused or mellow. Could she *really* say what she wanted? If she unwound her bruised heart, would it bleed all over him?

I want you to be here, she thought.

The words died on her lips. Had it come to that? Her shoulders shrank back. Of course it had. All these weeks that she'd been convincing herself they were only becoming closer friends, she'd been falling madly in love with him.

Now, Brecken was leaving.

Any hope of a relationship with him would likely disappear with his departure. He'd miss the Anniversary Ball and the beautiful ivory gown that she realized she'd been hoping all along would win his affection. In three months' time, they would grow apart. Nothing guaranteed he'd return to the castle once he finished, anyway. His contingent could be reassigned. Their duty extended. Anything.

Camille hovered on the brink of fear, empty and horrible.

Leda had been right; romance didn't really exist. Not the way the books wrote it. Despite Camille's best attempts, her war for affection had only led to heartbreak and confusion. But part of her, fostered by Brecken's attention and strange love for algebra, had kept hoping.

"Be safe," she said. "Please?"

His jaw flexed. He strode away. The heavy sound of his feet thudding across the floor disappeared into the background.

Camille dropped back to her chair, tears brimming in her eyes.

I am safe, she thought. Then she buried her head in her hands and let the tears fall.

* * *

Dear Brecken,

It's been two weeks since you left. Not much has changed. I passed the test on quadratic equations—barely. On my second attempt. Miss Scarlett said that "passing" was a generous grade. She gave me a 2+.

Maybe you were my good luck charm.

Hope the Borderlands are going well and you're staying safe. What's your schedule like? Are you enjoying the time in a new place? Hopefully bugs don't sleep with you at night.

Ugh. Don't tell me about them. My skin is crawling just thinking about it.

—Camille

* * *

Brecken,

Thought you'd like to know I re-took the quadratic formula test and passed with a level 4! It's not a 5, of course, but it's better than my previous score.

Are you proud? I celebrated with a fizzy drink. Or three.

Did you get my last letter? I sent it two weeks ago. I have so many questions about the Borderlands. Do you ever see West Guards? Are there cactus? (Or is it cacti? I can never remember.)

Luther and Zeke say you're probably bored out of your mind without burrowing gnomes to chase down there. I dumped my punch on Zeke's lap when he said it. He didn't speak to me for three days. A lovely time.

Hopefully my letter comes through.

—Camille

* * *

Breck,

It's been six weeks and I haven't heard from you. Luther says the reports look good, which means you're safe. I'm a little worried, even though Zeke tells me not to be.

Things were weird when we split, but not that weird.

Right?

Write as soon as you can. Even a few words. I miss laughing with you in the library.

—Camille

* * *

Breck,

YOU ARE THE WORST AT RESPONDING.

—Camille

* * *

Camille,

The Borderlands are hot. Even hotter than the castle.

And yes. Things were weird. I had a lot on my mind, and you didn't seem as surprised as I had expected at my news.

I felt annoyed that I'd overestimated your response.

—Breck

* * *

Brecken,

Good thing you didn't keep me waiting or anything. Your assignment is almost over, by the way.

You really won't make it to the Anniversary Ball? It's only a few days away . . . Luther said your contingent is preparing to return.

I'd love some good news.

—Camille

* * *

Camille—

This is not a variable that I can control, so I will not promise.

—Breck

* * *

Three days later, Camille bit back a delighted squeal.

A trellis of elegant white flowers bloomed over the door into the ballroom, beckoning her with its saccharine scent. Her ivory gown, with every seam straight and dart perfected, drifted around her legs in a gauzy, sleek waterfall. She patted her hair out of her face and bit back a sigh. Jikes, but violins made the air sweet enough to eat.

One could almost call it *romantic.*

Michelle advanced into the ballroom at Camille's side, her mouth hanging open. Paintings of Letum Wood alternated along the walls, blending with the subtle blooms and garlands crawling in between. A table burdened by an endless buffet of food filled the back wall. The High Priestess stood near the throne replicas at the top of the room, clad in a hideous lemon-colored dress.

Camille propped onto her toes. "Do you see Brecken?" she asked Michelle. "Is he here? I've asked around all day but couldn't figure out if he arrived or not."

"No. So many Guardians are here though."

Camille muttered under her breath, but pasted a smile on when two Guardians slid by, dazzling her in their handsome, crisp uniforms. On Brecken's wide shoulders and sculpted arms, the fabric would sizzle. Despite her most valiant efforts, she felt the giddy anticipation of seeing him again. *He's not mine,* she reminded herself. *He barely wrote.*

Her galloping heart didn't listen.

"It is beautiful," Michelle said, fidgeting with the folds of her pink-waisted gown. Baby curls and sprigs of white flowers decorated her hair with hints of summer. Next to her, Bianca filled the air with nervous tension. As usual, her hair flowed around her shoulders. A slight shimmer in the long strands from Camille's potion added a little dash of sophistication.

Jikes, Camille thought. Bianca looked lovely with her simple dress and shining hair. Even though her eyes darted through the room and fists remained clenched at her side. She walked like a coiled spring about to burst. Camille thought back to their skinny-dipping adventure the night before with a wicked blush, then a plunging despair.

What if she lost Bianca tonight?

No, she thought firmly. *Don't even think it.* The High Priestess would come through. She always did. Bianca wouldn't die.

"Really, Bianca," Camille said. "You should have let me do something more than just rub a potion into your hair. It's a ball, you know."

"My hair is just fine the way it is."

Camille let it go. Bianca hovered on a precarious precipice of life and death. If she wanted to wear her hair down, Camille didn't care. She turned her attention to the crowd while Leda and Bianca sank into conversation. Michelle attempted—unsuccessfully—to find a way to employ her hands.

The minutes of avid searching ticked by. Camille drank in the heady perfumes and layers of chiffon with delight. So many witches. So much elegance. She'd never seen anything like it in her life.

Eat your heart out, Bettina, she thought.

A familiar head of hair bobbed through the crowd, heading straight for her. Camille's heart sank. Brecken hadn't come. Why else would Luther approach her?

"Oh, no," she murmured. "Here comes Luther."

Bianca, Michelle, and Leda all turned at the same time to eye the approaching Guardian, who, despite himself, cleaned up well.

"You don't want to dance with Luther?" Michelle asked.

"No!" Camille cried. Her cheeks flushed hot as a sun flare. Pressing the backs of her hands to them didn't help. Oh, she wasn't being fair, of course. Luther did care for her as a good friend. There were worse Guardians to be asked to dance with than Luther. Brecken's bright eyes flashed through her mind. But there were better ones, too.

"I don't mind," Camille continued with a little sigh. "I-I just hoped to dance with Brecken first."

Bianca eyed Luther with a queer gaze. "Is Brecken back?" she asked, angling her body slightly so she stood between the crowd and Camille.

"I don't know!" Camille cried, turning her back to the crowd. "I haven't seen or heard from him."

Camille wondered if she could melt into the witches. Leave the Ball. *Romance,* she thought, *is a dirty old hag. Not real at all.*

Tears made her eyes hot as coals. She blinked the moisture back. Any second now and Luther would reach her. She didn't have the heart to say no, but she wanted to. Because even after months of almost total silence from him, she still wanted Brecken.

"Camille," said a familiar, rolling voice. "You aren't crying over me, are you?"

Camille sucked in a sharp breath. With a muted cry, she whirled around. Brecken stood behind her, seeming to glow in a crimson shirt and crisp, angled overcoat. Colorful emblems stitched to his shoulders and arms gleamed with every movement. The edges of his lips lifted into a full, devastating smile.

Camille's knees trembled.

"As if you ever doubted that I'd come," he said.

His hand claimed hers. He pulled her against his hard chest, wrapping an arm around her waist. Together, they circled into the bright shift and shuffle of the dance floor.

* * *

The second her breath returned, Camille's head cleared. She didn't even know the steps to this dance, but she glided in rhythm with him. She averted her eyes. The powerful line of his jaw and the muscled precision of his shoulders distracted her.

This is supposed to be romantic, she thought, viewing the whirling dresses. *I should be flying. But I just feel . . . jumbled.*

"I've never seen you speechless before," Brecken murmured.

"You said you couldn't dance."

"I said I didn't like it."

"You said you wouldn't make it."

"No," he drawled. "I said I wouldn't promise."

She blinked, looking away. They fell into silence. When the strains of violins faded, delicate as a gossamer thread, Brecken didn't release her. She tried to pull free, but he wrapped his fingers around her hand. They kept dancing into the next song. A waltz.

"Camille," he said in her ear. "Give me a chance to explain."

Her eyes narrowed. A shiver skimmed her shoulders and neck. "Explain why you ignored me for months?"

"Yes."

Camille swallowed. She lifted her chin. "Fine. I'll give you two minutes. It's more than you deserve."

"I felt sad."

She reared back. "What?"

"Sad. I felt sad."

She waited, meeting his intent gaze. "Well?" she asked when he said no more. "What else?"

"I wanted you to be sad when I told you that I was leaving. You didn't seem sad. So I figured you didn't really care."

"You assumed."

"Incorrectly. Yes."

His curls bounced as he gave a little nod. Her breath caught in her throat. Egads. Did he know the power of his crystal blue eyes? So many questions rushed her from all directions. She didn't know where to start. Why would he want her to be sad? Why did he ignore her?

Why couldn't men just *talk* about these things?

"But you didn't write."

He lifted an eyebrow. "Yes, well, working at the Borderlands with the West Guards so near is frantically busy on a good day. There wouldn't have been a lot of time to write letters anyway. But at first I was still angry." His brow furrowed. "Actually, I think I was jealous. I need to apologize for that."

"Jealous?"

He half-shrugged, looking like an adorable, lost boy. "Not sure. I'm new to this talking about feelings thing. You have so many Guardians talking to you. So many friends. Everyone at the castle knows you. I guess it made me jealous. Maybe. Not sure."

With a hand on her arm, he pulled her into an empty space near a painting of an oak tree that stretched into the rafters. Outside, shadows shifted in the distance. One window had been thrown open, spilling cool night air into the stuffy room.

Her mouth worked up and down.

"But if you were jealous, that means—"

A shriek shattered the jolly, bright air, cutting her short.

Camille whirled around. Violins squawked. The conductor's arms fell, his face elongated in a horrified expression. Brecken shoved Camille behind him. She peered around his broad shoulder to see Bianca pushing her way through the crowd.

"What—"

A *crack* behind her made her duck. Glittering shards of glass sprayed over her back, bouncing on the black-and-white tile floor. A strange flap of wings and high-pitched shrieks followed. Camille peeked out to find black creatures winging through the air in droves.

"What are they?" she cried.

Brecken placed one hand on the hilt of his sword and crouched down. "Bats."

The double doors to the ballroom slammed shut. Witches caught in the middle of the ballroom ducked as the bats whirled in black-winged funnels, cutting skin and ripping hair with their talons and razor-sharp wings.

"Leave!" the High Priestess commanded, her voice reverberating through the room. "All of you!"

"Not until I say so," drawled a familiar voice.

Camille's heart leapt into her throat. "No," she whispered, grabbing Brecken's arm. "Not her."

Only a few paces away, Miss Mabel strode forward, oblivious to the glass shards strewn across the floor. Billowing around her legs as she walked, a black silk dress undulated like liquid fire with every step. The garish diamond earrings—even her ice-cold eyes—glittered. She carried a tattered book in the crook of her arm.

"Isn't that Mabel?" Brecken whispered. "Head Witch of the Network school?"

Camille's mouth had turned to a desert.

"Yes."

"Merry meet, Mildred," Miss Mabel called.

Camille let out a faint cry. "Brecken!" she whispered. "She's right by Bianca."

Miss Mabel stood just in front of a trembling Bianca, who held her sapphire blue sword with white knuckles. If Mabel just turned to the right, they'd be eye-to-eye. Would Miss Mabel kill Bianca for good this time? Was Camille going to lose her best friend?

"What is she doing here?" Brecken asked as Mildred stepped forward to challenge Miss Mabel. Every witch in the room silenced, focused on Miss Mabel's awful beauty.

"I can't be sure." Camille shook her head. "But I think it has something to do with killing the High Priestess."

"Killing her?"

And maybe Bianca, Camille thought with a painful twist of her gut. She *had* to get to Bianca. Help her somehow!

"I'm in charge here," Miss Mabel cried, her voice ringing through the tomb-like air. "I came to accept your resignation."

The High Priestess didn't flinch. "You came to accept your own death," she said.

"Is that a no?"

"This is a no."

The chandelier burst into white flames. Heat rolled over Camille's face. Brecken swore under his breath. Flaming bats dropped in fiery plumes to the ballroom floor, crashing into frightened witches. The surviving bats swooped down, morphing into ghoulish, half-witch figures with long fingers and pitch-black plumes.

"Clavas," Brecken hissed.

"What are Clavas?"

"A strong magical army. Get down."

She shrank back against the wall. Half-formed Clavas landed on the floor with bony, bare feet so white they appeared blue. Slashing at witches with long nails and screaming with jagged, bloodstained teeth, they fought with vicious tenacity. Terror rendered her paralyzed for half a breath.

"Let's go," Brecken cried. "We need to find you someplace safe."

She hopped up, accepting his hand. Guardians leapt through the broken windows and into the ballroom from outside. Dragons roared with fire, swooping past the upper windows.

"There," Brecken cried, nodding to the other side of the room. "You can hide over there."

She followed. A Guardian locked in combat with a Clava stepped on her dress. A tear raced across the bottom hem. The long fingers of a nearby Clava sliced the back of Camille's arm as they attempted to dart through the packed room. She suppressed a cry. Her heart pounded, thudding with fear. Brecken dodged a bat, releasing her hand to fight another Clava.

Where was Leda? Michelle? What about Bianca? A cold, leathery hand grabbed her elbow and yanked her around. Camille spun to find a chilling face with gaping nostrils and an angular, half-human sneer. One claw grasped her dress while the other reached for her arm. The sharp bones dug into her skin. She wrenched free, grabbing a vase. The Clava ducked the wide arc of her swing, tightening his hold.

"Let me go!"

The Clava screamed, sending putrid breath and black spittle into the air. She cringed, scrambling back. The Clava jerked her close. Her sleeve ripped. She fumbled for the vase, but it had fallen out of reach. The bright flash of a familiar sword caught Camille's eye.

"Bianca!" she screamed. "Bianca, help!"

Like a savior from the good gods, Bianca dodged through the crowd, driving her beautiful sword into the Clava without mercy. Camille disentangled herself from the cold hand.

"Are you okay, Camille?" Bianca asked. She grimaced, pressing a hand to her head. Camille caught her before she fell.

"I-I'm fine, I think," Camille said. "Are we going to die? We're locked in!"

"No!" Bianca yelled. Flames sprang from Viveet, climbing high in the air. "You won't die! Come on. Let's get you somewhere safe."

"Where?" she cried. "Nowhere is safe."

Two Guardians slumped against the wall nearest them, their glassy eyes staring at nothing. Bianca nodded to couches lining the wall, where Brecken had been leading her.

"There," she said. "Hide behind those until you can get outside."

"What about Brecken?"

They both glanced behind them to see Brecken smite the leg from one Clava as another Guardian decapitated the second.

"He'll be fine," Bianca said.

"Where's Leda? I can't go without her."

"I'll find her!"

They pressed through the crowd together, dodging stray elbows and flailing torches swung in last-ditch attempts to kill the undead mercenaries. Sprays of blood flecked the couches. Bianca flipped one over, creating a small cave. Pools of blood leaked around her bare feet. Shards of glass glittered from the edges of her toes.

"Bianca! Your feet!"

"It's fine."

A body fell behind Bianca, splattering in a pool of ever-widening blood. Camille stared at his face, squashed into the black-and-white tile floor.

What is happening?

"GO!" Bianca yelled, shoving her behind the couch and pressing pillows against the top. "I'll find Leda."

The small cave enveloped Camille, blocking out the lesser sounds of the battle. For a moment, she drew in a deep breath, attached to reality by tenuous cords. Seconds later, Leda ducked behind the couch. Blood speckled her dress and cheeks.

"Stay here," Bianca said.

"Wait!" Leda reached for her as she left. "I need your dagger."

Bianca's brow furrowed, but she surrendered the small ankle dagger and pulled a few glass shards from her feet. When she looked back to Leda, her eyes had sharpened hard as stones.

"Use the dagger if you need to. Don't move until I come back!"

After calling for Bianca one last time, Leda sank back, cramped in the small space, face pale and sharp. Camille grabbed her hand. Relief at seeing her best friend made tears prickle in her eyes, but she blinked them back.

"Are you all right, Leda?"

"Alive."

Camille swallowed. "We're lucky so far."

The thud of a body falling on top of the back of the couch made both of them cringe. Camille let out a long, shaky breath.

"Think there's any chance we can help?"

"Staying out of the way is probably best." Leda met Camille's eyes. "We aren't fighters. We'll just be a distraction."

Camille swallowed.

"Yes," she whispered. Tears filled her eyes again, but she blinked them back. "But I wish I was a fighter."

Leda squeezed her hand. "Me too, Camille."

Several long moments passed while they listened to the battle waging around them. Camille's thoughts strayed to Bianca, to Brecken. She felt like a traitor, leaving them to fight alone. What would happen to the Central Network now? Would the High Priestess survive?

"Think Bianca will be okay?" she asked, her voice trembling. "Are we going to lose her tonight?"

Leda had fallen into a long stare. Her brow furrowed. She shook her head to clear it, but the glazed look returned. Her breath caught.

"Camille, I . . . I think I see—"

Leda dropped back into her haze, eyes distant. What felt like hours later, she blinked, nostrils flaring. Her grip on the knife tightened.

"We aren't going to lose, Bianca," she said. "Not if I can help it."

Without another word, Leda bolted back into the battle. Camille followed.

* * *

A sea of Clavas and witches littered the ballroom.

Camille wondered how many minutes had passed. It couldn't have been more than fifteen. Could it? Time moved so strangely now. The surge of Clavas left all the dead—Guardians, bat, and wraith alike—behind. Thanks to magical nets on the windows and dragons outside, this side of the ballroom had been abandoned. Nothing but a field of bodies and blood remained. The fight surged on the other end, near a wall of glass that ran from floor to ceiling.

Brecken stood on what had once been a dessert table, surveying the battle from above. Blood streaked the side of his face. He barked orders to surviving Guardians, pointing them to different places. They ran over the battlefield, throwing themselves into the melee. More came, seeking orders. Brecken's tactical mind viewed the field, barked more commands, and Guardians dispersed. Camille caught a glimpse of Luther's harried expression before he dove back into the fracas.

Camille and Leda picked their way over broken bodies and half-dead wraiths, dodging an occasional bat as they worked over to the window. Camille grabbed a small knife off a dead Guardian, and, with a shriek, stabbed a Clava hand that lifted toward her from the pile. A trickle of black blood flowed to the floor.

Even though he didn't reach out to her, Camille felt her courage grow the closer they came to Brecken.

Leda grabbed Brecken's arm, "I need your help now," she said, yanking him close. "I need to find a book. No time to explain. Trust me: this is the only way to really stop the battle."

Brecken commanded another Captain into his spot. He joined Leda, casting a concerned glance over his shoulder to Camille, wordlessly telling her in no uncertain terms not to follow. Camille nodded, and the two of them disappeared.

Camille skewered an annoying bat with a broken violin bow she'd found on the floor. Steeling herself, she used a spell to break a leg off an overturned table, and wielding it like a small club, she worked a path to the nearest wounded Guardian. Blood stained the bottoms of her slippers.

"I'm Camille," she said, leaning over him. He moaned, his right eye swollen shut. Fang marks pierced his cheek. "I'm here to help."

The battle waged on as she moved from witch to witch, propping them against the wall, conjuring cups of water, repeating healing incantations, and fending off the bats as they swooped down. She ignored the frenzy at the other end. Screams. Flashes of fire. Groups of fighting forms. All of it blurred into the symphony of death and dying. Only one layer of Camille's gown hung past her knees; the rest lay in shredded, ripped layers. Then an eerie silence fell on the room.

"An Apothecary will be here soon," she said, pressing a cool hand to the face of an Assistant with a deep laceration down his arm. "It'll be all right."

"Camille!"

Camille shot to her feet with a jerk deep in her belly. Brecken broke out of the chaos and ran toward her, limping. Crimson and black blood smeared his handsome face. Leda lay draped across his shoulders, her face slack, arms flaccid. Through strings of hair, Camille caught sight of her filleted skin.

"The Clavas attacked her," he said. "I couldn't get through the crowd. I-I tried."

Blood flowed from Leda's neck and face. Camille ripped the bottom of her dress off while Brecken lay Leda down. Camille bunched the material against Leda's neck and whispered every healing incantation she knew. The blood slowly staunched, staining Camille's fingers a vague pink. Clavas disappeared, diving out the windows in torrents. Their screams as they left set her teeth on edge. Outside, plumes of fire echoed in response.

Camille's head jerked up when a triumphant cry rose through the ballroom. Fists littered the air. Derek stood high above the crowd, his voice bellowing over the witches' cries.

"What is it?" Camille asked.

Brecken shifted, sword dripping with thick ebony blood. His chest heaved. "Mabel is captive."

Camille turned back to Leda.

Time passed with a strange unreality. Brecken veered off to help the dying Guardians calling out from the floor. She didn't leave Leda's side. A deep weariness plagued her. She'd never used so much magic. She wanted to sleep for days. Guardians called out. Bats flopped on the ground, half dead.

Finally, a hand landed on her shoulder, startling her. Camille whirled around to find Michelle and Nicolas standing there. Michelle only wore one shoe.

"Let's take her to an Apothecary," Michelle said, her eyes on Leda. "They've opened the ballroom doors again."

Apothecaries spilled into the room in droves. More Guardians. Protectors. Witches with fresh, horrified faces. A cold chill spread through Camille's body.

"Bianca?" she asked.

Michelle blinked. "Alive. Because of Leda."

Nicolas gingerly picked Leda off the floor. With one last glance over her shoulder, Camille followed them out of the room.

I'm safe now, she thought.

* * *

Camille waded through the layers of sleep slowly, like navigating a lush maze. Her body groaned with every little movement. She pulled in a deep breath. Her eyes fluttered open. Leda lay next to her, white as a sheet. Oh, lovely. Had they finally had a sleepover? Unusual. Leda never slept anywhere but her own bed, and she never even shared *that*.

"Leda?" she whispered.

"Yes, Camille. I'm okay."

Camille stretched her arms above her head, letting Leda's words roll through her mind. *Yes, Camille. I'm okay.* Of course she was okay. Why wouldn't she be okay? Camille's muscles protested as she stretched. Her brow furrowed. Why did she hurt?

The flash of a black wing in her mind's eye startled her. Clavas. Ballroom. Miss Mabel. Attack. Camille gasped, shooting up.

"Leda!"

"Calm down," Leda crooned. "I'm fine."

Bianca sat at Leda's side, her gray eyes bloodshot and drawn. The tears that had been sitting heavy on Camille's chest all night broke free. She buried her face in her hands. "Leda," she cried. "We've been so worried! I thought you'd died. I was so scared."

Leda patted her back. "It's okay, Camille. I'll be fine."

While she asked Bianca about Michelle, Camille bit the inside of her cheek until it hurt. *Get a hold of yourself,* she thought. *Don't lose it!* No matter how hard she tried, the dry hands and gaping nostrils of the Clavas raced back through her mind, and fresh tears spilled out.

Footsteps on the stairwell broke through Camille's internal nightmare. She wiped her cheeks with the back of her shaking hand. Leda's mother and Bianca's father spilled into the Witchery at the same time. Camille shrank out of the way, her heart crinkling, as both of her friends embraced their parents. Even Leda appeared relieved.

I'm safe now, Camille thought with stinging eyes. *I'm safe. Someone out there loves me and is happy I'm okay, even if I haven't found them yet. I'm safe.*

Hadn't she done wonderful things in a horrifying time? Camille thought back, startled at all she'd done to help despite her fear.

I'm stronger than I thought.

Bettina's severe expression sent another deep stab into her heart. Would Angie hug her with relief? Not likely. She'd flutter, offering her different types of tea and potions, but no real embrace. Bettina would demand an explanation.

No, Camille thought. Her aunts could never know about that horrible night. Perhaps they loved her in their own severe ways. But they couldn't impart peace. Her already sore heart trembled with pain. Oh, what she wouldn't give for a mother! She forced her hot, overwhelming tears back by sheer willpower, nearly choking on them.

"Camille."

Her head jerked up to find Bianca and Derek staring at her. She sniffled. Derek held Bianca with one arm, a half-smile on his chiseled face.

"There's a Captain waiting for you at the bottom of the turret," he continued. "He's concerned and wants to make sure you made it through the night. He said he won't move until he's heard from you."

"Really?" she whispered.

Derek grinned softly. "If I know Brecken, he'll wait all day."

Camille flung open the Witchery door and flew down the stairs. Just as she turned the final corner, Brecken came into view. He waited at the bottom, brow furrowed. Deep lines of fatigue left a heavy expression on his brow. His stormy blue eyes had never looked so concerned.

"Camille?" he asked. "I was so worried, I—"

She threw herself into his arms with a muted cry, sobbing so hard her stomach ached. Her heart throbbed with pain. Arms of steel wrapped around her, dwarfing her in his broad shoulders. She sank into the embrace with relief.

"It's all right, Camille," he murmured next to her ear. He leaned his head against hers. "You're safe now. I'm just glad you're okay after all that. You're safe now."

Her sobs faded to cries and then to hiccups. She pulled away. His concerned gaze made a fresh round of tears surface. He tucked a lock of hair behind her ear.

"Feel better?"

Dirt marred his face. Blood matted his hair. She suspected that his injured leg hadn't been cleaned or taken care of yet.

"Yes. Thank you."

He ran the pad of his thumb across her cheek, swiping at a long tear as it trickled free.

"What I was trying to say before we were *slightly* interrupted," he said, pressing their foreheads together, "was that I didn't want to leave you to go to the Borderlands. And I wanted you to miss me. Because I want to court you. And I don't want any other Guardian to tutor you or spend time with you instead of me."

"Brecken, I *did* miss you."

He cast his eyes down. "I realized that when I received your twentieth letter. And I didn't know what to say in response. Writing feelings down is so awkward." He grimaced. "So is speaking about them, actually. Don't know how you do it every other hour."

"Brecken, before we get into anything, you should know that I require *a lot* of patience. Bettina tells me all the time. Even now, and I don't live with her anymore. Angie scheduled time blocks with me only ten minutes long when I was growing up because I gave her a headache otherwise. Leda would probably tell you the same thing. I talk too much and—"

He frowned. "Camille, stop. I don't think any of that is true."

She paused, staring at him. "What?"

"Patience? I think you're perfect, Camille. Just being you. Open—sometimes irrational—emotions and all. I like that you talk, because I don't. And I don't want to. And I don't care if you do. Besides." He swallowed, meeting her gaze. "One of us could have died tonight. That made me feel . . ."

She lifted an eyebrow. He pressed a warm, gritty hand to the side of her face.

"Scared."

A thrill, long and deep, spiked through her. She sank into the feeling. His quiet, husky voice. The uneven patter of her heart. The way she wanted to just *be* with him, Clava blood and all.

It was so terribly romantic.

"So you're saying that I'm scarier than the undead?" she asked, cracking a grin.

His deep, rolling laugh echoed through her ribcage, sending waves right into her heart. Once he recovered, he pulled her close again.

"Yes," he said. "Which is just why I want to court you."

Camille entwined her arms around his shoulders and pressed her lips to his. Soft. Warm. Quiet. The mellow kiss had a spark of intensity, just like Brecken.

I'm safe now, Camille thought. *Someone is glad that I'm all right. I'm safe now.*

CHAPTER 6

Merrick

Merrick is one of my swoony crushes from the Network Series.
Derek aside, I have to say he's probably my favorite male
witch. Figuring out how Merrick's adventure began back in
the Northern Network—and continued in the Central Network—was a lot
of fun.

When I asked fans what stories they wanted, all of them said, "More
Merrick!" So here you are.

A lot more Merrick.

* * *

The silky brush of the bird feather on the back of Merrick's hand
reminded him of Ana, his little sister.

Quiet. Frail. Beautiful. The muted violet plume of the Northern
Sangrilly bird twirled between his thumb and forefinger. Lines of gentle
gray laced through the threads. Purple had been her favorite color.

He dropped the feather. It floated back to the table on an invisible
current, drifting with one last twirl to lay amongst the arrow shafts
waiting for completion.

No more, he thought.

A voice from just behind drew him from his thoughts. "Merrick." His mother, Kally, balanced a wooden bowl in the crook of her arm. Rich green leaves of high-altitude lettuce spilled over the sides. "We're out of firewood."

Merrick pushed the arrows aside.

"I'll chop more tonight. I also have traps out I need to check. Should get a hare for dinner tomorrow, if we're lucky. The roof leaked last night, so I plan on patching that this weekend once training ends."

Jacqui, his little sister, perked up from where she stood near the window. "Look!" she cried. "Wolfgang is coming."

Merrick and Kally spun to see a hulking figure striding up the trail, his short hair drifting in a cool summer breeze. Merrick's mind spun. Had he forgotten something at training earlier that day? He flexed his fingers, still sore from hours of archery practice. If Wolfgang climbed the mountain instead of transporting, he needed time to think. A sure bet he had something to say.

A thrill of anticipation—dare he call it hope?—ran through Merrick's arms in a streak of lightning.

Had his moment finally come?

Kally set the bowl on the table and wiped her hands on her apron. The scent of roses drifted by. Seconds later, a shadow filled the doorway. After a quick rap on the door, Wolfgang's low, rolling brogue filled the room. "Kally, Jacqui." He nodded to them. "How are you?"

"Welcome, Wolfgang," Kally said with a warm smile. She motioned to the table. "Would you like to stay for dinner?"

"No, thank you. I came to discuss a few things with you and Merrick, if you have a moment."

"Of course."

A look from Kally, and Jacqui scrambled upstairs, doll in hand. Kally pulled out a chair for Wolfgang. He shook his hand and remained standing. Pink scars puckered the right side of his face, casting his expression into greater shadow. The bright intensity of his left eye, unmarred by disfigured skin, seemed strangely intent in comparison.

Merrick met Wolfgang's gaze. His fingers curled into his palm. His heart started to pound.

Wolfgang broke the tense silence. "You likely know why I'm here," he said.

Merrick licked his lips, hating himself for feeling breathless. He'd been waiting for this moment since he turned seven.

"I have an idea," he said, forcing nonchalance.

Wolfgang let out a breath. "The Majesties have your first assignment as a Master."

Kally's hand clenched the back of a chair, blanching the knuckles white. Her expression didn't waver. Merrick pulled in a long, slow breath. *Assignment* could mean anything. As a member of the elite Master's for only two months, he had two lines associated with his name—sword fighting and archery. Most Master's with assignments had at least seven lines and a year of training.

On assignments *worth* having, anyway.

"Where is the assignment?" Merrick asked, swallowing.

"The Central Network."

Kally's hands relaxed slightly. Merrick's stomach tightened. *The Central Network?* What could possibly be happening there?

"Why there?" Merrick asked. Wolfgang propped his hands on his hips.

"Because we haven't sent a Master to do low-level reconnaissance in five years. We've been focusin' on the tribes in the Southern Network and the clans of the Western Network. There's trouble brewin' across all of Alkarra. We need to know how the Central Network is handlin' it."

Info gathering, Merrick thought. *That's it?*

Merrick would have to work his way across the Central Network, moving from village to village as a nomad while talking to witches. Reading news scrolls. Observing markets and town meetings and Guardian activity. Hardly as exciting as the rest of the trained Master's, who protected the borders or fought violent mountain dragons.

Merrick's disappointment quelled as a thought occurred to him. His shoulders tightened.

"This is because of Ana's death, isn't it?" he asked.

Kally sucked in a sharp breath. An awkward silence ensued. For a moment, Merrick's thoughts turned into images. A little hand against his palm. The curl of her tiny body pressed against his back in the middle of the night. The last, wispy breath of life as it fell from her lips. Merrick hadn't said Ana's name in months. The syllables made his chest ache.

The edges of Wolfgang's lips turned down. "The Majesties would never send a Master on any mission they didn't think fittin'."

Merrick bit his teeth together so hard his jaw ached. The idea that the Majesties would send him on a mission because his sister had died in his arms sent a shot of bubbling rage through him. He didn't need pity. He needed distraction. Danger. A fight. Something intense that couldn't be resolved, so he could press against it until Ana's memory faded.

"Tell me the truth," Merrick demanded, stepping toward him. "Is it about Ana?"

"I'd never lie," Wolfgang snapped. "You *can* do it. More than that, you need to do it, Merrick."

Merrick growled. "Then they *are* sendin' me out of pity."

"They're sendin' you out because of me!" Wolfgang cried, slamming a fist into the table. "I requested they send you. You need to get out of here, Merrick. You're drownin'. Ana's death is hangin' over you. It wasn't your fault! You couldn't have saved her *or* your father. You need to move on. You'll never do that here."

A long, tense silence filled the room. Merrick swallowed, averting his gaze. Tears glittered in Kally's eyes. Jacqui's shadow haunted the top of the ladder.

Merrick opened his mouth to say something, but closed it again. He clenched his jaw until pain radiated into his skull. How could he accept such an offer? Yet . . . how could he turn it down? He'd signed a binding to serve his Network. In honor of his father's memory, he'd worked until he thought his muscles would liquefy. Bruises colored his body. Deep fatigue kept him awake deep into the night. But still . . . Father's and Ana's memory fueled the insatiable desire to prove he knew more than grief.

He thought of escaping the burning torment and wondered if Wolfgang was right.

Wolfgang turned to Kally.

"Merrick is eighteen," he said. "By Network law, he's an adult at sixteen. Considerin' recent events with losin' Ana," Wolfgang cut Merrick a sidelong glance, "the Majesties wanted your blessin' to send him. It's a six-month assignment, and there's little danger. I have volunteered to be your Caretaker while he's gone in case you need somethin'. But you have the power to say no."

Kally fell into a long pause. Her eyes were drawn, bloodshot. For a moment, the sturdy mountain woman faded into an exhausted witch riddled with grief and the constant ebb of pain. The years hadn't been kind, but she still aged with a slow, lovely grace.

"You live amongst ghosts now, Merrick," she murmured with tear-filled eyes. "I think you should go. You'll never thrive here while blamin' yourself for their deaths."

Merrick winced and fell silent. The debate warred in his head. Did he *want* to leave his family? No. They needed him. Or did they? Kally cared for the garden. Wolfgang could provide game. An innate fear that more loss would come caught him by surprise. But leaving would provide freedom. A chance to prove to the Majesties that he could be as talented as his Father, whom they had loved. If he did this, perhaps more assignments would follow as he earned more lines.

In the end, Kally's pained expression made his decision. She clearly hoped this would be what he needed. He'd go for her.

I'll go, Merrick thought, his heart still laden with guilt. *Because I can't bear to stay.*

He crossed his left fist across his chest, resting it on his right shoulder in the symbol of agreement.

"I'll take it."

Wolfgang followed suit.

"Report in the mornin'," he said. "For the next two weeks, you'll sign a bindin' of secrecy and prepare to live there. You'll need language trainin' to get rid of your accent and to learn phrasin', like *merry meet* and *so mote it be* and *jikes.* You'll memorize the map, learn how to live off Letum Wood, and locate the political hot spots." Wolfgang released his hand. "Then you'll be on your own."

* * *

Summer in the Central Network felt like breathing through a hot, damp rag. Merrick stumbled through Letum Wood from day-to-day, annoyed by the early darkness and lack of direct sunlight. Did this green tunnel cover the entire Central Network?

Just keep movin', Wolfgang had instructed him. *Don't draw attention to yourself. You're gatherin' information, that's all.*

The weeks trudged by as Merrick meandered through Letum Wood toward the Eastern Border. He bought dinner for Border Guards, laughed with the locals, and helped an old woman dig for potatoes while discussing her disapproval that the High Priestess had cut funding to a small farming society.

In short, he learned nothing.

The sultry months faded into the cool mornings and tepid days of fall.

A month passed. *Nothing new,* he sent in a letter written in a wayside inn near the Southern Covens. *None of the foresters pay attention to anything but local politics. They don't even learn more than basic magic. I think I need to go somewhere else. Newberry, maybe?*

No, Wolfgang responded within the hour. *The Majesties want you in the smaller cities. Stick to your assigned course.*

Frustrated, Merrick pitched the letter into the fire with a growl.

Three months later, Merrick crossed an intersection in the heart of Letum Wood, a dusting of frost crunching beneath his boots. The crisp tang of fall turned bitter with the first month of winter. Above him soared a sparse canopy of butter yellow, crimson, and burnt orange. The unnatural stillness unnerved him, even though he'd been wandering through it for months. Did forests have eyes?

Merrick shuddered and pressed on to the small village of Timms.

Expect Timms to be a typical border town along the Eastern Network border, Wolfgang had said in his latest letter. *Small but growing. The Innkeeper at the Gray Goose Inn has a history of a loose tongue. See what you can find out from there.*

Four streets funneled into an open area with an elevated wooden stand in the middle. Two Guardians stood at the top, attempting to call over the mindless chatter of the crowd. Bodies blocked grocer stalls and shops, obstructing his view. Merrick slid past two shirtless witches grappling on the ground. He stood on his toes, attempting to peer over the heads of the crowd. In the distance, the clash of swords rang through the air.

Where was the Gray Goose Inn? And what could be happening in such a small village? The thin, corded arms and scraggly hair of the amassed witches meant *something* had drawn the foresters into a group.

Rare, indeed.

Merrick stopped when he saw three witches standing in a row at the beginning of a roped-off street section. Silence descended as all three witches drew arrows. At the other end, a single target hung from a tree. A Guardian in half-armor held out his arms, signaling for the crowd to step back. After a pause, he called, "Release!"

All three witches released their arrows. One flopped to the dirt. Another slammed into a branch on the wrong tree. The third hit the tree, but avoided the target entirely.

"Not bad," a Guardian said, twisting the arrow free. "Best we've seen today. At least one hit the tree."

Merrick stopped. Surely the Guardian jested.

"New recruit sign-ups are today," the Captain called as he collected the bows. "Prove your mettle against your neighbors. Win all the sweet dames. You know. All that stuff we promise but never happens."

Tempting, Merrick thought, studying the Guardians. If he wanted to know more about the Network, surely joining the Guardian force would be the way. His fingers twitched with the temptation to show them how to *really* shoot a bow and arrow. Brushing both temptations aside, he resumed his search. Wolfgang would never approve.

A head of rugged locks of ebony hair stepped into his path. Merrick stopped, nearly crashing into the green-eyed witch with a plethora of freckles. A red ribbon draped the left shoulder of his half-armor. A Captain. The bright eyes darted over Merrick, as if taking inventory. Maybe this wasn't just a competition.

The Guardians were recruiting.

"You have the look of a good Archer," the Captain said to Merrick. He nodded to the lane. "Why don't you give it a shot?"

"Not interested."

The Captain surveyed him with a narrowed gaze. "You sure?"

Merrick's hand balled into a fist at his side. He hadn't shot in months. Getting a bow in his hands again would feel wonderful. The *thwhack* of an arrow hitting the wrong tree resonated behind him. As if he sensed Merrick's weakening, the Captain extended an arm.

"I'm Damen," he said. "A Captain in the elite contingent of Archers."

The hair on the back of Merrick's neck stood up. *Elite contingent of*

Archers. He'd never heard of such a thing. Merrick accepted Damen's arm, gripping it in his own.

"Merrick."

Damen motioned behind them. "Give it an arrow. See what you can do. The Guardians have a way of bringing out potential, so don't feel bad if you aren't as handsome as the rest of us yet."

Merrick wove through the crowd behind Damen and accepted a bow. *So close,* he thought as he studied the distance. Fifty paces at most. Damen passed him an old bow with waning tension and a grooved grip. The feathers on the arrow had seen better days, as had the mostly-blunt tip.

He nocked the arrow and adjusted his left hand, shifting the grip until it fell into a comfortable groove. He closed his eyes and drew in a deep breath. The outside world quieted. For several heartbeats, his own breath filled his ears. The middle of the target loomed large in his mind's eye.

No wind. Short arrow. Soft cord.

With instinctual adjustments, he lined up his sights, pulled the bow until his hand pressed into his cheek, and let the arrow fly. The crowd cheered. He dropped his arms to his side. The arrow hit the exact middle of the target.

Damen rolled his lips. "As I thought," he murmured. Merrick handed the bow to a waiting Guardian. "Forester?" Damen asked Merrick.

"Yes."

Damen's brow furrowed. "Don't look like one." He frowned. "Too clean."

"More like a wanderer, I suppose."

"You must hunt a lot."

Merrick's mind spun back to the North, where he had trapped for furs and meat but shot large game with his bow.

"Yes."

Damen nodded. "Want it?"

"Want what?"

"A slot to join the Guardians."

Merrick chuckled, turning away. "No, thanks."

"No problem." Damen shrugged. "Probably not for a witch like you anyway." He turned away, pointing to a gangly witch with cut-off sleeves despite the cold weather. "Oy, you! Want to shoot an arrow? Prove you're a better witch than your friend there. Archers are the most handsome witches in the Guardians, you know."

Merrick stopped mid-step. He *knew* what mental manipulation game Damen was playing. Plucking at the strings of Merrick's pride just to get him to do what he wanted. The knowledge didn't stop it from bothering him.

Not for a witch like you.

Merrick's fingers tightened like coiled springs. He ground his teeth. He *shouldn't* do it. But he did. His legs moved. His mind honed in on Damen, who laughed with another forester attempting to nock an arrow.

"How long is the agreement?" Merrick asked Damen's back. Damen spun around, a subtle smirk on his lips.

"Two years if you pass the Wringer."

Merrick's eyebrows lifted. "The Wringer?"

Damen grinned. "You didn't think we'd just let you in, did you? You have to work for it."

Wolfgang would never allow this. The Majesties would call him back—evict him from the Masters for breaking the rules. But wouldn't he commit a greater service to his Network by garnering *actual* information?

Wolfgang isn't here, a little voice in his head whispered. *Sometimes you have to take matters into your own hands.*

Damen lifted an eyebrow. "You in?" he asked.

Merrick blew out a fast breath.

"Yes."

Damen grinned. "Good choice. Follow me. We'll get your binding signed." He clapped a hand on Merrick's back and steered him toward the platform in the middle. "Don't worry—if you don't pass the Wringer, you're free."

"What's the pass rate?"

"Two in ten. It's gotten easier over the years."

* * *

Two days passed in a blur of contract review followed by travel along lengthy highways. The journey ended at Chatham Castle, a bulwark of soaring turrets and stone hidden by freezing cold drizzle that smudged Letum Wood into dreary bruises of green and gray.

Eighty recruits turned out with Merrick in the lower bailey, shivering beneath their coats. Merrick stayed on the edges, arms folded across his chest. He'd received a letter from Wolfgang that he'd shoved in his pocket and attempted to forget. Merrick pushed the North from his mind. He'd think about that later.

A thickset witch with wide shoulders, a paunchy belly, and a scraggly auburn beard loomed on top of the Wall, a three-story structure ringing the lower bailey.

"Recruits!" he bellowed, stacking his hands on his hips. "You will now remain silent and will not speak without permission."

The low simmer died into instant silence. Merrick squinted against the freezing rain and suppressed a shiver.

"I am Tiberius, Head of Guardians. You have been recruited into my house. Welcome. Now you will be tested. If you pass, you'll start training. If you don't, you'll go home. Each of you will pass through the Wringer. If you fail, merry part. Come back when you've grown a pair of big boy parts. If you pass—I'll see you soon. Follow Daniel, the Captain of New Recruits."

Two massive wooden doors groaned open, emptying the lower bailey onto Chatham Road. A witch with blond hair slicked out of his face waited with a line of Captains flanking him on both sides, hands clasped behind their backs. Their crimson ribbons sagged over their left shoulders in the rain. Daniel's piercing gaze seemed to cut right through the mist.

"Come with me," Daniel called, magnifying his voice with a spell. Tiberius disappeared from the top of the Wall, but not before Merrick caught his gaze. Merrick left the lower bailey with a chill, convinced that Tiberius's beady eyes had been staring into his soul.

The Captains spread out along the group of recruits as they followed Daniel around the edge of the wall toward the back of Chatham Castle. Water dripped down Merrick's neck as he stepped into the foliage behind another recruit, winding through the twisted forest path until they stopped at an open clearing.

Branches had been hacked off trees to create a long rectangular space.

Guardians dotted the perimeter, busy with intermittent tasks. Merrick's stomach dropped when the witch behind him let out a long, low whistle.

The Wringer.

An obstacle course lay on the muddy ground. A balance beam at least forty paces long led to a drop into a pond with chunks of ice floating across the top. A steep bank of mud slaked the other side, just before a bed of sharp boulders and rocks at least fifty paces across.

Sandbags lined the rock field. Guardians were warming up to swing them back and forth as the recruits crossed. The course disappeared into the bushes. Given the shouts of Captains in the distance, Merrick felt a tinge of uneasiness regarding what lay unseen.

Daniel stepped forward, his striking gaze moving from face to face. A nearby recruit gulped.

"Get through this obstacle course, and you'll be accepted into training," Daniel called over the drop of rain on the dry leaf skins. "Fail and you'll go home. First recruit, you're up."

A thin eighteen-year-old with knobby knees stepped forward. Two Captains ushered him to the balance beam, half as wide as Merrick's palm.

Too fast, Merrick thought, watching the speedy swish of the boy's legs. Halfway across, he tumbled to the spongy moss below. The recruits groaned. The witch straightened, lips pressed tight, and scrambled off to the side with his head hung.

The second recruit managed the balance beam with more ease and then paused, eyeing the icy pond. The autumn chill would intensify after a jump into water—especially a half-frozen pond. Frosted edges and floating chunks of ice awaited him. With a deep breath, the witch threw himself into the water and surfaced with a flailing shout.

"Can't . . . feel . . . bottom," he gasped.

"Too far down." Daniel yawned. "Gotta swim."

"Can't!"

His head drifted under and then back up with another gasp. A Captain tossed him a rope and towed the witch back to safety. His teeth chattered as he stumbled to the side of the clearing. A bluish tinge shadowed his lips.

Recruit after recruit attempted the Wringer. One fell off the rope climb and jarred his back. Another passed into the forest. Then a second disappeared, and a third. The remaining strained to see what happened through the bushes. The line winnowed down until Merrick moved into the next slot. He yanked his shoes off and set them off to the side, then peeled off his shirt and folded it on top. He rolled his pants up to his calves. Daniel's all-seeing gaze flickered his way and then back to the course.

Just like walking the ridge. Jumping in the glacier pools. Climbing the rocks. Merrick shook his arms as he peered into the course. *Nothing new here. Nothing but winning this challenge. I can do this.*

When the Captain signaled him to start, Merrick climbed on top of the beam. He maintained a steady pace across the precariously thin ledge and threw himself as far across the icy pond as he could. The slushy water hit him like a slap. He gasped and started swimming. Four strokes later, he broke out of the water, scrambled through the mud, and stood at the field of boulders and rocks. His fingers and toes numbed with a frozen burn. A wave of cold fire prickled across his skin, and the chill pierced deep into his bones.

Eight Guardians lined either side of the rock field, swinging sandbags back and forth. Merrick's muddy feet slid over the rocks as he scrambled across the first section.

The nearby Guardian released a bag, and Merrick flattened on top of a boulder. Edges poked his ribs as the sandbag passed overhead. He leapt to his feet and stumbled forward. A sandbag angled from an unexpected direction slammed into his ribcage. He wrapped his arms around the bag in a tight clutch, letting it drag him a few paces until his ankle sliced open against a sharp rock. A collective *ooh* sounded behind him.

Ignoring it, he scrambled forward, slithering through the uneven terrain without stopping. He dodged the remaining bags and jumped free of the rock field. Around the corner lurked a long tunnel of empty space. He sprinted through and skidded to a stop at a rope on the other side.

Blood buzzed through his veins now, warming his frozen fingers and toes. He wrapped the rope around his feet and climbed, hand over hand, until he stopped at a platform thirty paces up. Fifteen metal bars bridged a gap between trees. Merrick ignored the lofty drop and swung from bar to bar, moving with the focused determination he loved so much from his work with the Masters.

Finish strong, he thought, sinking into the new challenge with relief.

The metal bars ended on another platform where a Captain waited. He handed Merrick a small piece of knotted rope.

"Glide down."

A long rope stretched from above the platform all the way to the ground in a gentle slope. Merrick tossed the small rope on top of the other, grabbed each side, and jumped free of the platform. His weight sunk for two seconds in an almost free-fall. The rope caught him, jerking his shoulders before he reached the ground seconds later.

Once he released the smoking rope, he stood at the foot of a massive tree.

"Jikes," he muttered.

The towering tree disappeared into the canopy of leaves, sprawling with branches so wide a house could perch among them. Recruits littered the front of the tree trunk, in various stages of climbing. Their feet slipped often; the trunk had been stripped smooth by thousands of attempts to climb it over the years.

One witch fell, plummeting toward the earth. Within a second, the screaming recruit slowed, stopped, and landed on his feet in the bare dirt.

Tiberius and four other older Guardians—as grizzled and thick-bellied as Tiberius himself—ringed the bottom of the tree, no doubt using incantations to stop anyone who fell. Merrick stepped back to study the tree front and then moved around the tree in careful study. When no Guardian stopped him, he kept going.

Textured bark still littered the back. He'd have to climb in an upward angle, but the grooves should give him adequate handholds. He reached down, dug below the mud until he reached dry dirt, and covered his hands. He mapped out his initial moves and grabbed the first handhold. A flicker of movement in the bushes caught his eye. Tiberius, arms folded across his chest, stepped out of the trees with tapered eyes.

Merrick ignored him and climbed on.

With firm fingers and a fast mind, he maneuvered his way up the trunk. The rain made the pillows of moss slick. Fog obscured the light filtering through the dense canopy, and his fingers slipped often. By the time he reached the first branch, his forearms and thighs burned like hot coals. He shook them out but didn't waste time on a reprieve.

After mapping out his next moves, he pressed on, working a slow crawl to the left and up. The quiet of the backside of the tree gave him more room to think.

When he reached the platform, he rolled onto his back, chest heaving. The climb had been brutal: a worthy test of skill. Merrick hadn't looked down, but he imagined a chasm separated him from the earth.

A Guardian with short-trimmed hair and buggy eyes leaned over him, lifting one eyebrow.

"Stand up, recruit," he said. "You're not done yet."

Merrick's eyes narrowed in silent question. The Guardian grinned, his rows of teeth gleaming, with the glaring exception of the missing tooth on the bottom left side. He motioned off the ramp with a jerk of his head.

"You gotta get down, right?"

Merrick pushed onto his hands and peered down. Even the hulking Tiberius appeared small from this distance. Fog curled in wisps along the ground. Off to his right, another recruit's legs trembled as he peered down, eyes wide. Merrick sucked in a breath.

"Jump?" he asked.

"Test of trust," the Guardian said, shrugging. "Hardest kind. You have to jump to complete the Wringer."

Merrick stood up, brushing his hands against his grimy pants. The skin had torn off two of his finger pads, and the top half of one nail dangled free, leaving a thin streak of blood at the top.

"No way."

The Guardian turned his back to him, pointing. "There's a rope ladder. Merry part, quitter."

Merrick ground his teeth, blowing a hot breath that turned crystalline. The advancing rain increased, sluicing down the sides of his face and bare chest.

"Fine," he muttered. "Fine."

The Guardian whipped back around. "It's not as bad as it seems. You can't join the Guardians if you don't trust the leadership. Common sense. Jump."

Merrick hesitated. The height didn't bother him—he'd grown up on mountains this steep and infinitely more dangerous. But the *landing* made him nervous. He stepped forward, curling his almost-numb toes around the edge. If Tiberius didn't see him, Merrick would die.

But at least it'd be fast.

"Ready?" the Guardian asked. Merrick nodded. The Guardian stepped to the side and whistled, high and clear.

"Recruit jumping," he called. A low shout responded.

With a growl, Merrick stepped off the platform.

* * *

The wind whipped past his ears.

The gray of Letum Wood moved in a strange blur for several seconds. His stomach lurched. His mouth filled with blood from biting his tongue to keep from shouting. Instead of slamming into the earth, he slowed, like something held him from above, until he hovered just above the patch of dirt where he would have slammed into a root.

Tiberius stared at him from the swath of fog, condensation forming on his ragged beard. "Fastest time on the Wringer we have on record," he said. "How'd you do it?"

Merrick swallowed and set himself on his feet. Now that his frantic motions had stopped, the chill set back in. He tried not to tremble.

"I've climbed trees since I was a kid."

Tiberius's eyes slitted. "And the rest of the Wringer?" he asked.

Merrick's heart pounded from an entirely different set of fears. *Cripes,* he thought with a flash of horror. In his haste to complete a challenge, he'd exposed his skills. Put himself at the center of attention. Why hadn't he thought of it sooner? He should have struggled. Been just mediocre enough to make it without drawing attention to himself.

Merrick cleared his throat. "I'm an active witch, sir."

"That can shoot an arrow into the heart of a target."

"I hunt for food."

"You took your shoes off."

"Yes, sir."

"Why?"

"Better grip and control."

"And your shirt?"

"Less resistance in the water."

Tiberius paused. "Why are you here?"

Merrick hesitated for half a breath. Did Tiberius know? Impossible. Merrick scrambled for the first answer that came to his frozen, frenzied mind. "To be useful, sir."

Tiberius didn't move, hardly seemed to breathe. After an impossible pause, his arms released. "No forester or wanderer comes to the Wringer that talented just because they shot a few squirrels for food. Go stand with the rest of them. If you're lying to me, I'll turn you in to the High Priestess. And trust me, I always find out who is lying." Tiberius jerked his head to the side. "I'll see you tomorrow."

Tiberius stalked away, fog swirling behind him. No further recruits raced toward the tree from the Wringer. A mournful horn from the Guardian at the front broke the air.

Behind him, a group of haggard, but exultant, witches stood near the base of another tree. The idea of a two-year contract binding him to the Central Network Guardian force loomed heavy in his gut. A wave of panic followed.

What have I done? he thought, blinking.

Wolfgang was going to kill him.

* * *

Merrick,

I received your letter regarding your idiotic idea to bypass our approval and make your own decisions. I sent it to the Majesties.

Meet me tonight in Letum Wood near the Forgotten Gardens. Things don't look good for you.

—Wolfgang

* * *

That night, Merrick stared deep into Letum Wood with a tight stomach. A thick wool coat encased his arms and torso, warding off the deep chill of the night. In the distance, lights flickered along the Wall where torches burned in yellow halos. He'd transported away from his room in the Ranks once the other fifteen recruits settled into sleep after an exhausting day of first lessons. Wolfgang's letter lay heavy on his mind.

Your idiotic idea to bypass our approval.

He prayed to the god of mercy to calm Wolfgang's temper.

Merrick's breath misted in front of him as he shuffled to keep warm. Once the sun sank, the intermittent rain froze into ice balls that dropped into his hair and melted. The briefest whisper of leaves, so subtle it could have been a squirrel, caught Merrick's attention. He straightened. Seconds later, Wolfgang stood in front him.

"What were you thinkin'?" he barked. "You put this entire operation at risk."

Merrick swallowed, forcing himself to meet Wolfgang's furious gaze. "No real information came from the villages, and we haven't had scouts down here in—"

"That wasn't your call to make," Wolfgang snapped.

Merrick flinched at his tone—cold, hard as stone. Screaming rage would have been preferable to chilling disapproval. When Father died, Wolfgang had stepped into that gap for Merrick. Shame burned hot at the back of his throat. He hated disappointing anyone.

Merrick opened his mouth to counter, but stopped. What defense could he make? Everything that ran through his mind made him sound arrogant, as if he knew more than the three High Priestesses. *The Guardians challenged my pride. Seeking political information from villagers is a wasted venture. I don't want to come back with nothing to show.*

"Yes, sir."

Wolfgang let out a sharp breath, ropes of tension tightening in his neck. A question hovered on the tip of Merrick's tongue, but he bit it back.

"Farah wants to exile you for riskin' the safety of the Network."

Merrick bit the inside of his cheek, Tiberius's dubious gaze flashing through his mind. He didn't blame her. He had put them at risk. At least he hadn't told Wolfgang about Tiberius's suspicion.

Wolfgang folded his arms across his chest. "But I convinced her not to cut you off. Yet. She's livid, I'll have you know. Havin' to spend time down here will keep you alive. She hasn't exiled you, but she will kick you out of the Masters."

Merrick let out a long breath. His shoulders slumped. The dishonor of being shunted out of the Masters was the least of what she could do.

"Thank you, Wolfgang."

"I did it for your father," he said. He drew in a deep breath. "And . . . because I don't think it's the worst idea."

Merrick's head jerked up.

"What?"

Wolfgang ran a hand over his weary face. "I've wanted to integrate more into the Networks for years, but Farah has resisted. You forced her hand. Doesn't bode well for you . . . unless—maybe—we can prove it's a good thing."

The stirrings of dread that had been weighing him down released. Merrick straightened. "Are you serious?"

Wolfgang frowned. "I think we could work the situation to our advantage if you find the right information. Information we would never have obtained from villagers."

"I will."

"You *hope* you will. This will have to happen carefully. There is much at risk, Merrick. If you are found out, do you realize what you've broken?"

Centuries of safety and anonymity, Merrick repeated a line from the Master's Oath in his head. He hadn't directly broken the Oath—there was no line in there that said he couldn't join the Guardian force of another Network. But he'd broken the trust of his leaders.

"Yes," Merrick said.

Wolfgang let out a long, weary breath. "Continue on, Merrick. Be very careful. You have signed a bindin' to the Northern Network and to the Central Network. Find somethin' to redeem yourself, and you have a chance of retainin' your honor. If not . . ."

The words trailed into the bitter night air. Wolfgang disappeared, leaving Merrick to think about his mother, his sister, and the ghosts of those he'd left behind.

*　*　*

For the next two months, Merrick slid into the Central Network Guardians with careful calculation. He ran forest trails, feigned ignorance of sword work, and worked closely with Damen to qualify for the elite contingent of Archers. Subtle adjustments continued to improve his distance accuracy.

We've underestimated the cohesiveness and attention to detail of the Central Network's Guardian system, Merrick wrote in a letter to Wolfgang. *Tiberius is well respected. Derek, the Head of Protectors, is spoken of often. I haven't met him yet, but his talent in leading the Protectors and his close relationship with the High Priestess cannot be understated. Should the West decide to take action, the Central Network will be a worthy foe. Though quiet, they have means of mounting an impressive offense.*

We've already surmised much of this, Wolfgang said. *We need more.*

Merrick burned the letter with a frustrated growl.

The final month of Guardian training descended with the cool clutch of freezing cold and crystals of ice. Merrick woke in the middle of the night, huddled under a pile of heavy blankets. The frost seemed to bore into his bones. His cramped stone room radiated the cold howling outside. At home, snow buried them inside their log cabin several times every winter. He used to hate the shrill way the wind screamed. But now he wished for the familiar sound. The Central Network's wet winters crept by in the strange silence of Letum Wood.

Just as Merrick sank back into a light slumber, a resounding horn echoed down the Ranks hallway. Merrick groaned. What were they thinking? It had to be the middle of the night. Not even the dead felt this cold. With stiff fingers, he dressed and hustled into the hall, where other bleary Guardians with half-lidded eyes shuffled by in the narrow space.

Tiberius and Daniel waited in the lower bailey with bright torches burning high despite the heavy snowfall. Petite gusts of wind drifted by, teasers for a real storm. Despite the skin-numbing cold and occasional snowflakes, the air seemed clear. Merrick wondered what time it was. It couldn't have been later than two in the morning.

"Recruits," Daniel called, bright-eyed and boisterous. "Line up."

Loaded packs formed a line behind Daniel and Tiberius, both of whom were draped with heavy furs. A weight sank into Merrick's stomach. The hope of a warm breakfast faded into dreams.

"The time has come to test your knowledge and skills," Daniel said. "The day to prove yourself has arrived."

Low grumbles echoed Merrick's silent opinion. Daniel and Tiberius had probably been waiting for this weather. He could just fail this last task and be released from the Central Network Guardians and return home to the North.

Or could he?

Daniel grabbed a pack and lifted it into the air with one arm.

"Every one of you will take a pack and a map. Each map has an end point where you will find a painted square token. Collect the token and return in three hours. If you return without your token, or after three hours, you have failed. We'll weigh your packs before and after you return. If you lighten it, you fail. If you transport back, you fail. If you're injured or frozen, return. We'll discuss the situation before making a decision."

Merrick almost snorted, but no amusement flickered in Daniel's eyes. Merrick frowned. So, freezing was an option.

Cripes.

A long pause filled the lower bailey while the recruits soaked that in. Merrick's teeth chattered. Daniel hadn't specified what happened if they failed. He pushed that aside, too laden with other questions.

What is a token? Could it be buried in snow? Is it heavy? Am I going to die from snow dropping from the boughs overhead?

Daniel tossed the pack at the feet of the nearest recruit.

"Grab a pack," he said. "Make it fast. A storm's coming. Trust me. You don't want to be caught in it."

* * *

The gentle snowfall turned into a blizzard thirty minutes later.

Daniel released the recruits in waves of five. A Captain standing next to Daniel recorded names, pack weights, and routes on a scroll with each wave. His hand quivered, skewing the letters. Merrick waited for the final wave.

Tiberius growled as the last of the recruits waded into the knee-deep snow. "Let's go inside and warm up," he muttered. "It's getting blasted cold."

Merrick shuddered and pressed on.

At first, snowy Letum Wood reminded him of home. Thick layers of piped frosting lined every branch with intricate precision. All the creatures had burrowed away into their trees and homes. Not even gentle tracks showed on the drifts.

The map of the main trails was easy to follow at first. But after he worked through already trodden paths, the snow cover coated the undisturbed ground, and it grew increasingly difficult to orient himself. Had he followed a game trail? The real trail? Merrick floundered in the deepening drifts, sinking from the weight of his pack. A mental clock ticked the minutes away. He didn't have time to pause in uncertainty, so he checked the map and pressed forward.

The winds increased from gentle breaths into gusts, then billows, reminding him of the haunting melodies of home. He squinted against the storm. He should go back. He should transport to the Gatehouse and safety. Surely some of the other recruits had done so. He couldn't feel his toes. His fingers ached. Just when he felt re-orientated on his path, it would bifurcate in the wrong place, and he'd second guess himself all over again.

He pressed on.

What felt like an eternity later, the snow broke beneath his feet. He pitched to the side, unable to pull his hands from his pockets to break his fall, and sank into a stream. The pack pulled him under, and water splashed over his head.

The bite of the freezing water raced down his back and into his nostrils. Merrick released a breath of surprise. Flailing to free his hands, he wrestled the pack off, rose to the surface, and clawed up the bank. With a spell, he called the pack out of the stream. It fell onto the bank with a wet *squish*. He rolled onto his back with a gasp.

I'm going to die.

A piercing wave swept through him, so cold it felt like heat. The water dripping off his nose rolled in a freezing drop toward his ear. His hair started to ice over in clumps.

Transport back, he thought. *I can do it.*

But his mind wouldn't focus on the incantation. The sound of shifting snow beneath him sent a streak of panic into his heart. With lightning speed, he rolled to his hands and knees and crawled free of the stream just as the rest of the snow collapsed. Finally safe on the bank, he stared at the churning, black water. His mind raced, unable to settle.

"Who's out there? It's a bloody blizzard, you idiot."

At first, he thought he imagined the voice. The trees were more open here, allowing thicker gusts of snow. A trick of the wind, surely.

"You aren't another bloody Guardian lost during a Qualification, are you?"

Merrick squinted through the snow frosting his eyelashes to see hints of a cottage through the swirls. The outline of an old woman, bent with age, stood on a porch.

"Well?" she demanded, shouting. "What's wrong with you? Transport home. Unless you're one of those idiotic foresters that don't learn magic. Fools!"

Shoving free of the snow, he pushed up and stumbled toward the witch. His body trembled. Every thought felt sluggish. When he approached the little house, the old woman's foggy eyes, staring at nothing, caught him by surprise. She wore no shoes on her knobby feet, and only a light shawl covered her shoulders, even though the wind blasted her face and sent two white braids flying behind her.

"Who are you?" she asked.

"M-m-merrick."

She jerked her head. "Get inside. You fell in the creek, didn't you? Thought I heard a splash. Go sit by the fire. Can't have a Guardian dying near my cottage again. Too much work."

* * *

Merrick didn't feel the warmth of her cottage on his face at first. Once inside, he tried to peel his coat off, but his fingers wouldn't move. The fire flared brighter when the witch slammed the door shut behind her. The noise of the howling wind rescinded.

"Well?" she asked. "Aren't you going to take your clothes off?"

"C-c-c-can't."

Ice cracked as the coat dropped off his shoulders and drifted next to the fire, freeing his limbs from its heavy weight. He eyed her, but she'd settled into her chair and stared at nothing.

"Can't see a thing," she muttered. Her upper lip curled over her teeth. "Wouldn't want to even if I could. Strip down. Get warm."

Merrick eagerly stripped his clothes off, draping them on the hearthstones. Something heavy hit him in the back. He reached behind him and caught a blanket before it fell.

"Warm up. I'll send a note to Daniel. I'm Sanna, by the way. Qualifications must be going again," she said.

Merrick wanted to ask if she had panther-like hearing, but couldn't get his teeth to stop chattering. How had she heard him fall in the creek over such a storm? She had to be well over a hundred years old with her wrinkled hands and blind eyes. Dismissing the thoughts, he wrapped himself in the blanket and sank to the floor on a braided rug. He'd think later.

A quill scribbled across a nearby scroll that disappeared when she murmured a transportation spell. Merrick stared at the empty spot with a numb feeling of apathy. He didn't care about the Guardians. Or the Central Network. Or the Masters. He just wanted to be warm. He turned away. Maybe he did care.

Failure stung.

After a few minutes, prickles replaced the numbness of his feet. A good sign—albeit painful. Outside, the storm howled with a sinister ferocity, as if angry at losing its rightful prey. Sanna leaned back in her rocker with the slow back-and-forth creak of wood. His wet clothes had started to steam. He studied the room, his eyes flittering to the walls. Except for one or two random adornments, nothing else filled the sparse cabin. Then again, what blind witch needed decorations? Merrick leaned back and then stopped. He blinked. Hold on.

Was that a dragon talon hanging from her wall?

His eyes narrowed on the crescent-shaped fixture. Veins of lavender ran through it with marbled wisps of color. Weren't they supposed to be black ivory? A flash of light caught his eye as Sanna leaned forward to cough. The faintest hint of an orange dragon scale hung from a necklace around her neck. A thrill shot through him.

Interesting.

The Dragonmasters are still alive, he thought. The Majesties didn't know. If the Central Network had dragons, they *needed* to know. They thought all the Dragonmasters had been killed long ago, back when they lived near the border of the Northern Network. Before the formation of the inane Mansfeld Pact. But apparently not *all* of the Dragonmasters.

He thought of Letum Wood with new eyes. Had there been any subtle signs he'd missed? Burn marks? Fire? The faint hiss of a tea kettle pulled Merrick from his thoughts. Surely this would be information Farah appreciated.

"Tea's almost done," Sanna said.

With perfect command of magic, Sanna orchestrated the pouring of the tea into two separate cups. One floated to her side, where she reached up and plucked it from the air. Merrick accepted his cup, sipping at the warm tea with relief. The liquid rushed into his stomach, spreading warmth into his deepest belly. He downed it in two long draws. The cup zipped back to the kettle and refilled. Merrick repeated it four times before setting the half-full cup on the floor.

"Feel better?" she asked.

"Yes." He cleared his throat. "Thank you."

"What's your name?"

"Merrick."

She tilted her head back and forth. "Huh. Not a sissy name."

He lifted one eyebrow. "A sissy name?"

She sipped at her tea and then rolled her eyes. "So many young men with weak names. What's the point, eh? They need strong names." She waved a hand through the air. "Witches just aren't the same anymore. Too much magic for stupid things."

"Like pouring tea and transporting messages."

A hoarse, barky laugh caught him by surprise. Sanna slapped her knee. "Oh, you're a feisty one. I like it."

Relieved, he sipped again at the tea. His feet and hands hurt in earnest now.

"Are you always up this early in the morning?" he asked, hoping to distract himself from the pain.

"Don't sleep well. I've always been an early riser, anyway." Sanna leaned back in her chair. "So . . . you're qualifying."

"How could you tell?"

She snorted. "Some Guardians are idiots and can't follow a map. Run into my house. Daniel plans it during bad weather on purpose, you know."

"I'm not surprised," he muttered.

"You've failed, haven't you?"

"Yes."

"Should have transported back."

He shook his head and then realized she couldn't see it. "Not my thing."

A toothy grin split her wrinkled face, appearing more like a grimace. "Not one to give up, eh?"

"Not really."

She fell into silence.

He swallowed a sip of tea. "How many Dragonmasters survived the massacre?"

The stillness that came to her expression gave him pause. For half a second, he wondered if he'd startled her into a heart attack. He felt a bolt of panic—the massacre of the Dragonmasters was common lore, wasn't it? Had he just betrayed himself in the worst way? In his travels, no one had ever mentioned dragons. He shouldn't have jumped so confidently into that conversation.

To his immense relief, she relaxed. "Still surviving? Only my sister, Isadora, and me. A few others lived through the massacre, but have since died. The pure blood is gone. I keep to myself. On purpose."

"But you still display a talon?"

She flashed another strange grin. "Why not? It's a special talon. Ivory instead of black ivory. Extremely rare. Besides, no one visits me except Isadora and the dragons."

He nearly choked on another swallow of tea. Of course the dragons visited her, the Dragonmaster. Still, imagining the giant creatures tromping around Letum Wood gave him pause.

"Do you own this property?" he asked, studying the walls anew. The close, thick walls of the Ranks suddenly felt secure and downright cozy when he imagined dragons prowling around outside.

"Letum Wood owns itself," she quipped. "And to answer your next question, witches haven't seen the dragons in years because Letum Wood protects them. Just like Mildred does," she added quietly.

Merrick's brow furrowed. Such a simple detail, yet so many complicated effects rippled from it. "Why doesn't Mildred want witches to know?"

Sanna scowled. "Protect them from poachers seeking black ivory. Letum Wood protects the dragons most of the time, but witches still slip by. Pah. Doesn't matter. The dragons take care of them if Letum Wood doesn't."

Merrick lifted an eyebrow. "What do you mean?"

She snapped her teeth together. "Lunch."

"Of course."

Sanna held up a finger. "If you think you hear a dragon, just transport away. It's the dragons you can't hear you have to worry about. The end of your life will be a blanket of fire or basket of teeth. Either way—you'll go fast." She chortled. "Not a bad way to go, really. I've seen worse."

Merrick flexed his hand, his thoughts racing. The chills had subsided, leaving him weak and wrung out. With no clock, he had no idea how much time had passed.

They fell into casual conversation—she said no more about the Dragonmasters, and he asked no more questions. He sliced a few pieces of bread, rooted cheese out of a cold box, and they ate in cordial silence. The food restored his energy. Time passed in a strange way. It felt like minutes, but hours slid by while the storm raged itself out. When her pile of wood dwindled, he wrapped the blanket around himself more tightly and stepped outside. Her pathetic pile was on its last pieces. But the wind had calmed.

"You're almost out of wood, Sanna," he said, closing the door firmly behind him, sending new firewood to the hearth with a spell. Fat snowflakes still drifted from the sky, settling in his hair like flecks of glitter. He brushed them free. The pressure on his tingly feet felt uncomfortably sharp still, but his blood seemed to move more freely.

"Tiberius normally provides it for me," she said. "Mildred's order."

He tested his clothes. Mostly dry. He murmured an incantation under his breath to finish the job and shucked the blanket off. The dying winds would clear up his visibility so he could find his token now.

As if she read his mind, she said, "You can't be thinking of going back out there."

"I'm not. I'm planning on it."

Her frown morphed into candid amusement. "You've already failed."

"Doesn't matter."

Her brow furrowed. "Then why are you doing it?"

"I don't leave a job unfinished."

"I like you, Merrick. You've got spunk. You're clearly an idiot, but at least you have spunk. Come back and chop my firewood tomorrow. You won't have a job, so might as well do something productive."

"Sure, Sanna," he said, sliding his shirt over his head. "I'll be back in the morning."

"You owe me at least that much for drinking all my tea and finishing off my food."

"I agree."

She scowled. "Not too early. I don't wake much before noon, mind you. I'll curse you if you wake me up too soon."

* * *

His pack had solidified into a ball of canvas and ice during the storm, which had frozen it to the ground. With a couple of incantations and sturdy kicks, he broke it free. Although twice its original weight now, Merrick cleared the snow and ice crystals and heaved the pack onto his back. He staggered under the weight and then headed toward the bridge.

Thanks to Sanna's revelations, Merrick eyed the murky depths of Letum Wood with newfound respect as he stumbled around the quiet forest. Half an hour later, he found the right trail. An hour later, a square of bright color winked down at him from halfway up a thick tree.

He let out a heavy sigh. All that work for such a small thing.

Ten minutes later, he set off for the castle, token in his bag. The thick clouds and dense canopy blocked the morning light. Snow poured off the boughs in glittering waterfalls as he trudged past.

Within an hour, he broke through Letum Wood and into an empty field outside Chatham Castle. No waiting Guardians. No recruits. No Daniel. Without Letum Wood looming large overhead, the world seemed lighter. Yet gray. Dismal. Only a few turrets of the castle were visible through the soft-falling snow.

He tromped through the field, up the Wall steps, and over to the Gate-house. The sound of heavy laughter came from inside. Daniel. Tiberius. A few Captains. With his breath billowing in plumes, Merrick pounded on the door. The laughter stopped. Heavy footsteps trod to the door. The door cracked open, revealing two confused eyes and a burst of heat from within. Daniel blinked.

"Merrick?"

Merrick dropped his pack with a *crunch,* yanked the token free, and held it out. "I know I'm late," he said, sniffling. "But I didn't transport. My pack is twice the weight now."

I almost died, he thought of adding, but bypassed the melodramatics.

Daniel stared at the wooden square. His mouth bobbed open and closed. Tiberius appeared behind him.

"Sanna wrote," Daniel said. "Said you fell in the creek."

"I did."

Daniel lifted an eyebrow. "Why did you go back for your token?" He glanced down, nudging the pack with a foot. "The rest of the recruits have been back for hours."

Merrick hesitated. Had he missed something? Why *wouldn't* he be here? A hint of tension in Daniel's expression caught him off guard. He wouldn't be a bit surprised if they were playing some sort of game. Maybe the time limit had been a farce. Maybe they just wanted to test his mental limits.

"I never leave a job unfinished," Merrick said, forcing himself to meet Tiberius's beady eyes. The morning of the Wringer flashed back through his mind. Tiberius's distrust hadn't waned in the interim. If anything, Merrick's tenacity had just made it worse.

Daniel studied him for a long pause.

"Then, congratulations. That's what I like to hear. Time limit didn't really matter—not in weather like this. Welcome to the Guardians, Merrick," he said with a nod. "Go get something to eat and take the rest of the day off. You'll receive your first assignment in the morning."

* * *

Merrick,

Farah accepted your Dragonmaster report.

I will look in more detail at what we know, but I am happy to hear that the Dragonmasters continue. I congratulate you on obtaining new information.

The potential for it to impact us directly is small, but it's still important to understand.

Keep going.

—Wolfgang

* * *

On a calm day in the late spring, Merrick hung his bow on the peg designated for him within the elite contingent of Archers. The rest of the elite Archers milled in conversation behind him, stuck in an age-old war over feathers.

The conversation slid in and out of his mind like Jacqui and her girlish antics used to. He missed her persistent requests to play dolls or carry her on his back. Nine months had passed since he'd seen her. Merrick turned his back to the calendar and pushed away the fact that it was also his nineteenth birthday. Kally had always made him fat, stuffed pastries for breakfast. The sweet raisins and creamy insides filled his belly with a long-lasting sweetness.

He shucked off his boots, thick with the warm mud of early summer. The deluge of recent rain intensified the already stifling heat. He longed for a cool burst of mountain air.

A voice called above the din as he stripped off his half-armor.

"Merrick. Rolph wants to see you."

The entire room silenced. Damen—the newly appointed Captain of the Archers—filled the doorway. The Archers gave Merrick a sidelong glance. His infamous trek through the snow had earned him notoriety that he didn't want. Only he and one other recruit had returned with a token. The rest of them had retested and passed under calmer skies. Now they regarded him with a weird mix of camaraderie and awe.

"Yes, sir," Merrick said. "I'm on my way."

The door slammed shut behind Damen. A chorus of *ooh* morphed into guffaws and rising questions. Merrick shot a few quips and disappeared outside leaving them rolling with laughter. A wave of heat hit him like a boulder.

Rolph, the Captain of Advancement, stood with his hands folded behind his back. He extended an arm, which Merrick clasped.

"Good to meet you, Merrick. Join me at the top of the Wall, will you?"

Damen nodded as Merrick followed Rolph up the stairs. In the distance, the sunset lit Letum Wood on fire. Sweat trickled down Merrick's back. When the sun went down, everything humidified. He hated it.

"How can I help you, sir?" Merrick asked when they reached the top. Rolph folded his arms across his chest.

"I've been observing your work in the Archers. You show talent and skill as a Guardian. Excellent run times. No disciplinary action. You've set yourself apart from the rest of your cohort with leadership skills." His eyes narrowed. "Although I never see you with them in the pubs at Chatham City. Why is that?"

Merrick rolled his lips. Ipsum didn't exactly mix well with keeping secrets, although he couldn't deny an occasional desire to lose himself in something that would take the edge off his memories.

"No, sir. Losing control and inhibition doesn't appeal to me."

Rolph's upper lip wrinkled. He shrugged. "Me either. Never saw the appeal in pissing all over the place." He reached into a leather vest and removed a scroll tied with twine. "I want to invite you to apply for a Captain's slot."

Merrick stared at the scroll. *Captain?* Rolph managed the career progression of Guardians and Captains alike. But Merrick didn't think he'd been in the Guardians long enough for something like this.

"Sir?" he asked.

"The minimum requirement of service is six months. You've served six as of yesterday. We need good Captains." He frowned. "Trouble may be stirring in the Borderlands, and Tiberius wants to be prepared."

Merrick's interest stirred as well.

Advancing to Captain would be better than continuing association with Guardians that only wanted an easy guard duty job. It might open up new opportunities to garner pertinent information. But it would prolong his time in the Central Network, and he didn't have permission to stay.

Trouble may be stirring in the Borderlands, Rolph had just said. Merrick bit his bottom lip. Staying meant he'd walk a traitorous ledge; accepting further responsibility without permission could cement his exile. He thought of Jacqui and Mother again with a sharp pang.

Having a leader invite a Guardian to advance was a high honor— rejecting it would give him a reputation as a low life weasel in the Ranks, effectively erasing the last nine months of careful work. Rolph's intent gaze meant he wanted an answer now.

Merrick's silence continued.

"Captain training is less about brawn and more about brain," Rolph said. "In order to qualify for training, you'll face mental tests more than physical challenges. If you accept my offer, you'll be given a Qualification test. If you pass, you're accepted into a six-month training phase."

Merrick clenched his jaw. The shimmering top of Letum Wood wavered in the distance. Rolph paused, his eyes glowing with a blunted reflection of the sunset. Wolfgang would agree to Merrick's advancement. The Majesties might not. But he'd have to take that chance, even as a young Master with only two lines and certain dishonor.

"Thank you, sir," he said, sticking out his arm. "I accept."

Rolph grasped his proffered arm. "I'm happy to hear that. Tomorrow, be in the lower bailey at six in the morning for the Qualification."

Merrick's forehead furrowed. "What does the Qualification entail, sir?"

Rolph smiled and released Merrick's arm.

"You'll find that out when you get there."

* * *

Merrick stepped into the lower bailey the next morning at sunrise. Light suffused the sky, illuminating the stones and chasing away the shadows. Birds twittered past; an earthy, sweet scent filled the air. The chatter of Guardians coursing into the castle for breakfast hummed in the background.

Rolph waited in the middle of the lower bailey.

"Welcome to your Qualification," he said. "My Assistant will be here shortly with four Guardians. They will be your contingent for this exercise."

Merrick frowned. A five-witch contingent? Exercise? The hair stood up on the back of his neck. He shifted. An interesting morning, for sure.

"Yes, sir."

Rolph folded his hands in front of him. "Your task is to retrieve a token from a Guardian leader."

Merrick's mind whirled back to the Guardian Qualification. *Of course it's the same,* he thought with a little snort. Neither the North—nor the Central—Networks seemed inclined to change the predictability of tradition.

"Is that all, sir?"

Rolph smiled. "Tiberius has volunteered to harbor your token."

Merrick's mouth slackened. He blinked. Obtain the token from Tiberius? A door leading into the lower bailey slammed open, and his thoughts froze.

Four Guardians spilled out. Two of them shoved at each other with irreverent guffaws. Jack and Pete. A theatrical pair of twins from the Eastern Covens. A skinny witch with buck teeth and gangly arms followed behind them, his left wrist bound with a white cast. Neilsen. He'd broken his arm during a shield exercise, just weeks after slicing off a little toe during a sword fighting accident. A dark-skinned witch with only one eyebrow and a slash of healing pink skin over his left eye brought up the rear. Miller. A known fire lover.

Four Guardians Merrick would never have chosen as a well-functioning team stood before him. The dismal outlook left Merrick momentarily stunned. They had physical strength—no one passed the Wringer without it. But their youthful antics had caused multiple lapses in judgment. With a couple of sturdy Guardians, he could likely pull a plan together to complete his task.

But these?

"Your goal is to use your team and retrieve the token. Simple as that. No magic once you enter the forest. No leaving Letum Wood. You have two hours to find and retrieve. You may use magic to prepare, but not once you advance. Your team has to work for you. If you win, they will receive a ten pentacle bonus."

Jack and Pete high-fived. At a quelling glare from Rolph, they ducked their heads.

"You have one hour to prepare." Rolph handed him a scroll tied with twine. "Here is your map to Tiberius. He'll be mostly stationary. Best of luck."

Merrick ran a tongue over his front teeth. Having Tiberius stationary made it more difficult. They were testing Merrick's ability to make decisions under pressure with a less-than-ideal team. He doubted the token mattered as much as the method. Rolph and his Assistant disappeared into the Ranks.

"Oy, Merrick." Jack stepped forward. Pete followed. Their jet-black eyebrows both lifted high into their foreheads. "Let's win, yeah? We gotta bet we need to cover with a couple extra pentacles, if ya know what I mean."

"We need the element of surprise, yes?" Miller said, beating his thumb against his leg in a fast staccato. "Scare Tiberius out of his pants. I can do a massive fireball. Tons of concentrated ipsum. Boom. Huge."

"Let's just get naked and run at him," Jack said. "That'll startle him."

The four of them cackled with laughter.

"Needs to be something new," Neilsen murmured, rubbing his injured arm. "Tiberius knows everything. We have to be really . . . unexpected."

Pete nodded. "Pentacles on the line."

Merrick's mind spun with ideas as the Guardians asked Neilsen to describe—in gruesome detail—the sound of his arm snapping. "Not so bad." Neilsen shrugged. "I've broken lots of bones."

"Did you scream?"

Neilsen laughed. "Like a girl."

Merrick caught snippets of their conversation, clumping them into a train of thought, then an idea, and then a plan. *Element of surprise. Unexpected. New.* He yanked open the map, and his heart hiccupped. The spot marking Tiberius wasn't far from a very familiar stream by a very crotchety old witch.

A wild idea ripped through him, spreading heat into his very bones. Rolph hadn't set a limit on *what* or *who* he could use once they entered the forest. His blossoming idea could work—likely wouldn't. He'd need Sanna, perfect cooperation from four Guardians who didn't focus for more than five seconds, and a whole load of luck.

He straightened, clapping Pete on the shoulder and nearly knocking him down.

"Lads," he said with a broad smile. "I have a plan."

* * *

After gathering a few supplies, transporting once into Letum Wood and back, and reviewing the plan for the fifth time, Merrick and his contingent advanced into the forest. According to the map, Tiberius waited in a circular meadow amidst the thicker parts of the forest. The contingent agreed he'd probably wait in the middle of the open space. He wasn't the sort to hide, and he'd make very sure no one could ambush him.

They moved north of the meadow and then east, giving it a wide berth until they faced its northeast corner. The stream bubbled on their left. The Guardians had sobered, falling into unusual restraint.

Merrick closed the distance to the stream and peeled off his shirt. He'd worn dark pants and his hair tied into a queue.

Jack lifted one eyebrow in silent question.

"So, we *are* getting naked and running at him after all?" Pete drawled. They dissolved into muffled chortles. Merrick glared them into silence.

"Cover me with mud," he said, lying on his back in the moist stream. They stared, wide-eyed, as he rolled around the slippery embankment.

Once Merrick scooped up a handful and smeared it on his face, they fell into action, slinging handfuls onto his shoulders, neck, and pants. Once finished, Merrick stood up, covered any bare spots, and then rolled in the leaves coating the forest floor.

"Jikes," Miller said, recoiling. "He's dedicated, all right."

Merrick stood. The mud and sharp leaves itched. He wanted to jump back into the stream and wash the irritants away. Instead, he motioned with a jerk of his head.

"Let's go."

Slipping through the forest with his natural camouflage proved more difficult than Merrick had expected. Flakes of mud and leaves peeled away as he moved. When he arrived at a thinning in the bracken, he paused. The lay of the trees would determine how this scene played out.

Pete tapped on the map where he thought they stood. Merrick nodded and pointed to Miller. Miller craned his head back, surveyed the branches, grabbed one, and disappeared into the tree. A thin bottle of clear liquid strapped to his hip sloshed. A heavy, weighted pouch dangled from his neck.

Merrick kept a fist in the air until three pinecones dropped to the forest floor. *Miller's ready.* He motioned the rest of the contingent toward the southeast corner for twenty paces.

The trees protected them from Tiberius's gaze, but twigs snapped and leaves rustled in their wake. Tiberius would hear. Merrick didn't care.

When they stopped again, Neilsen stepped up to Merrick's side.

"You ready?" Merrick mouthed, pointing to the south. Nielsen grinned and faded into the trees, the cast on his injured arm flashing as he strode. On Merrick's signal, the twins rustled through the brush on the right. Within minutes, everyone was in position.

Merrick pulled in a long, slow breath. "Be good to us, Sanna," he murmured. "We need you."

His heart jumped into his throat and lingered there with dull, empty thuds. *Do your job the way I told you,* Merrick thought, staring where the twins had left. *Just do what I said.*

What felt like hours later, a rustle of branches and the hiss of two subdued voices carried through the near-silent forest.

"Quiet, Pete."

"That's the wrong way."

"You stepped on a damn branch. The—"

Merrick's stomach turned cold as their voices grew in volume. It felt so counterintuitive. He clenched his fists. *Not too loud, boys . . .* The twins left a short span of silence, then shuffled forward again.

"Are you kidding?" Jack hissed.

"My stomach growled! It's not my fault. I didn't eat breakfast."

Easy, Miller, Merrick thought, his eyes darting to the tree tops. His fingers wrapped around a rock. *Wait for Neilsen's signal.*

Merrick lobbed the rock into the trees where Neilsen had disappeared. Seconds later, an ear-splitting scream rang through Letum Wood. Birds scattered. A burst of heat flashed on the back of Merrick's neck, surging from the tree tops twenty paces away. Branches turned to crackling flame and gray smoke.

"That was Neilsen!" Jack hissed from nearby.

"A damn lion's eating him!" Pete shouted.

"Lions don't breathe fire. It's a bloody forest dragon!"

The sound of their feet running through the underbrush passed right by Merrick. *Yes,* he thought. *Just as planned.* The twins screamed Neilsen's name as they streaked by, pounding past with running feet and fading voices. Heart pounding, Merrick lay on his stomach.

Come on, Sanna, he thought. *Come on.*

"Hey!" a gravelly, old voice rang through the trees. "Get outta here, you rotten lizard. I told you to stay away from witches!"

Merrick almost shouted in relief. *Yes!* Sanna had come! Tiberius would never suspect a trick now.

Neilsen screamed again. The shrill, pained sound grated on Merrick's nerves. Fire billowed from the branches above a second time, leaving an acrid scent of smoke on the air. Merrick's heart leapt into this throat when the crashing sound of something heavy moved through the trees behind him.

Tiberius.

"Neilsen!" the twins screamed, their voices farther away. "Where are you? We can't see you."

"Dragon!" Neilsen yelled. His voice squeaked with fear. "There's a forest—"

The final burst of fire cut him short. Sanna's answering bellow rang through the trees. As expected, Tiberius sprinted through the bracken, shoving branches and trees aside. "Guardians!" he bellowed. "Where are you?"

Merrick crouched low in his spot. The natural lay of the land would funnel Tiberius right past him. Then came the not-so-easy task of getting the token. From Tiberius.

While in motion.

The natural path split in two. Tiberius would slow down to decide where to go next, which is when Merrick would reach up and grab the token. Tiberius sprinted faster than Merrick had anticipated. Merrick drew in a deep breath. *Just grab the token,* he thought.

Tiberius didn't slow. He bypassed Merrick on the ground, covered with leaves and forest debris, by veering—correctly—to the left on the game trail without stopping.

"Guardians!" he bellowed. "Make yourself known."

Neilsen screamed again. Merrick shoved off the ground in a panic. As soon as Tiberius found the Guardians, he'd know. Miller wouldn't have enough concentrated ipsum and fire powder to do another burst of flame. Tiberius disappeared into the trees, and Merrick followed. The token bounced around Tiberius's chest, suspended from a thin piece of twine.

Neilsen's gut-wrenching screams of pain grew louder as Merrick followed Tiberius through the bracken. Tiberius, a surprisingly quiet runner for such a giant body, slowed. Merrick's heart nearly stopped as Tiberius spilled onto a strange sight. Merrick skidded to a stop, remaining back in the trees.

Pete, Jack, and Neilsen sat on the ground, leaning back against a tree trunk, their lips pressed together in silent laughter. The moment Tiberius burst through the trees they stopped, eyes wide, and stared. Tiberius's brow grew heavy.

Merrick sprinted, threw himself on top of Tiberius's back, and thrust his arm forward. His fingers closed around the twine. When he yanked, the frail string snapped. Tiberius dropped to his knees. The token popped free. Sparks erupted from the square in long strands of light.

Victory.

Tiberius shoved to his feet, his eyes narrowed into dangerous slits. He whirled around, hand on his sword.

"What the hell just happened? Where's the damn forest dragon?"

Neilsen averted his eyes. Pete pointed to Merrick, and Jack put a hand over his eyes and cleared his throat, tilting his head in Merrick's direction. The sound of running feet interrupted the deafening silence. Miller raced into the clearing with a wild grin, a curl of smoke spiraling above his right ear. His gaze darted to Tiberius, then the twins. He shrank back. Merrick pushed back to his feet while Tiberius glowered, swinging his sword in an arc.

"There was no dragon," Tiberius bellowed. "Was there?"

Merrick swallowed.

"No, sir."

Several seconds passed while Tiberius's hot bursts of breath calmed. He opened his mouth, then closed it. His nostrils flared. The token burned in Merrick's hand, smoking from the display. He couldn't even feel gratified that he'd just bested the Head of Guardians—who didn't like him anyway. He might not live to survive it. What if he'd broken some sort of rule? Could Tiberius declare this unethical?

Tiberius sucked in a deep breath through his nose, snatched the token from Merrick's hand, and muttered, "Visit the Gatehouse in the morning." He ground his teeth. "You pass."

His footfalls disappeared into the leaves as he stalked through the forest. Merrick held his breath until he felt dizzy and then let it out in one great *whoosh*. The Guardians waited until long after Tiberius left to explode in a chorus of victory.

Merrick pounded all of them on the back with profuse gratitude but stared at the spot where Tiberius had stood with deepening fear. He'd just passed, accepting a position that would keep him in the Central Network for two more years.

Without permission.

* * *

Wolfgang,

I have been invited to—and qualified for—the Captains of the Guard.

The training begins next week in the Borderlands, where I can do more reconnaissance on the Western Network activity I'm hearing rumors of.

This extends my obligations by at least two years. I understand that it may also sign my exile order.

For now, I feel the ends justify the means, and I apologize for having to act without seeking your permission.

—M

* * *

M,

What the Majesties don't know won't hurt them for now. Continue your work.

For both of our sakes, I suggest you find something to report that will impress them.

—W

* * *

Merrick squinted, one hand shielding his gaze from the fading glare of the sun. A bead of sweat trickled down his neck in the increasing almost-summer heat. Twentieth birthday, and he had to stand in the broiling sun, peering at . . . well . . . nothing.

"Ah," he muttered. "There it is."

In the distance, a small red circle, no bigger than his palm, hung from a tree on the outskirts of the forest. Letum Wood cast a long shadow this late in the day, bringing an early darkness to the meadow.

With long strides, he returned to the contingent of Guardians hoping to become elite Archers. They stood in a straight line stretched across the middle of the outer meadow, hundreds of paces from their target. When he glanced back, a hint of red flickered from the depths.

"All right, Guardians," he said. "Your final Qualification test begins. I want your arrow in the middle of that disc. You have three tries. If you hit it during one of the three, you pass."

The Guardians didn't respond. They stared downrange with assessing eyes, listening to the sounds, analyzing the strength and timing of the breeze, and becoming one with their targets. Just as he had taught them. He paused, soaking in the wet silence of the meadow. Almost two years in the Central Network, and he still couldn't get used to the humidity.

Merrick folded his hands behind his back.

"Draw."

Without a sound, each Guardian nocked an arrow, pulled their bow strings back to their cheeks, and assumed the correct stance.

"Release!"

A volley of arrows raced through the air, disappearing in a hiss. The Guardians released their second, and then their final arrows. The distance was too great to tell whether they'd made it.

"At ease."

Just as he opened his mouth to release them, a black scroll drifted in front of his face. Merrick blinked. Only Tiberius used a black scroll, and a black scroll meant he wanted something. Merrick snatched it from the air with a growl. Why would Tiberius send a message at the end of all day Qualifications?

Merrick shoved the scroll into his pocket.

"Retrieve."

While the Guardians transported to their targets, Merrick glanced over his shoulder. Tiberius stood on the Wall, his arms folded across his chest. He could feel his piercing glare even from this distance. Tiberius disappeared.

Merrick couldn't explain the gut-punch he felt when Tiberius left, but it felt as if all the air had left his chest. Several Guardians returned, exultant. Merrick shoved Tiberius out of his mind.

He'd deal with him later.

* * *

Twenty minutes later, Merrick ducked into the Gatehouse. Tiberius sat at the table, scrolls spread around him. Crumbs littered the coarse curls of his coppery beard. A warm fire crackled in the hearth.

"Did you need something, sir?"

Tiberius frowned.

"No."

Merrick pulled the scroll from his pocket. "You sent this message."

"I didn't send that. I'd never interrupt a Qualification."

Merrick moved to open the scroll, but an unexpected voice from behind stopped him.

"I sent it."

He whirled around to find Derek Black, Head of Protectors, standing behind him. The lamplight flickering on the walls cast his face in shadow, highlighting lines of fatigue that seemed deep as canals. Derek propped his hands on his hips, his dark hair skewed as if he'd recently run a hand through it. Merrick had seen Derek several times but never interacted with him.

"*You* sent for him?" Tiberius asked, setting both hands on the table and pushing himself up. "Why?"

"To talk."

Derek's easy reply dissipated some of the building tension. Tiberius growled. "We've talked about this. You know how I feel about—"

Derek waved him off. "Later, old friend. Come, Merrick, into my office."

Merrick licked his lips and forced his feet to follow. Behind him, Tiberius sputtered into silence. Within ten strides, Merrick stood in Derek's office, alone with the Head of Protectors. One of the most famous and revered witches in the Central Network. Merrick's palms started to sweat.

Derek stood behind his desk, but didn't sit. Instead, he leaned back against the wall, studying Merrick with a shrewd gaze.

"You didn't come right when I summoned," Derek said.

He said it so matter-of-factly it didn't sound arrogant or perturbed. If anything, Derek seemed curious. Merrick clenched his fists. A low current of energy had started to hum in his veins. The Head of Protectors summoned a Captain for a one-on-on conference for only one reason.

"My Guardians were qualifying for the Archer's contingent. If I had left, their testing work today would have been wasted."

"You stayed even though Tiberius could have demoted you for the delay?"

"Yes, sir."

"Why?"

"It wouldn't have been fair."

Derek paused, then straightened. Merrick's heart beat so hard it made his ribs ache. "I called you in here to extend an offer," Derek said.

"An offer, sir?"

"To try out for a Protectors slot. Are you interested?"

A brief shot of panic made Merrick pause. What would Wolfgang say? Her Majesties? He dismissed it. Derek wouldn't take kindly to hesitation.

"Yes, sir."

"Good. Be in the upper bailey tomorrow morning. 5:30. Meet me at the white circle."

Merrick's stomach clenched like a cold fist. The white fighting circle. He hadn't been there since Guardian training, and he didn't relish returning. He'd walked away with a healthy dose of humility, a sore jaw, and a black eye.

"Yes, sir."

And just like that—he'd been invited to prove himself for a slot in the most secretive, talented Brotherhood in all of Alkarra.

"Oh, and Merrick? Be there on time." Derek smiled in wry amusement. "The Brothers don't wait."

* * *

W—

Derek Black asked me to try out for the Protectors. I accepted the invitation, but can withdraw. I await your orders.

—M

* * *

M—

Proceed.

—W

* * *

Merrick retched three times that night.

Every time he closed his eyes, the white circle filled his mind. He woke up in a cold sweat around three in the morning, kicked the covers off, changed, and transported out of the chilly walls of the Ranks. The excitement of Derek's offer had quickly spiraled into an oblivion of anxiety. When it came to proving himself for the legendary Brotherhood, no previous training could prepare him. Not even the Masters—certainly not a measly two lines.

Merrick stalked up the Wall stairs and into the cool morning air. He wanted to climb. He wanted to dig his fingertips into ledges of rock and move from shelf to shelf. He longed for the snow-drenched peaks of his mountain home. He satisfied himself with sitting on the edge of the Wall, overlooking Letum Wood until the sun peeked above the skyline. With a knot in his stomach, he headed for the upper bailey. Eleven witches milled around the white circle. The low murmur of their voices died when he approached.

A broad chap the size of a bull waited in the middle of the circle. Balfrey. Famous for tearing a strip of thick leather in half with his bare hands. Derek stood off to the side, arms folded across his chest.

Merrick kept his chin high.

"Early this morning," Derek called with a jaunty grin. "A wise decision." He spread his arm toward the white circle. "Meet the Brotherhood."

All of them stared a hole right through his chest.

"The rules are simple," Derek continued. "You fight the Brotherhood. No magic. No cheating. Your challenge begins with Balfrey."

Merrick stepped into the circle and tucked his hair into a tight bun against the nape of his neck. The strands pulled against his head. Balfrey grinned, crouching, the bulging muscles of his arms rippling beneath his tight shirt. "You ready?" he asked.

How could I be?

Merrick nodded.

Balfrey charged.

Merrick ducked out of the way just as Balfrey's hand reached out, grabbed his shirt, and yanked. Merrick stumbled, caught himself, dodged a blow, and fell on his back from a swift sweep of Balfrey's massive leg. Seconds later, a beefy arm wrapped around his neck. He clawed for freedom. His vision turned to fog and then darkness. The pressure around his neck released. Merrick rolled away, sputtering.

Balfrey seized Merrick's shirt and yanked him to his feet. He clapped him on the back, nearly knocking him over. "Good try," he said, brushing him off. "But you don't stand a chance."

"Yanno," Derek called. "Your turn."

Merrick attempted to pull his mind back together, but a short, lean witch with dark skin and bright eyes replaced Balfrey. He cracked his knuckles with a maniacal smile.

Gods of mercy, Merrick thought. *They're enjoying this.*

"Ya ready?"

Yanno plunged into the circle. No matter how quickly Merrick slipped away, Yanno followed. Yanno danced on the balls of his feet, fists flying into Merrick's ribs. The sudden shock woke him out of his previous haze. He crouched into a fighter's stance. They sparred for several minutes. Yanno darted back and forth, moving in and out with ease. If Merrick struck him—which he couldn't be sure—Yanno gave no sign.

I'm going to die, Merrick thought, ducking a wide swing. Something hit the side of his head, and all went black.

Merrick emerged from a shallow darkness within seconds. Voices wavered over him. With a groan, his eyes fluttered open. Pain reverberated through his head. Yanno stood above him, grinning.

"I won. Ya lost."

He disappeared. With a growl, Merrick pushed to his feet. The Brotherhood murmured in the background, silencing when he straightened. A witch with short gray hair and a furry mustache stood in the ring, waving him over.

"Merrick, meet Terry." Derek motioned between them. "Please, get to know each other."

Merrick pulled in a deep breath—wincing from an ache in his left rib —and prepared to spar again.

The Protectors showed no mercy. He accepted none. With every blow, Merrick's abilities waned. His energy flagged. He stumbled from one opponent to the next in a tortured haze until Derek stepped into the ring.

"You lost, Merrick. To every single Protector." Derek's gaze moved around the circle. "There wasn't even a moment when we thought you *might* win. That's pretty bad. Maybe the worst I've seen so far."

"Yes, sir."

Merrick peered at him through a swollen eye. He shifted his weight to his other leg, certain he'd sprained his right ankle. A rib on his left side smarted with every breath. Blood filled his mouth.

"Now you fight me." Derek tilted his head back. "Do you want to fight me?"

Merrick swallowed.

"Yes, sir."

Derek's eyebrows rose in amusement. "Really?"

He nodded, afraid that if he spoke, he'd quit. The slight movement sent his balance reeling. One more blow and he might never rise again. But he wouldn't quit.

Fight until you can't fight anymore, son, his father would have said. *Fight your heart out.*

"A wise decision," Derek said, rolling his long sleeves back. "Let's fight."

Derek stooped, hands at the ready. Merrick's mind spun. He needed to do *something,* he just couldn't remember what. Did he wait for Derek to attack? Rush first? The artistic form of hand-to-hand combat eluded him. It had rules. Best practices. Methods. He'd forgotten all of it.

Something in the glint of Derek's eyes caught Merrick's gaze. In his hazy state, it looked like a challenge. Merrick raised his hands to guard his face. He'd probably die.

But at least he'd die fighting.

Summoning the last of his energy, Merrick released a guttural yell and charged. Within three strides, he slammed into Derek, taking them both to the ground. His breath left him. Merrick's fists flew in a fast staccato against Derek's chest. He became a seething ball of desperation and pain.

Derek's fist connected with Merrick's jaw. A spray of white lights broke before his eyes. His body went slack. He disappeared into the waiting oblivion for the second time.

This time, he welcomed the reprieve.

* * *

Merrick woke to the sting of a slap.

His arms, heavy as iron, struggled to move. When he moved, his muscles clenched. Snippets of recollection came back at him one at a time. *Derek. Fighting. Blackness.* Mortification swept through him.

I lost, he thought. *I lost horribly.*

"Ah. The handsome lad is awake again. He's never looked better, has he, Brothers?"

Merrick's right eye flew open—the other wouldn't respond. A blur of faces floated over him. Derek emerged from the hazy mass, wiping a bloody nose with the back of his hand.

"You lost, Merrick."

Merrick nodded. His jaw ached too much to speak. Derek grinned.

"But you punched my pretty face. That's impressive enough."

"And knocked you to the ground!" another voice called, amidst a ripple of laughter. Derek grunted.

"Impressive enough. What do you say, Brothers? Shall we let him try to be one of us for a couple of years?"

A low murmur rippled through the crowd. The Protectors backed away. Derek extended a hand to Merrick. Tentatively, Merrick reached for it and stood. A buzz took the edge off the swarming pain. He'd lost consciousness twice, possibly a tooth, and wanted to die. Not a bad start before breakfast.

Derek motioned to the Brotherhood with a jerk of his head. "You lost to every Protector, including me. But we weren't expecting you to win. Hell, if you did, we'd have to replace *that* Protector as well."

Derek slapped him on the shoulder, nearly knocking him to his knees. Merrick grunted, nostrils flaring in pain.

"Just wanted to make sure you'd get back up once you'd fallen down," Derek said. "Most who try out don't keep going. We value determination over raw talent. In the beginning, anyway. We'll see if you can keep it up."

"Yes, sir," Merrick mumbled, a hand on his jaw.

Derek held out his hand.

"Welcome to Protector training, Merrick. It'll be fun trying to defeat you a second time."

* * *

M—

The Majesties were pleased to hear of your successful entry to the Protectors' training program.

Farah appreciates the difficulty of your task and the decisions you made while under uncertain pressure. Although you face a disciplinary council upon your official return, she will allow you to remain without dishonor.

She expects you to continue placing your home Network above the Central Network and providing us with needed information. Your binding of silence is still active.

You are welcome to visit home on your first available break.

—W

* * *

Answering a summons from the High Priestess made Merrick's heart spin like a top.

Too early, he thought, ascending the black-and-white marble stairs two at a time, passing Guardians on each floor. *Derek can't be kicking me out of Protectors' training yet. He wouldn't need the High Priestess to do that. And it's only been a year and a half. I have six more months.*

The cumulative logic didn't ease his nerves. Why else would he be summoned to the High Priestess's office? He hovered between worlds here. Not a Captain anymore, but not a Protector either.

He hurried down the Royal Hall. A girl with wild black hair and bare feet stood at the High Priestess's door, her ear pressed against the wood. Merrick stopped.

Ah, he thought with a glimmer of amusement. *This has to be the infamous Bianca Monroe.*

He'd seen Derek's daughter around the castle—when he'd sought Derek for help with a mission gone awry or attended meetings with her father in their apartment. But they'd never spoken or made eye contact. She'd walked around in a bit of a daze since she'd come to the castle. Derek had told all the Brotherhood—Merrick included—the truth about Mabel murdering Marie, even though the *Chatterer* reported it as an accident. Whispers of Marie's death swirled amongst the servants in Bianca's wake. He thought of his own father's passing with a pang of understanding. Even Ana's memory didn't hurt so much anymore.

"Merry meet, Bianca."

She whipped around so fast it would have startled him if he hadn't expected it. Like Derek, she had a natural, athletic finesse with honed instincts and a sharp edge. A hand flew to her chest.

"Oh. You startled me." Her eyes narrowed and darkened at the same time. "What are you doing here, Merrick?"

A very good question, he thought, wondering if he should ask the same.

"The High Priestess summoned me."

He withdrew his hand from his pocket, producing the note from the High Priestess. If Bianca lingered outside the door, eavesdropping on whatever went on inside, perhaps he hadn't been called for dismissal.

Would it be disloyal of him to hope that someone caught her? One flash of her gray eyes—such a strange mix of shadows and a hint of sorrow—made him regret the thought. Bianca fulfilled her reputation of a wild young girl raised in the forest, but he admired her spunk. Who else would have the courage to eavesdrop on the High Priestess in broad daylight?

He certainly wouldn't.

"What are you doing here?" he asked, looking to the door. In the distance, he could just make out a shuffle of sound. With a quick, silent spell, he expanded his hearing. Footsteps closing in.

Bianca's mouth bobbed open and then closed. She hesitated, studying him.

"Ensuring the success of my future," she quipped. He smirked. Whatever that meant, it would soon be comical if she remained this distracted.

"You may want to step back then," he said. "Or else your future is going to involve a black eye."

She stepped back just as the door cracked open, sending him a grateful look that took him by surprise. A flash of curiosity stirred within him. Who was this girl indeed? She had Derek's spunk and drive to prove herself, only in feminine form.

The High Priestess's voice spilled into the hallway, pulling him from his thoughts.

"Both of you may enter."

Merrick stepped back, allowing Bianca to go before him, and followed her inside.

Plucky, he thought as he closed the door behind them. *She'd make a great sword fighter.*

Sneak Peek from
HAZEL

CHAPTER ONE

Papa stared at the table.

Hazel stared at him.

Angry gashes welled blood onto his cheeks. His shoulders lifted and fell as if he were still running for his life even though he sat in a rickety chair. No, he hadn't run for *his* life. He'd run for the orphans' lives, to protect them from the Guardians slaying innocent witches in the street.

A tear rent his shirt almost in half, and blood stained the neck. His beard was singed on one side, where his jaw twitched as he tightened it.

Ragged came to mind. As torn up as ivy in a windstorm.

Mama hardly looked better, with a bruise forming below one eye, her hair mussed to all ends and a slight limp on her right ankle. Hazel looked better, but only because her parents had insisted that she stay inside, hidden in the attic. She'd crouched behind a screen of dry wood sorrel she'd harvested a few weeks ago and waited for the destruction to stop.

Papa's hand twitched as his thoughts moved, a silent storm in the back of his eyes. The rage rolled off him in languorous waves. She shrank back a little.

Of course, Papa wasn't angry at *her*.

Papa was never truly angry. Not like Mrs. Sauers down the street, a bitter old woman. Not like Mildred either, filled with righteous indignation. No, he was too gentle for such a visceral emotion. As such, being a leader in the Resistance against High Priestess Evelyn had left its mark on him. Deep lines fanned his eyes and face.

The Guardian attack on Stilton Covens tonight had only cemented his angst. Total Network corruption led to this atrocious night, thanks to the High Priestess Evelyn's order to draw Mildred out of hiding by killing innocent witches.

Bodies lay in piles. Houses set on fire. The hiccupping sobs of witches still rang in her ears from outside.

Of course, tension had simmered in the Central Network for ages now. First the almost-riot over the new Central highway tax that Mildred managed to stop. The Resistance growing. Secret classes in the castle.

Now, if Mildred truly did come to power, those Guardians would probably die for treason.

If she didn't?

Well, they'd all probably die.

"Here." Mama set a cup in front of Papa, breaking Hazel's thoughts. "Have a drink, William. It will make you feel better."

"Thank you," he murmured.

Mama set a glass of tea in front of Hazel. No honey. Hazel hadn't found any in a while, despite searching her usual places. She needed to go deeper into Letum Wood for that. Something she hoped would happen soon enough. There just wasn't enough vegetation here.

The three of them studiously avoided any discussion about the attack. Instead, they sat calmly around the table with the snap of the fire to fill the silence. Hazel's parents, William and Lily, wouldn't leave the Stilton Covens office where they lived even after this attack.

They want us to hide, Papa had said. *They want us to be afraid. This is our home. The Resistance is our life's work. We won't be scared away.*

Hazel swallowed hard. *Life's work.* The words stuck in her throat.

Papa rotated his glass around and studied the smooth liquid but didn't drink from it. Mama kept her trembling hands in her lap. Hazel could only think about the attack.

"It won't be long now before Mildred makes her move," Papa said quietly. "I'm certain it's almost time. Then all this hell can end, and we can get on with our lives."

Mama nodded.

Hazel's stomach tightened.

Everyone spoke of "the time." *The time is coming. The time is almost here. It's not yet the right time, but it will soon be time.*

This elusive time should come already.

Hazel had met the leader of the Resistance—Mildred—briefly. Mildred was an intense thundercloud with eyes that snapped like lightning. But she hadn't been unkind, nor without power. If Mildred could undo what Evelyn had done, then Hazel didn't care about her personality.

If Hazel could *just* make it back to school, she could be back with growing things again. There was no real greenery here, at the Coven office. Thus, no reason for her to stay. She longed for life again.

At school, she could educate herself on the best gardening methods, deftly prune and sort through her favorite plants, and be happy. With her extensive knowledge of herbs, she could really get back to the earth there. Afterward? Maybe find a place in Letum Wood and surround herself with all the greenery she could find.

"Hazel?"

She startled out of her thought, blinking. "Yes?"

"Are you all right?"

"Yes."

Mama and Papa exchanged a dubious look. Hazel swallowed a little tea, but it didn't have a drop of flavor.

"Well, what do you think then?" Mama asked.

Too late, she realized she'd been lost in thought and missed something important. Her brain felt sluggish as she attempted to extract herself from dreams of living in the depths of Letum Wood.

"Think about what?" she asked.

"About not going back to school in a few days," Papa said. "Will you be upset when we pull you out?"

"What?"

His expression hardened. "It's not safe anymore."

"It's never been safe," she said, then clamped her mouth shut when his nostrils flared. Wrong thing to point out. "I mean yes, I'll be upset. I'm so close, Papa. You can't pull me now."

Schools as far safer—far more normal—than here. Thanks to Evelyn's reign of terror, the dividing line between the rich and poor had become far more pronounced. In the Stilton Covens, the depths of poverty were deeply felt in the swollen bellies, rubbish streets, and haunting eyes of those that lived around her.

At school, they all wore the same uniform and ate the same food. She wouldn't have to worry about walking down the street and running into a beggar who turned out to be her old teacher.

"May is Evelyn's right hand," he said. "She owns the school, which likely means she'll be there. You may already have been flagged as a Resistor. What's to stop her from giving you an inheritance curse?"

"May is hardly ever there," she said quickly. "Miss Mabel runs it, and she's in the Resistance."

He sent her a wary glance. "Rumor has it."

"Papa, please. Tabitha is going as a first-year! If *her* parents are letting her go, it must be safe."

"You'll have time after things settle down to finish your education. What if Guardians come and ask you questions?" Mama said. "Especially if they start to suspect us of anything. We couldn't protect you. Something like this could happen again. Evelyn specifically authorized inheritance curses for the Network School students that are *suspected* of being in league with Mildred. They don't even need proof. She wants the results to linger. Do you want that?"

"No, of course not. But we don't know that it's unsafe. If I can just finish, then I could really serve the Resistance. I know you think that Mildred will fight Evelyn soon, but maybe not. She hasn't yet, right? And now Guardians are attacking witches. Plus, there's more that I can do there than just graduate."

She let that thought linger. Mama sent her an uneasy look. Attending school meant Hazel could also provide further insight into well-to-do families in the Network. In a world of subterfuge, information was power.

Because there was no guarantee Mildred would win.

Silence fell on the three of them. Papa stared at his glass. He tipped it from side to side again, watching the liquid swish around the bottom. The blood on his lip had dried now, turning to a sticky ebony.

Just when Hazel wasn't sure she could stand the silence, Papa picked the glass up, gulped it in one swallow, and slammed it on the table.

"You're almost an adult. It's your choice. But know that we don't like it."

* * *

HAZEL is a short story that I'd *love* for you to read. For fans of *Mildred's Resistance* and all things Bianca Monroe, you'll love the dive back into history to find out what happened that fateful night.

Just visit www.katiecrossbooks.com. Type HAZEL into the search bar and the paperback will pop right up. It's the only place you can get this super special story.

Join Other Witches

Merry meet!

There is more epic magic and wild places waiting for you.

If you want to stay in-the-know about new releases, get awesome discounts (IE—more books, less money), and have free novels and short stories land in your lap, I've got your back.

Go to www.katiecrossbooks.com to join the other witches on my email list, where you get exclusive, can't-find-anywhere-else kind of stuff.

(In fact, I'll send you some free stories right away—first email!)

Or you can go to The Witchery, which is my Facebook group of other readers just like you. Please visit www.facebook.com/groups/thenetwork series to learn more!

There, you'll see more images of Alkarra, join all your witchy friends, and go to lunch with me on my weekly Coffee With Katie calls.

(No, seriously. I will Uber-Eats you lunch!)

Can't wait to see you there!

—Katie

Also by Katie Cross

The Dragonmaster Trilogy

FLAME

Chronicles of the Dragonmasters (short story collection)

FLIGHT

The Ronan Scrolls (novella)

FREEDOM

The Dragonmaster Trilogy Collection

The Network Series

Mildred's Resistance (prequel)

Miss Mabel's School for Girls

Alkarra Awakening

The High Priest's Daughter

War of the Networks

The Network Series Complete Collection

The Isadora Interviews (novella)

Short Stories from Miss Mabel's

Short Stories from the Network Series

Hazel (short story)

The Network Saga Suggested Reading Order

1. The Parting (novella #1)

2. The Lost Magic (full-length novel)

3. The Lamplighter's Daughter (novella #2)

About the Author

Katie Cross is ALL ABOUT writing epic magic and wild places. Creating new fantasy worlds is her jam.

When she's not hiking or chasing her two littles through the Montana mountains, you can find her curled up reading a book or arguing with her husband over the best kind of sushi.

Visit her at www.katiecrossbooks.com for free short stories, extra savings on all her books (and some you can't buy on the retailers), and so much more.

CPSIA information can be obtained
at www.ICGtesting.com
Printed in the USA
BVHW061922170223
658735BV00007B/755